MANU

Recent Titles by Christopher Nicole from Severn House

The Secret Service Series

ANGEL FROM HELL
ANGEL IN RED
ANGEL OF VENGEANCE
ANGEL IN JEOPARDY
ANGEL OF DOOM
ANGEL RISING
ANGEL OF DESTRUCTION
ANGEL OF DARKNESS

The Jessica Jones Series

THE FOLLOWERS
A FEARFUL THING

The Arms of War Series

THE TRADE
SHADOWS IN THE SUN
GUNS IN THE DESERT
PRELUDE TO WAR

The Historical Romance Series

DAWN OF A LEGEND
TWILIGHT OF A GODDESS

MANU

Christopher Nicole

This first world edition published 2011
in Great Britain and in the USA by
SEVERN HOUSE PUBLISHERS LTD of
9–15 High Street, Sutton, Surrey, England, SM1 1DF.
Trade paperback edition first published
in Great Britain and the USA 2012 by
SEVERN HOUSE PUBLISHERS LTD

British Library Cataloguing in Publication Data

Nicole, Christopher.
  Manu.
  1. English–India–Fiction. 2. Missionaries' spouses–
  India–Fiction. 3. India–Kings and rulers–Fiction.
  4. Princesses–India–Fiction. 5. India–History–
  British occupation, 1765-1947–Fiction. 6. Historical
  fiction.
  I. Title
  823.9'14-dc22

ISBN-13: 978-0-7278-8073-4 (cased)
ISBN-13: 978-1-84751-386-1 (trade paper)

All Severn House titles are printed on acid-free paper.

Severn House Publishers support The Forest Stewardship Council [FSC],
the leading international forest certification organisation. All our titles that
are printed on Greenpeace-approved FSC-certified paper carry the FSC logo.

MIX
Paper from
responsible sources
FSC
www.fsc.org   FSC® C018575

Typeset by Palimpsest Book Production Ltd.,
Falkirk, Stirlingshire, Scotland.
Printed and bound in Great Britain by
MPG Books Ltd., Bodmin, Cornwall.

'To be a queen in bondage is more vile
Than is a slave in base servility;
For princes should be free.'

Henry VI, Part 1, William Shakespeare

Manikarnika, known to her intimates as Manu, daughter of Brahmin Moropant Tambe, was married at the age of thirteen to Gangadhar Rao Newalkar, Maharaja of the northern Indian state of Jhansi. She was officially renamed Lakshmi Bai after the goddess of beauty. At the age of eighteen she was forced by circumstances to become queen regent of the state in one of the most turbulent and important moments of Indian history. Her beauty, courage and determination in the face of endless adversity have made her the most iconic heroine the subcontinent has ever known.

This is a work of fiction. However, most of the characters are real and the Rani of Jhansi did live, and love, and fight, and die like the heroine she was.

The Road from Cawnpore

1849

'Oh, Sergeant Hopkins, it is so terrible,' Mrs Caldwell gushed. 'This poor, dear girl, so lovely, so innocent, in the hands of murdering thugs . . . the ordeal . . . what was done to her . . .'

I have always found being referred to as if I wasn't there, when I *was* there, most irritating. But I had found Mrs Caldwell most irritating from the moment of our first meeting two days earlier. She was large, stout and perspiring; clearly the heat of central India did not agree with her. I doubted that she was as distressed as she was trying to appear, but what had happened was certainly a huge source of gossip for the foreseeable future. All she required were the hideous details, and these she had not yet obtained.

'Now, I know it will be a ghastly ordeal for you,' she continued, 'Emma.' An experiment this, to see how I responded to the use of my Christian name. 'But this gentleman needs to know exactly what happened. Exactly,' she added with relish.

The man in the blue uniform and the little moustache touched the brim of his peaked cap. 'It is necessary, Mrs 'ammond, if we har to appre'end these criminals.'

The cockney police officer was no less agog and anticipatory. If I say so myself, I *am* a handsome woman, and at the age of twenty-three was at my best, despite my recent privations and somewhat sunburnt features. I was tall, and what is best described as buxom, possessing a mass of chestnut hair which curled damply down the back of my borrowed and ill-fitting muslin gown – I had recently had a bath. The thought of so much voluptuous femininity in the hands of slavering alien beasts was obviously having a powerful effect on his endeavour to appear calm and businesslike.

I was, however, not in the mood to assuage the obviously overheated imaginations of either Mrs Caldwell or the sergeant. My sole desire was to escape their company as rapidly as possible. So when he suggested, 'Begin when you left Cawnpore,' I replied,

'We left Cawnpore a week ago. My husband felt that he had completed his work there and we were returning to the Deccan. As we knew that it was going to be a long journey, when our caravan-master suggested that we take a shortcut that he knew of, through some hills, my husband agreed, but soon after we left the main trail we were beset by bandits, who took us by surprise. My husband died gallantly fighting to protect me, and thanks to his bravery I was able to escape. With my life,' I added for good measure.

'How terrible,' Mrs Caldwell said. 'You must have loved him very much. As he must have loved you.'

'Oh, indeed,' I agreed, sadly wiping away a non-existent tear.

Of course there was almost no word of truth in my statement. We were not suddenly beset by bandits; in our innocent ignorance we invited them to join us. It was they, not our caravan-master, who suggested we leave the main and well-used trail and go into the remote fastnesses of the hill country. As for my husband, I have no idea whether or not his was a gallant death, but I do know that he did not die attempting to save me; I had to accomplish that entirely on my own. And as regards loving each other, I had long come to regard him with utter loathing, while he had always regarded me as nothing more than a receptacle for his lust, one that also washed his clothes and oversaw his meals.

I will admit that I owed him a great deal – my life, to be precise. But that had been six years before the events of the previous week, and I had expiated, on my back, any gratitude I might have once felt, as I had come to realize that he had acted not out of any desire to assist *me* but to get his hands on my body; he had spent his life in vain attempts to reconcile his calling as a man of the cloth with his desires, which were excessive.

My father was, and perhaps still is, the vicar of the village of Lower Stapleton in Hampshire. As his stipend barely kept him and our family out of indigence, as soon as I reached the age of fourteen and having survived, he would have it miraculously, an attack of smallpox which had left me virtually unmarked, it was necessary for me to earn, and this I did by finding a position as housemaid to Lord Stapleton, who to all intents and purposes owned the village, and whose manor house dominated it.

I worked at Stapleton Manor for three years. I did not enjoy one of them, as I intensely disliked being treated as an inferior by the other servants. Thanks to Papa I was reasonably well educated and in fact earned additional funds, when I had the time, teaching in the village school governed by Mr Estrich. I should make it perfectly clear here that I went to the Reverend Hammond's bed a virgin, despite the efforts of the village youth, not to mention Mr Estrich.

As I have always been big enough and strong enough to take care of myself, my principal concern during this time was the increasing penury of my parents, and I watched with dismay Papa gradually sinking into debt as he attempted to maintain a certain standard of dress and visible family comforts. But there was nothing, on my meagre wages, that I could do to assist him. Until the fateful morning when, in pursuance of my duties, I entered his lordship's bedchamber to tidy up and make the bed, and saw, scattered across the dressing table, more than twenty gold guineas.

The careless manner in which this, to me, small fortune had been thrown down left me in no doubt that he had gone to bed drunk – which was common enough – after an evening spent gambling, and thus probably had no certain idea of how much was there. I stared at the coins. Just five of the glittering objects would settle my father's debts, and such a small proportion of the whole would surely never be missed.

Thus I succumbed to temptation and, having done so, hurried from the bedroom to gain the privacy of my own small chamber, there to secrete my ill-gotten gains until I could safely take them home. But at the top of the stairs I encountered Mrs Houston, the housekeeper, and without thinking curtsied, as we were required to do in her presence. And my apron clinked.

She raised her eyebrows. 'What have you got in there, Weston?' she demanded.

Already in a state of some agitation, I lost my head entirely. Once she looked in my pocket, my job was gone and I would almost certainly go to prison. But if my position was definitely lost, if I could escape the house and regain the rectory I could at least provide Papa with the money before it was missed. So I mumbled something and made to step past her.

'Stop there,' she commanded, and caught my arm. My response was instinctive. I made to push her aside but used too much force, with the result that she lost her balance and fell down the stairs, rolling and bumping all the way to the bottom . . . To arrive, even more calamitously, at the feet of Plumpton the butler.

He bent over her then straightened, a look of the most complete horror on his face. 'Help!' he bawled. 'Murder! Police!'

Mr Plumpton had a loud voice, and footmen and housemaids emerged from every doorway; even Mrs Lustrom, the cook, came steaming in from the kitchen. Unable to believe what had happened, I was stumbling down the stairs, to realize at a glance, although I had never seen a dead body before, that Mrs Houston was very definitely not living. She seemed to have hit her head on just about every step, and there was blood everywhere. 'Oh, my God!' I gasped. 'Oh, my God!'

'Arrest her,' Mr Plumpton commanded, and two of the footmen grasped my arms.

'No, no!' I shouted. 'I didn't mean to. It was an accident.'

Which was of course a confession of guilt, as I had not denied that it was my fault. But worse followed immediately. One of the footmen holding me had heard the clink from my apron, and he thrust his hand into my pocket, an outrageous act as my pocket was situated against my groin, although I have no doubt that it was something he had wanted to do for some time.

I was speechless, but he was not. His hand emerged holding two of the guineas. 'Mr Plumpton! Guineas.'

'She's a thief!' screamed one of the maids.

'And a murderess!' shouted someone else.

At this moment, as I supposed I might be about to be lynched, we were joined by Lord Stapleton, who had apparently been having a meeting with some gentlemen in his study. He was a large and habitually red-faced man. 'What the devil is going on?' he demanded.

'It's Mrs Houston, my lord,' Plumpton explained. 'Weston had apparently been robbing the bedrooms, and when Mrs Houston attempted to stop her, pushed her down the stairs and she split her head open.'

'What?' Lord Stapleton dropped to his knees beside Mrs Houston. 'She can't be dead. Sophie! Wake up, Sophie!'

The staff exchanged glances. Lady Stapleton preferred living at their London home to, as she put it, burying herself in the country, and it had long been whispered that Mrs Houston performed more important duties than merely overseeing the household.

'It was an accident,' I babbled. 'I only tried to push past her. I didn't mean to hurt her.'

Lord Stapleton slowly straightened. 'Murderess,' he hissed at me. 'Thief! A parson's daughter, by God! You'll hang, miss. Oh, you'll hang. I'll see to that.'

As his lordship was chairman of the local magistrates, this seemed an entirely likely prospect. I burst into tears.

'Send for Constable Briggs,' he now commanded.

'Ahem!' said another voice. It was a somewhat harsh voice, although fairly quiet.

'No claptrap, Reverend. She is guilty, and must suffer the penalty.'

'Indeed, my lord,' the parson said. 'But to take a human life, especially one so young and . . . ah, vibrant, is a very serious matter.'

I froze, as I remembered who the speaker was. His name was Charles Hammond and, being on a fundraising tour of the south of England in search of support for the mission he maintained in some distant land, he had actually dined at my parents' house a week earlier, obviously not in the hopes of obtaining any funds from them, but in order to ascertain where and whom would be the best objects of his appeal; Lord Stapleton had naturally been at the top of the list. I had not liked him. Like Lord Stapleton, he was a big man, but much younger, and unlike his lordship was quite good-looking, in a forceful sort of way, while his colour was much better. But he had looked at me like a wolf on the prowl and, although saying nothing more than a greeting, had seemed to strip away my clothing with his eyes – a most embarrassing experience. But now . . .

His lordship was not to be mollified. 'May I point out that this "vibrant" young woman has just committed murder?'

'She claims it was an accident. She could be telling the truth.'

'Balderdash! What about the money in her possession?'

'That is a serious matter, I agree. But hardly a hanging offence. A few years ago she'd have been sent to Australia.'

'A few years ago,' Lord Stapleton sneered. 'They don't do that any more.'

'Suppose, my lord, that the girl be removed from England for an appropriate length of time. Perhaps not to Australia, but . . .?'

'What the devil are you talking about?'

'As you know, I am about to leave England to establish my mission in India. I could take her with me. Ten thousand miles away.'

'You . . . you . . .' his lordship was nearly as speechless as I. 'A man of the cloth, proposing . . .'

'No, no, my lord. You misunderstand me. I would be prepared to marry the girl.'

'Bless my soul!'

I would have chosen a far stronger remark. Marriage? Even if I had been prepared to consider such a step, marriage . . . to this unpleasant man? *No,* I wanted to scream. *You cannot permit this.* But then, I reflected, what was the alternative? To have my life ended? To stand before a mocking crowd while a rope was placed around my neck? I found myself gasping again.

'Would the parson accept this?' Lord Stapleton inquired, obviously interested.

'I am sure he would, my lord. Both to save his daughter's life and to avoid a scandal which could well involve his ministry.'

'Hm. Hm. It would be irregular, to be sure.'

'It would save you a possible scandal as well, my lord. If the case came to court, well . . .' he paused, meaningfully, while Lord Stapleton's always red cheeks turned puce. 'Who knows what might come out. Her ladyship would certainly wish to discover the facts of the case. Whereas . . .' he looked around the servants' faces. 'If it was put out that Mrs Houston simply missed her footing and fell down the stairs . . .'

'Hm,' Lord Stapleton remarked, also looking over his staff.

'I suggest,' Mr Hammond went on, 'a gratuity for everyone, and instant dismissal for anyone who attempts to reveal the truth.'

'Hm. How long is your ministry for?'

'Ten years, my lord.'

'Ten years.' His lordship pointed at the reverend. 'I'll have no subterfuge, Hammond. You'll marry the wench and you'll take her to India, and you'll keep her there for ten years. If she ever sets foot on these shores again in one day less than that I'll have her hanged, scandal or no scandal.'

And so, quite against my will, I embarked upon a long sojourn in purgatory that had, no doubt appropriately, ended in hell. I accepted it because my upbringing and background convinced me that I deserved punishment for my crime, even if that crime had been undertaken for the best of motives, and had been compounded by an accident. Ten years! But only six had elapsed when we left Cawnpore on that fateful August morning.

We had left the city early, proceeding to the south; in August it was extremely hot, thus most of our travelling had to be done before the sun's rays became oppressive. Our destination was the Deccan, and we were expecting a long journey ahead of us.

As was usually the case, we had not been in a very happy state of mind. Our six months in Cawnpore had been both unproductive and socially difficult. Although set in virtually the heart of the subcontinent in what was known as the Bundelkhand, and on the edge of the great state of Oudh, Cawnpore was a very British town in which both the considerable military establishment and the even more considerable civilian establishment was dominating and wished to be seen to be dominating. This was most evident in the attitudes of the memsahibs.

I should mention that these memsahibs were a recent phenomenon in India. The steady advance of the East India Company, also known as the John Company, and the success of Lord Wellesley in particular, had allowed the Company to spread its tentacles until it ruled a third of the peninsular, and controlled, by means of political agents foisted on the various rajahs, as well as those pensions and subsidies it allotted to favoured local rulers, much of the rest.

His successes had appeared to make at least southern and central India safe for that most protected of living species, the English wife and daughter and, by projection, mother. Thus they had begun following their menfolk east, bringing with them English customs and worse, English attitudes, dominated by an immense arrogance. Great Britain controlled the greatest Empire of recent times; Great Britain was ruled by a woman, thus it followed that British womanhood was the greatest and most important asset of that vast Empire.

The arrival in India in droves of these formidable females was not universally applauded. The Indians themselves, with their concept that a woman's true place belonged in a respectable purdah, were at once scandalized and amused. Accepting with

weary resignation that there might be some worthwhile assets to
be gained from John Company's rule, they now had to come
to terms with the realization that behind the administrator who
told them what they could or could not do and the magistrate
who punished them when they did or did not do it, there stood
a terrifying figure in white muslin and button-up boots, a broad-
brimmed straw hat and impenetrable veil, who told both magistrate
and administrator what *they* could and could not do, and who
was not to be crossed.

I cannot pretend that I was aware of this situation when I
landed in Madras in the spring of 1844. Nor did my position, as
the browbeaten young wife of a despised missionary bring me,
at that time, into contact with any of these dominating females.
Rather it was responsible for my having to sit on a mule on a
boiling summer's day, wending my way over some very desolate
country. I rode immediately behind Mr Hammond, and thus
found myself inhaling his dust through my veil. At least the rest
of our party was behind me; the only other company we enjoyed
was that of several large vultures circling overhead, almost as if
they could foresee our future.

We had not been *expelled* from Cawnpore; the British would
never be so overt in their treatment of a missionary. The missionaries had followed the memsahibs, once assured of their personal
safety, and their invasion of the subcontinent had been welcomed
and supported by the British Government in London, who steadfastly adhered to the opinion that the only good Indian was a
Christian Indian, regardless of what the Indians might feel, or of
the fact that their home-grown religions were far older than
Christianity, and in the main had worked very well for several
thousand years.

From the beginning we had been less well received by the
English community. They didn't care what image of God the locals
worshipped, so long as they provided a profit for the Company.
Missionaries too often got in the way of that, if only by interfering
with the business of making money by requiring the workers to
spend some time listening to the word of God. My husband, sadly,
had always compounded the innate dislike his calling incurred by
being a difficult man to get on with, and I speak as his wife. He
had, however, been inclined to blame me for our social ostracizm,

for my unladylike delving into Indian customs and affairs and expeditions in both Delhi and Lucknow over the previous two years with Allia, my maid and servant, which had rapidly become known to the community at large and had made him furious.

I do not have any evidence that the memsahibs played any part in our departure, but they had made it very clear that they would be happy to see the back of us and I could really not see why we continued to waste our time in this unprofitable pursuit.

I had often found myself thinking in a similar vein about our marriage.

No doubt I am prejudiced by disappointment. When I had fled Stapleton six years before, in the company of a man who had quickly revealed that the only thing about me he wished to get close to was my body, my innate optimism had yet convinced me that with the passing of time we would settle into a domestic routine of mutual respect and understanding. This had not happened, owing to his nature, and our relations had steadily deteriorated.

Thank heavens, perhaps because our love-making, if it can be so-called, was so one-sided and perfunctory as to be meaningless, our union had produced no children.

I was therefore nothing more than an appendage, attractive and to be displayed, to be sure, and certainly useful as I darned his socks, washed his undergarments, prepared his meals, arranged his texts and dutifully stood at his side looking enthusiastic when he delivered his sermons. This, even though I did not understand, and certainly did not agree with, nearly all of his tenets; he belonged to some obscure brethren who regarded the world as having no more than another fifty years to survive, and promised those that did not immediately enter his communion a most miserable fate which began with fire and brimstone. I had been brought up in the Anglican faith, and although this could be severe enough, it was a paradise of goodwill when set alongside Mr Hammond's beliefs.

Obviously these beliefs did not make him any more popular with his fellow ex-patriots, whose only god was Mammon, and who believed that the attainment of this state of grace should be accompanied by as many pleasures as possible, while I reflected on more than one occasion that even if I was little more than an unpaid servant, this had to be preferable to being hanged. Besides, there was India!

'There are some people up ahead, Sahib,' Lall said on our third morning out of Cawnpore. Lall was our caravan-master from north of Delhi, and was taller and more powerfully built than those from the south. He was also a Muslim but the religions of India had become, over the centuries, so interwoven and subdivided into differing sects – very much like Christianity, to be sure – that this was no longer held against him even in a mainly Hindu area. Lucknow, where we had first met him and employed him, was situated in the state of Oudh which, although predominantly Hindu in population, was ruled by a Muslim family. He certainly knew about horses and mules, and apparently men, and could control them all. He also spoke some English, which was useful, although he preferred to use the local tongue, Marathi, as he did now.

'Men?' Mr Hammond asked, reining his mule and thus allowing me to catch up with him. 'What sort of men?'

'I think they are religious,' Lall said.

'Are they armed?'

'It does not appear so, Sahib. They beg only to be allowed to join your caravan as far as the next town. They are afraid to travel by themselves.'

'Well, why not?' Mr Hammond asked. Having taken the decision to abandon Cawnpore, he was in one of his jovial moods.

It did occur to me that for men who were afraid to travel by themselves they seemed to have come a good way from civilization on their own. But I had learned never to question any decision of my husband's, at least in public.

And certainly not in front of an Indian.

'I do not like these men, Memsahib,' Allia said.

Allia was an attractive girl, small and dark-skinned, to be sure, but well-endowed physically with a wealth of midnight hair and very good-humoured, which made a great difference to our unhappy domestic life. Part of her good humour was because she had no caste, and therefore very little place in Indian life except as a servant; that she had become a servant to a memsahib had been a great cachet to both her and her family; that I had taken such a person into my employ had been another count against me in the eyes of Cawnpore society.

I entirely agreed with her opinion of the travellers who had now joined the caravan. They looked very poor in that they wore only dhotis, a sort of loin cloth that left their torsos as well as their legs bare, but every man also had a thick shawl which he wore over his head and shoulders, in the main concealing his features, and which gave him a sort of secretive look.

But again, I was not about to raise the matter with Mr Hammond, who rode serenely on his way. However, I began to remember what I had been told in Cape Town.

Our arrival in Cape Town had given me my first glimpse of that Empire into which I was plunging, and it was to be our first sight of land since leaving the Channel five weeks earlier. I had been in a constant state of wonderment during this time, the only travelling I had ever previously done being my hasty departure from Stapleton. I had never seen a ship close to, much less set foot on one, and had spent the first week of our voyage in varying degrees of sickness.

We spent only a few days in Cape Town harbour, mostly replenishing our supplies of fresh food and water, before we were away again, once more plunging into a vast ocean, but this one so different to the Atlantic, filled with Eastern promise.

However, a group of Dutch ladies I met in Cape Town, several of whom had relatives or acquaintances who had travelled and settled farther east, and who spoke sufficient English to carry on a conversation, were full of the most startling old wives' tales. 'The Indians *worship* the phallus,' one confided in hushed tones.

At that stage of my life – I was just eighteen – I had no idea what a phallus was.

'They actually have it in their temples,' another told me. 'Carved!'

Still in a state of bewilderment, I attempted to look suitably shocked.

'And the women,' my first informant continued. 'They depict them absolutely naked! In their temples!'

This *did* shock me. The only naked woman I had ever seen in my life was me, in a mirror, and every time I looked at myself I had a feeling of guilt, a sense that I was venturing into forbidden territory. This was encouraged by my husband, who held that nudity in any shape or form was obscene and un-Christian. Thus at night he never entered the bedroom until I was wearing a thick flannel nightgown, as he himself was similarly encased. At the moment he showed amorous intent I always closed my eyes and kept them firmly shut until his weight had departed, and so I had never actually seen a male member, or phallus as these excited ladies would have it.

'And then,' said another lady, 'the thugs!'

The very word sounded sinister, especially as the 'h' was dropped and yet remained as a sort of aspirant; the pronunciation, t'ug, promised all manner of evil.

'They roam in bands, pretending to be innocent travellers and join caravans, and then in the dead of night they reveal their horrid purpose and murder everyone they can lay hands on. As to what they do to the women . . .' she rolled her eyes.

By now I was beginning to suspect that these good ladies were indulging in hyperbole, but I was sufficiently alarmed to raise the matter, tentatively, with my husband.

'Oh, yes, indeed,' he said. 'It is a totally indecent society. This it is our business to correct.'

I wondered how he proposed to go about accomplishing that with a carved statue?

He could obviously read my mind. 'But their temples are best avoided,' he told me. 'They are heathen places, and obscene with it.'

'And are the thugs also real?' I ventured.

'Oh, indeed. Or they were. A menace to society. But they were all rounded up and hanged a few years ago.'

It did strike me that 'all' is a somewhat indefinite word.

I took his word for it, as I took his word for most things. But I also took Allia's instruction in most of the things I found on the ground, as it were. The most important instruction she gave me was in the Marathi language, an essential part of the education of any educated Indian of the Maratha region, second only to Persian, which was the diplomatic and court language. I learned this also, not that at that time I had any idea that I might one day be either a diplomat or belong to a court.

Allia also taught me the intricacies of Indian cooking. To be sure, we had encountered curries almost from the moment of landing. Then we had been so anxious to improve on the very restricted shipboard diet, especially at the end of a long voyage, that I suspect we would have eaten anything. But we soon had to accept that food in India means curry. This is not only for the flavouring, but for the far more important reason that the various spices, certainly when combined, form a preservative, and this is essential in a climate so hot and moist that food can go off in a few hours. Cholera was also an ever-present threat.

By this time, sadly, Mr Hammond had determined that he did not like curry; as there was seldom anything else on the menu he had to eat it or starve, but every meal was accompanied by recriminations. Allia taught me the specifics of the spices, how they should be mixed and in what proportions, and how the word curry actually covers a huge range of dishes with widely differing tastes and appearances. I found it fascinating and endeavoured to reclaim my husband's appetite, without much success.

Allia equally indulged my passion for exploration, of the senses as much as my physical surroundings. Mr Hammond's warnings regarding the obscenities that might be found within Hindu temples was an irresistible magnet to my curiosity. Under Allia's guidance I explored several of these religious edifices and found them quite as explicit as my Dutch friends had suggested. But although my initial reaction was one of terror and confusion, I could not deny their beauty.

Not all were beautiful, however, and some were profoundly disturbing. The goddess Sita, mother of all things, was presented as a gentle and generous creature, to be admired as she was respected. But the goddess Durga, who ruled over death and destruction, was a terrifying figure, and her even more sinister offshoot Kali, the black goddess, could make one shiver just by looking at her contorted features, dripping blood, her eight hands clutching swords and knives.

'Kali is the goddess worshipped by the thugs,' Allia whispered, fearfully.

'But the thugs have been suppressed,' I said.

She gave me what had best be described as an old-fashioned look.

I thus observed the men who had joined us on our journey with more than an ordinary interest. They were certainly obsequious enough, bowing and pressing their hands together whenever they found me looking at them. I reflected that I was merely being nervous and took comfort from the fact that the caravan route we were using was a popular one, and that we were continually passing other groups of travellers, as well as, from time to time, bodies of red-coated soldiers, a very reassuring sight.

But I was not alone in feeling insecure. All of British India was at that moment in a state of apprehension. This was mainly because of the method of government which had developed out of the original trading stations.

The enormous wealth of this country had led to a system of graft and corruption on an immense scale, which had convinced the British Government that a handful of merchants interested only in profit were incapable of ruling such a vast accumulation of latent power and wealth, and so, while officially leaving the Company in control of its affairs, had imposed above it the rule of a governor general, whose powers were virtually unlimited. British India was, in reality, converted into a kingdom, ruled absolutely by a man representing the king, or as it now was, the queen, in England.

Monarchies are by definition capricious. But, for better or worse, they are usually consistent during the lifetime of each ruler; this may last twenty or thirty years, or even longer. However, the Indian governor generals were usually appointed for no more than five years at a time, and each new one arrived with fresh instructions from England as to how the Indian Empire was to be administered and with his own ideas, based on his character, of whether to be aggressive or passive, sympathetic to Indian history and customs and aspirations, or hostile, and above all with the expectation that, by whatever means, he would uphold the power and grandeur of Great Britain: the Raj.

This had inevitably led to a mishmash of conflicting decisions. Hardinge, the current governor general and a hero of Waterloo, had arrived only a month or so ago and had immediately managed to stabilize the spiralling Afghan situation, but had in turn got himself involved with the militant Sikhs of the Punjab, who had had the temerity – in British eyes – to refuse passage through their country to an English army bound for the relief of Kabul, and where a bloody war was clearly about to commence.

As for this poor unwanted housewife, she was, as I have

indicated, only aware that she was suddenly surrounded by an immense unease, which she herself felt in her bones.

Possibly the only person in the country *not* affected by the news from the north was my husband, except for a somewhat unpatriotic and certainly un-Christian reflection that it served the Raj jolly well right for not being more sympathetic towards his own aspirations.

That night he was in a remarkably good humour as we sat around our campfire. 'A good day's journey,' he said. 'In another two days we shall be in Indore.'

Indore was our immediate destination. But I found this difficult to accept. 'It looks further than that on the map,' I suggested.

'Ah, that is following the caravan route,' he said. 'Our new friends know of a shortcut through the hills which will save us at least two days.'

'Are you sure these men can be trusted?' I asked.

'God save me from frightened women,' he declared. 'What are you afraid of?'

I chose my reply with care. 'This alternative route will undoubtedly be more difficult.'

'Are you afraid of a little rough terrain? Pull yourself together. What you really mean is that you are afraid of these fellows. Really, my dear. There are twelve of them and twenty of us. They are not armed; we are. They are paupers; we are of the ruling elite. What is there to fear?'

The word thuggism hung on my tongue, but I sadly lacked the courage to use it. Instead I dutifully mounted my mule the next morning and took my place behind my husband. I observed that he was having an animated discussion with Lall and the leader of our 'new friends', as he described them. This fellow had, at least temporarily and for the sake of the discussion, removed his shawl from his head, exposing his features. They were not something I was ever likely to forget, for although he was quite young, he had an enormous beak of a nose and tightly pressed lips, however often he tried to smile. Lall was obviously objecting to leaving the route he knew so well but he was overruled, and a few miles farther on, where the road bifurcated, we took the path to the right. Ahead of us were some considerable hills; the caravan route penetrated these by means of various passes and valleys, which would undoubtedly add considerable time and distance to our journey. This new path led up into the hills themselves, which meant a good deal of huffing and puffing, both going up and coming down again into the next valley, but was far more direct.

It was not a route commonly used, that was obvious. We not only failed to encounter any other caravans, but also did not see a living creature – save for the vultures – nor was there any evidence that anything living had ever passed this way. But our new guides seemed to know exactly where we were going, and in the late afternoon we arrived at a rushing stream in another shallow valley. This we forded, and then climbed the slope on the other side, at the top of which, on a small tableland, we camped for the night.

The Survivor

I was utterly exhausted, so much so that I did not even wish to chat with Allia, who seemed to have a great deal on her mind. Instead, after a quick and frugal supper, I watched our tent being pitched and took myself to an early bed. As was customary when on the road, I did not completely undress or change into a night-dress but merely disrobed to my shift and lay down in this. To my weariness after another long day on the road was added the discomfort of the heat and the dust. Fortunately Mr Hammond apparently felt the same and did not come near me.

I fell into a slumber straight away, but awoke with a start. It was a very dark, moonless night, and for several seconds I could not determine what had disturbed me. Then I decided that it must be a full bladder. I threw back my blanket – however hot during the day the nights were distinctly cool – and rose to my knees. On the far side of the tent Mr Hammond was snoring gently.

I rose to my feet and moved to the canvas doorway, looking out at the darkness. I thought I saw, or perhaps felt movement, but when I looked again there was nothing, save for some rest-lessness from the line where the horses and mules were hobbled.

There was, of course, a member of our party required to be on watch during the night, and I had no wish to encounter him when on such a private mission, but as I did not see him I assumed that he was on the other side of the encampment. I therefore made my way round the tent, seeking a convenient bush. There was a clump of them only a short distance away, and somewhat farther down the slope; I went towards them, moving very slowly and carefully as I was barefooted; I had now been in India long enough to be sure that there would be no snakes in this empty wilderness, and while scorpions were to be found everywhere, one was as likely to encounter one in one's own bed as out of doors – they were an ever-present fact of life.

I rounded the bushes, crouched and lifted the skirt of my shift, and realized to my horror that I was gazing at a body lying at my feet, hitherto invisible in the gloom. I gulped, and instinctively stretched out my hand to roll the man on to his back, recognizing him as one of our people, almost certainly the watchman.

I was stunned. I could see no blood, yet his flesh was already cold. I looked this way and that, and again heard that stealthy movement. There were people all around me, awake and going about their deadly business.

Thugs!

I had no idea what to do. There was so much I needed to do, at least to give the alarm, but I had no doubt at all that to reveal myself would be to die. While I continued to crouch in an agony of fear and indecision, I heard a shout from Mr Hammond, followed by the explosion of his pistol and a ghastly choking sound.

I realized then that I was a widow. I wish I could say that I was overcome with grief but that would be to tell a lie, and however often I have been forced to lie just to survive I have never lied to myself. At that moment I was more concerned with what might be happening to Allia, and what might soon be happening to me.

Other sounds soon filled the night: cries and grunts, mostly muted. I could not doubt that very shortly the thugs would be looking for me, not finding me beside my husband. And I was alone and unarmed, and wearing only my shift.

Again I looked left and then right. There did not appear to be anyone immediately close to me. I rose to my feet, although still crouching so as not to appear above the bushes, stepped over the dead body of our guard, and made my way as quickly as I could away from the camp.

Now the ground was sloping downwards towards the stream. The stones were sharp and hurt my feet and I had to move slowly, less from the pain than the fear that if I cut or even scraped myself the thugs would be able to trace me from the bloodstains. Nor did I know how long I had before daybreak.

I reached the water, sobbing as I stumbled along, and splashed into it. Here I knelt again, scooping it up to drink as I suddenly discovered a tremendous thirst. I then paused to listen, but the sound of the rushing stream obscured all others. I realized I could see my hands in front of my face.

Desperately, I scrambled up again and out the far side. I could make out a clump of trees about a hundred yards away. I made my way towards them before checking myself; was that not where any pursuers would search?

I looked back up the hill at the encampment and thought I could discern the tents, and also movement. There were as yet no shouts to indicate that anyone had seen me, but I realized that the thugs did not shout or make any noise while going about their ghastly practice.

I found that I was panting as well as weeping, but I had every intention of surviving if it were possible. It was necessary to make a decision, so I turned back towards the stream, going beside it towards some tumbled rocks through which it bubbled. I went into the water, to these rocks, and there lay down so that only my head was showing. The water was cold enough in the dawn to have me shivering, but at least it would provide me with some sustenance if I had a long wait.

Slowly the darkness faded and to the east I saw, beyond the hills, the glow of the rising sun. From where I lay I could no longer see the camp, and for a while I had no idea what might be happening there. Then, about half an hour after full light, I saw several men at the foot of the slope, casting about and occasionally signalling to each other.

I waited, the water flowing past my cheeks and trying to get up my nose, not daring to move, while the men slowly came down to the stream and then waded across it. On the far side they paused to discuss the situation, and then, as I had suspected, they went towards the trees and indeed disappeared from view for a few minutes. Then they were back, but this time hurrying to regain the slope and their comrades. The sun was now above the hills and glaring down, and I guessed the thugs would be anxious to be far away from the scene of their crime before any other travellers happened upon it.

As I could not tell exactly what they were doing once they disappeared from my line of vision, I could do nothing more than remain where I was for the next hour. Truth be told, I hardly wanted to move. The water was soothing and my brain was only just beginning to work again. But there was nothing I dared think about until I had discovered exactly what had happened at the camp. We had been a party of twenty. It was not conceivable that nineteen of us could have been killed. It wasn't as if we had been obviously wealthy, and only two of us had been European.

I watched the sun slowly making its way higher. It was at about three quarters towards overhead, which I estimated to be after ten o'clock, before I made myself move, first rising to my knees and then standing up in the knee-deep water, my soaking shift clinging to my body but drying very rapidly when I left the stream.

I crawled on to the bank, the shift pulled up around my waist – decency or modesty hardly seemed relevant in my circumstances – and slowly made my way to the foot of the slope. There I crouched in the shelter of some bushes while I looked for any sign of movement. From here I could see some of the tents, but as far as I could make out there was no one there. Yet to stand up and expose myself required an enormous act of will; if the thugs *were* still there, waiting for me to return . . .

I drew a deep breath and stood up, prepared to take to my heels, even if I knew there was no hope of my outrunning any Indian; my feet were in any event so badly bruised I could only hobble. I must have stood there for ten minutes before I began to climb the slope, moving very slowly as before, not only because each step was so painful but because I dreaded what I was going to find at the top.

I already had some idea, for the vultures were circling and several of the huge, ugly birds were descending to caw and flutter their great wings as they searched for food. There was obviously plenty of that; the stench of death was already hanging in the air.

I reached the level ground and paused for breath, while being afraid to inhale too deeply because of the smell. Now the birds were very close, peering at me almost censoriously, as if asking, what are you doing here alive?

I went forward even more slowly. The man on whose body I had stumbled during the night had a bird sitting on his chest, pecking at his eyes. I waved my arms and it flew away, but only circling to return as soon as I had moved on. I entered the alley between the tents, looking left and right; bodies were sprawled in every direction, all very clearly dead; there was a remarkable absence of blood, yet the faces were hideous with their protruding eyes and tongues.

The mules and horses were all gone, taken by the thugs.

I reached our tent and had to brace myself before looking inside. Mr Hammond lay on his back, his face blackened and his eyes and tongue also bulging. I stood above him and realized that he, and all the others, presumably, had been strangled. The motive for this horrendous series of murders appeared to have been, very simply, robbery. Our boxes had been torn open and the contents scattered; of my clothes only one or two items remained. Our small store of money had disappeared, and with it Mr Hammond's books and papers, save for some torn scraps.

I found the fact that the tent was still standing very odd, but then reckoned that the thugs probably did not wish the fact that we had been massacred to be observable from a distance.

I returned outside, my head swinging and feeling very close to fainting. The scanty belongings of the rest of our people had also been looted. Now I was searching with a purpose; however a growing tide of sickness was building within me. I came across Lall's body, crumpled and hideous, and soon afterwards I found Allia.

Like all the others, she had been strangled, but to my great relief there was no evidence that she had been violated beforehand: her clothes were disarranged but intact. I do not know why this was such a relief to me; if one is about to be murdered does it really matter what happens to one first? Perhaps it was a second-hand relief, in the feeling that had they captured me they would merely have strangled me rather than first inflicted the rape of which I had been even more terrified.

It was now quite impossible to remain in the camp any longer.

It was coming up to noon and the heat was making the stench unbearable, while to the vultures there was now added a horde of flies, buzzing loudly in their eagerness to feast and joined by lines of no less voracious ants.

I climbed further up the hill and sat there, panting and again weeping, and becoming more and more aware of the dangers of my situation. I was alone, half-naked, in a country which was apparently empty save for those villains who had just departed. I had seen no evidence of any food left in the camp, not that I had looked very carefully, nor was I inclined to return and do so now. I could not have eaten anything anyway.

I was very thirsty again, and was prepared to return down the hill to the stream whenever I could summon the energy. But after that, what? I could not hope to survive for more than forty-eight hours, nor could I hope to protect myself from any wandering marauder, be he thug or not. As far as I could make out the thugs had taken all of our few weapons.

I almost felt that my best course would be just to lie there on that hillside and die as rapidly as possible.

But then I mentally squared my shoulders. I had survived the thugs by sheer determination to do so, as I had survived the catastrophe at Stapleton, no matter what I had had to endure. It made no sense to curl up and die now. I got to my feet, went down to the stream for a last drink, then climbed the hill again, looked at the camp for the last time, from a distance, and then set off in the direction we had been following the previous afternoon.

It would, of course, have made more sense to find some shade and wait until the heat had left the sun, but I was desperate to get as far away as I could from the stench and the dead bodies, the flies and the vultures. So I plodded on, the heat pounding on my scalp, until I fell down from a mixture of exhaustion and despair. I must have lain there for several hours, and might have lain there for ever, had I not been aroused by the sound of a shot.

My head jerked as the noise reverberated and echoed through the hills and gullies; it seemed to have come from all around me. But then there was another, and that had definitely come from behind me. From the encampment!

I scrambled to my feet and started back. The heat had now

left the sun, and I felt almost energetic. I had retraced my steps for perhaps a quarter of a mile when I checked. I had no certainty that the shots had been fired by a friend. And if the thugs had not appeared to use firearms, they were not the only robber bands roaming the Indian countryside.

Thus I stood and stared at the pass I was approaching, and beyond which I was sure lay the encampment, and watched a horseman emerge from the shadows thrown by the setting sun. My knees became weak, and I fell to them . . . and realized that the man wore the blue uniform of a Bengal Lancer.

Apparently I fainted. Certainly my memory of the next few days is totally unreal. I knew people were fussing around me. I knew that my shift was removed and I was bathed in cold water; it appeared that I had a fever and, as there was no medical unit with the patrol, this all had to be done by a pair of highly embarrassed sergeants while their men carefully looked the other way. As I had very little idea of what was going on I was not at that time the least embarrassed. Perhaps fortunately, one of the sergeants had some medical knowledge and was able to apply various salves to my torn feet and then bandage them up.

This all took place while my new escort, which was a company of soldiers attracted to the scene of the massacre by the inordinate number of vultures they could see wheeling in the sky, and having buried the dead regardless of the fact that your average Indian prefers to be cremated, proceeded on its way. Naturally, as soon as I was somewhat recovered, the commanding captain rode beside me; apart from my other ailments my feet were too painful to fit into stirrups and I was travelling in a litter between two horses.

'Captain James Dickinson,' he introduced himself. He presented a most attractive picture, at least to my eyes at that moment, his close-fitting blue uniform indicating a splendid body, while he had a handsome face, even if somewhat contorted with embarrassment: I was wearing only a blanket. 'May I ask your name?'

'I am Emma Hammond.'

'Hammond. Ah.'

I understood that if, as seemed obvious, he and his men were out of Cawnpore, he would have heard of my husband.

'One of the dead bodies we found in the encampment was that of a white man. Would it have been . . . ?'

'That was my husband, yes.'

'I am most terribly sorry.'

'Thank you.'

He digested my rather obvious lack of grief for a few moments, then ventured, 'Can you tell me what happened? Did your servants mutiny?'

I told him about the thugs but he did not seem convinced and suggested that I had not yet fully recovered my senses. I was far too exhausted to take offence, but I did understand that these good fellows, although no doubt pleased enough to have rescued me, had no idea what to do with me, and became somewhat offended themselves when I refused to elaborate my tale that I had left the camp in the middle of the night and had thus escaped the massacre. They were quite sure I had at least been raped, and refused to believe that I had not.

There was also the matter of my non-existent clothes; I spent the next few days wrapped in the blanket. Thus we came to Indore, and I was delivered into the hands of the wife of the commissioner, Mrs Caldwell.

This, at least initially, was to her delight. I was a toy, sent to relieve her boredom. She had bathed me as tenderly as if I were a babe, removed the dressings from my feet and clucked knowingly before adding some more salves but leaving them exposed, which she explained would make them heal more quickly.

But from the start she was disappointed by my lack of communication which, as with the soldiers, irritated her husband, the commissioner. Thus he had turned the matter over to the constabulary. Mrs Caldwell and the police officer listened to what I had to say with even more scepticism than Captain Dickinson, certainly when, in view of the repeated questions and the antagonism I could feel building around me, I felt called upon to expand my story.

'Thugs, you say,' the police officer remarked when I had finished. 'There 'as been no instance of thuggism for nearly ten years. We 'anged them hall.'

'Then these must have been their sons,' I retorted.

'Can you describe them to me?'

I shrugged. 'They were Indians.'

He looked to Mrs Caldwell for support.

She was determined to remain sympathetic, sure there was a

great deal more to be got out of me in the course of time. 'The poor child is still not herself,' she explained. 'You must give her time, Mr Hopkins.'

Mr Hopkins snorted and left, muttering 'T'ugs,' to himself in utter disbelief.

'Policemen,' Mrs Caldwell remarked. 'Everything must be now, to them. Now, my dear, I want you to just rest, and eat some sherbet, and tell me . . . well, anything you think I should know.'

I certainly felt like eating some sherbet; my mouth was continually dry and hot. As for my body . . . exposed to the sun as it had been for only a few hours, it was yet reddened and beginning to peal.

'That will soon fade,' Mrs Caldwell said, reassuringly. 'Now, my dear, would you like to talk about your husband? I know it must be very difficult for you, but perhaps . . .' she paused, hopefully.

'I don't even want to think about it,' I said.

She was not to be put off. 'Did you love him very much?'

'No,' I said.

She had not expected such honesty. 'You had been married for . . .?'

'Six years. And now I am a widow. Believe me, Mrs Caldwell, I am very sorry for his death. It was a horrible way to go, and it was horrible for me to see, but . . .'

'You mean you actually saw him die?'

'No, I didn't.'

'You mean, while they were murdering him, they were . . .' she paused, even more expectantly.

'I don't know what they were doing, Mrs Caldwell,' I said. 'I was not in the encampment at that time. I have explained all this.'

'Yes,' she said doubtfully. 'What will you do now?'

'I have no idea,' I said.

She wasn't too happy about that, especially as it was obvious that I was quite indigent as regards both clothes and money and, as it turned out, immediately began making plans for getting rid of me. But for the time being possessing me was a social cachet. She had her various friends round for tea so that they could look at me and make pointed remarks, because of course she couldn't actually be rid of me until I at least had something to wear, and she put her seamstresses to work to create me a wardrobe.

The ladies of Indore were not the only people interested in me. The commissioner spent a great deal of his time sitting with me and asking probing questions – if manners prevented him from ever using the word, like his wife he could not accept that I had not been raped. The local doctor came in to examine me almost every day. Unfortunately, Mr Hammond, as was his custom, had been at me on the night before the thug attack, and thus the doctor, with his knowledge of anatomy, could tell that I had recently had sexual contact and no doubt made his observations known.

And of course there were the young men of the city, both soldiers and civilians, who felt it their duty to entertain me and show me the sights. Fortunately, Captain Dickinson and his squadron had done no more than deliver me before moving on; I felt that, attractive as he might have been, the captain had seen altogether too much of me during the two days we had been thrown together – a woman is always at a disadvantage when wearing only a blanket, unless she is doing so deliberately. But there were sufficient replacements, as soon as I could be decently dressed, all anxious to show me the sights, such as they were. Indore was that rarity in India, a city that was hardly more than a hundred years old. It was situated in the heart of the land once ruled by the Maratha Prince Holkar, just north of the River Narmada, and had been created as a trading centre for the wheat-filled country with which it was surrounded. On overrunning the Holkar's lands the British had found it convenient to upgrade the town into an administrative centre and it was a thriving, bustling, but not very interesting place.

I suspect that my arrival in extreme déshabillé was about the most exciting thing that had happened there for some years, but I am afraid that I provided very little excitement for my would-be escorts. For one thing, I was a recent widow, a fact that was accentuated by the clothes Mrs Caldwell had had made for me, in which black and dowdiness were the dominating factors; she even had my bonnet dyed black, although this set off my red-brown hair rather neatly. For another, none of the young men had the slightest idea how to treat me. Like everyone else, they supposed I had been raped, but did that make me more or less approachable when it came to a flirtation?

As I regained my strength and health, the future suddenly loomed very large and somewhat grim. For six years I had given very little thought to it. As I had been married to a man I did not love and could not even like, contemplating ten years as his wife had always been too depressing. As for my situation when my ten-year exile came to an end, which was now only four years away, because I am a woman, and perhaps because I had been brought up by my parents to believe in such things as marriage vows, however forced, the idea of rebelling against my fate had no longer appealed to me; I had rebelled once, which was what had landed me in my present situation. Besides, I had sworn certain oaths I was determined to keep, and did. I had known Mr Hammond would never agree to a divorce or even a separation, and as I had been transplanted to a strange and utterly alien land, running away from him had been even less practical. Even if it could be done, there was nowhere for me to go. After the Stapleton catastrophe, compounded by the fact that I had been caught stealing which had led to my 'assault' on Mrs Houston, my father had made it plain that he had no room for me at the vicarage, now or ever. My mother had wept and hugged me, but I knew she would never oppose Father.

Well, the problem of my marriage had been resolved in a way I had never contemplated, but the more urgent consideration of my future had suddenly become immediate rather than a distant nightmare. The only possible solution to my problem seemed to be to marry again. But this was simply not on. In the first place, I had no desire to marry again; the thought of surrendering myself and my body again to a man, even one as attractive as Captain Dickinson was, at this moment, nauseating. In the second, I was quite sure none of the men to whom I was introduced in Indore had any desire to marry me: from their point of view, no matter how attractive I might be, quite apart from the rape factor, I had no money to bring to the marriage bed, and every European in India was on the lookout for a fortune.

However, aware of only the visible aspects of my situation, my poverty and undeserved reputation, Mr Caldwell, encouraged by his wife, had been beavering away on my behalf, as he saw it, and so he invited me into his office for a chat a month after my rescue.

'My dear Mrs Hammond,' he said. 'May I say that black becomes you.'

'Why, thank you, sir,' I replied. There was no risk of a flirtation here; his wife would soon have put a stop to *that*.

'Of course, the circumstances . . . but . . .' he brightened. 'You will be pleased to know that I have been in correspondence with Calcutta.'

He paused, portentously. But the only thing I knew about Calcutta was that it was the seat of British Government in India; I had never been there.

'It has taken some doing, I can tell you,' he went on as I did not show sufficient enthusiasm. 'Your husband . . . your late husband . . . well, he was not in any way accredited to the government or the Company.' Another pause.

'I understand that,' I said.

'So you will also understand that neither the government nor the Company feels that it has any responsibility towards him . . . or his family.'

'Does the government, and the Company, also feel that they have no responsibility for the safety of people who travel across the country they claim to rule?' I asked.

He glared at me. 'Your husband's murderers will be apprehended and hanged,' he assured me.

'I am sure that will be most gratifying, to my husband.'

Another glare. Then he arranged his features in a smile. 'However, as I was saying, the government, and the Company, did not, in the first instance, feel that they had any responsibility towards you, Mrs Hammond. They felt, correctly, I am sure you will agree, that your future movements and, er, upkeep, are the responsibility of the parent body of your husband's church.' Another pause.

'I'm afraid I know very little about my husband's church, Mr Caldwell,' I said. 'And certainly not where its parent body may be located.'

'Quite so. I, we, have also found it difficult to make contact with these people. I have, therefore, pursued the matter, right up to the governor general, I may say, and I am sure you will be pleased to know that I have at last obtained a judgement which I know will be a great relief to you.' Yet another pause.

I could only wait.

'This judgement is,' he went on, 'that the Company will finance your removal expenses: in the first instance, from Indore to Calcutta; in the second instance, your passage on the first available ship to England; and in the third instance, your removal expenses from the port at which you arrive to your parents' home, wherever that may be. Now, is that not most satisfactory? And, I may say, most generous.'

I stared at him.

'Are you not pleased?' he asked.

'I cannot go back to England,' I said.

He raised his eyebrows. 'You mean you do not wish to?'

I had to make an instant decision. But there was nothing for it; my position was becoming desperate. 'I mean I cannot. I will be sent to prison.'

'Why? Have you committed a crime?'

Time to start lying again; there was very little likelihood of anyone in India ever going to the trouble of ascertaining the truth. 'My husband, the Reverend Hammond, was engaged in some fraudulent activities, which is why we left England in some haste. There is a warrant out for his arrest. Unfortunately, at his bidding, I signed certain documents without realizing what they were. They turned out to be part of the fraud. And so there is a warrant out for my arrest also, should I ever return to England.'

He had assumed a formidable frown. 'You have never made this known.'

'There has been no reason for it. I did not wish to impugn my husband's reputation.'

'Remarkable,' he commented. 'You understand that you are confessing to being a criminal.'

'I was hardly more than a schoolgirl. And I was obeying my husband's wishes. We had only recently been married.'

'No doubt. Well, you will have to see what view the government takes of your situation.' Clearly he was now in a desperate hurry to get rid of me.

'You cannot send me back,' I protested again. 'You would be condemning me to prison.'

'I'm afraid you should have considered that before agreeing to assist your husband in his crime.'

'You cannot send me back,' I said again. 'I would rather die.'

His expression indicated that I had had the opportunity to do that, and rejected it. 'Now you listen to me, young woman. I had no idea that you had a criminal past. You say your husband forced you into it. If he did, I'm sorry for it, but I'm afraid that is the line anyone in your position would attempt to take. Now, I and my wife have gone to a great deal of time and trouble, and expense, to help you. I have already explained that no one in India feels responsible for you. That includes me. But I have done everything I can to assist you. I will see you safely to Calcutta and into the hands of the authorities. I will of course have to acquaint them with the facts, but I shall do so in confidence, and request them to respect that confidence to save you from embarrassment, and if possible to refrain from locking you up as there is no warrant against you here in India. But I can go no further than that. You leave tomorrow morning.'

I like to think that my later experiences have proved that I lack neither courage nor spirit, but I will admit that at that moment both all but failed me. I was sent to my room like a delinquent schoolgirl, which I suppose is how the Caldwells considered me, and told to pack my few belongings. This I did, and waited for the house to settle for the night, almost determined to flee there and then and take my chances. At what? The whole idea was absurd, but in any event when I tried the door it was locked, while I already knew that my bedroom windows were barred, ostensibly to keep out burglars.

Despite Mr Caldwell's promise I was, in effect, under arrest.

Next morning I departed in a caravan for Calcutta, being bid an effusive farewell by Mrs Caldwell. This was a large and well-guarded caravan, and any hopes I may have had of escaping from it were dashed when I discovered that I was virtually at the mercy of a gaoler, a hard-faced woman named Ross who had also lost her husband, due to fever, and was also meaning to take the ship back to England, or in her case, Scotland, to rejoin her relatives.

'I'm sure we shall get on very well,' she told me. 'As long as you behave yourself.'

Indicating that she knew all about me.

But I was already forming a plan.

It is roughly four hundred miles due east from Indore to Calcutta, and it was some three weeks before we finally descended into the valley of the mouth of the Ganges. The country through which we passed varied from cultivated fields to almost desert and some quite thick forests. We saw a variety of birds and animals, a large number of elephants and watched cows being ceremonially worshipped, as is the Hindu way; we were frightened by the occasional tiger and even more so by the great crocodiles we observed during our river crossings. The human habitations also varied from pitiably poor villages to sizeable towns and one or two cities; we were always well received by the locals. There were many old and interesting buildings, and of course a multiplicity of temples, but I was not allowed to investigate these. 'Horrid places,' Mrs Ross declared.

In her company, what should have been a fascinating journey turned into just about the longest three weeks of my life, certainly to that moment. We plodded along, through a succession of rainstorms or a scorching sun, we ladies either riding when it was fine or in one of the wagons when it was not. We sweated and suffered from prickly heat and general discomfort, while from my point of view the company was entirely lacking in the slightest levity. The younger officers of our escort showed some interest in the beginning but were rapidly put off by Mrs Ross, who reminded them not only that I was a recent widow but that I had also suffered most grievously at the hands of the natives, leaving them to decipher the true meaning of the word grievously.

I could only possess my soul in patience. And at last, we arrived in Calcutta; as I have said, during the long journey I had formed a plan of campaign. It was desperate, but then my situation was desperate.

Calcutta, the capital of British India was, like Indore, by Indian standards, a recent excrescence, having been built by the early Company traders, firstly as a fort and depot, around which the town and then city had grown. I had little time to enjoy whatever beauties it might contain, however, as Mrs Ross informed me that the ship on which we were to sail was leaving in two days' time.

'Then I must attend Government House immediately,' I said.

'Attend Government House? You? Whatever for?'

'I have an acquaintance with Lady Hardinge,' I lied. 'I cannot be in Calcutta, and leaving again so soon, without paying my respects.'

'You, have an acquaintance with Lady Hardinge?'

She clearly could not believe her ears, which was reasonable enough.

'Yes,' I said coolly. 'So if you would kindly arrange a carriage . . .'

Mrs Ross did this, as it was not part of her plan to risk antagonizing the wife of the governor general, supposing I was telling the truth. She would have accompanied me but I absolutely refused, so she contented herself with instructing the carriage driver to wait for me and bring me back directly to the hotel where we were staying.

I was of course in a state of some nerves as we entered the grounds of Government House. But if this was a most unlikely gamble, I kept reminding myself that I had nothing to lose.

I negotiated the major-domo in the front hall without difficulty; it was not his business to reject a white lady who was obviously a widow. I was thus shown up a flight of stairs into a large and airy office where there were several secretaries. One of these was a young man who greeted me courteously, directed me to a chair before his desk and inquired after my business.

'I wish to see Lady Hardinge,' I explained.

'I see. Do you have an appointment?'

'I'm afraid I do not. It is rather urgent.'

'I see. Does Lady Hardinge know you?'

Obviously to continue the lie would get me nowhere. 'We have never met.'

'Ah. Mrs Hammond, is it? Well, you see, Mrs Hammond . . .'

'But I have something very urgent to communicate to her.'

'I see. He glanced at a file on his desk, which he had extracted from a drawer. 'Would you be the widow Hammond?'

'I would have supposed that was fairly obvious.'

He raised his eyebrows at the tartness of my reply, but continued urbanely enough. 'Your husband died . . .?'

'Just over two months ago.'

'Then please accept my sympathy. Is your husband's death what you wish to see Lady Hardinge about?'

'Indirectly.'

'Well, I think you should tell me the exact reason you wish to see her ladyship.'

'I will tell Lady Hardinge.'

'Well, you see, I'm afraid that will not . . .'

There was a small commotion, with everyone in the room rising together. My interrogator glanced at the door and did likewise, so I rose also, and turned as I did, to observe that a lady had just entered the room and was chatting with the secretary nearest the door.

I estimated that she was perhaps forty years old, stout without being in the least fat, very well if quietly dressed, and with an air about her which, added to the deference shown by everyone present, left me in no doubt as to who she was.

It was necessary to act immediately. I hurried towards her.

'Here, I say,' said the man to whom I had been speaking, coming round the desk. But I had too great a start, and as no one else in the room knew my business and therefore made no attempt to stop me, I reached the governor general's wife without being interrupted.

'Milady,' I said, giving a brief curtsey.

She turned to look at me; her eyes were soft and I felt a surge of confidence. But her eyebrows were raised as she looked past me at the secretary.

'I do apologize, milady,' he said. 'This woman has been asking for an interview.'

Lady Hardinge subjected me to a quick inspection, taking in the fact that I was wearing black.

'Her name is Hammond,' the secretary continued.

'And are you a widow, Mrs Hammond?' Lady Hardinge asked.

'Of two months, milady. If I could just have a word . . .'

'I see no reason why not,' she agreed.

'But, your ladyship,' the secretary protested.

'If it so concerns you, Mr Loveridge, you may also attend. Come with me, Mrs Hammond.'

She led me along the gallery to a much smaller but more comfortably furnished room and gestured me to a settee. 'Will you take tea?'

'That would be very kind of you, milady.'

I sat down while she rang a bell. Mr Loveridge, having received a nod from his employer's wife, sat in a straight chair looking embarrassed. An Indian servant bustled in and Lady Hardinge, having commanded tea to be brought, to my surprise and great gratification seated herself beside me on the settee.

'Now,' she said. 'Tell me your problem.'

This I did, beginning with the thuggee attack and everything that had followed. Lady Hardinge listened in silence, although Mr Loveridge shifted restlessly in his seat. Tea was brought and Lady Hardinge poured. Then she said, 'What a tragic tale. Do you not agree, Mr Loveridge?'

'Certainly, milady. I should point out, however, that thuggism was eliminated, oh, several years ago now, during the terms of office of Sir Henry's predecessors.'

'I am aware of that,' Lady Hardinge said. 'At least officially. I will speak to my husband to make sure that there is no risk of any large-scale recurrence. But that will be of small solace to you, Mrs Hammond. Are you now, therefore, on your way home to England?'

I drew a deep breath. 'I am being *sent* home to England, milady.'

Once again the eyebrows arched. 'Do I understand that you do not wish to go?'

'If I return to England, milady, I shall be sent to prison.'

'Good heavens! What was your crime?'

I repeated the story I had told to Mr Caldwell. I had rehearsed this so often I was almost coming to believe it myself.

Lady Hardinge looked at Loveridge.

'Well . . .' he remarked.

She looked at me again.

'If I could be allowed to remain here,' I said.

'My dear Mrs Hammond,' she said. 'Have you friends, or relatives, in India, who could look after you?'

'I'm afraid I do not.'

'In any event,' Loveridge put in, 'we cannot be seen to be sheltering wanted criminals.'

'I am not a criminal,' I snapped. 'I acted as my husband required. Demanded. Is that a reason for me to be locked up for . . . I don't know how long?'

'It does seem harsh,' Lady Hardinge agreed.

'With respect, milady,' Loveridge said. 'Were Mrs Hammond an Indian . . .'

'She would probably be hanged. I cannot say I would be very happy about that, either. But what can we do with you, Mrs Hammond? If there is no one to look after you?'

'I can look after myself, milady. If I could be given employment . . .'

'What sort of employment?'

'Well . . . I could be an interpreter. I speak Persian and Marathi fluently.'

'Do you? Good heavens.'

'I am also studied in history and arithmetic.'

If only briefly, before my world had collapsed.

'I was trained as a schoolteacher,' I added. If one is going to lie, one should do so convincingly and on the largest possible scale. 'But I married Mr Hammond before I took up my first position.'

'A schoolmistress. Now that is very interesting. And, of course, you know the scriptures,' she suggested.

A trap?

'I have studied the Holy Bible, yes, milady.'

'You say your husband was a missionary. May I ask what society he represented?'

'Something entirely obscure, milady. To which I did not personally subscribe.'

She studied me for several seconds. She could tell that I was desperate, and I could tell that she was sympathetic. As to what she could do about it . . .

But it appeared that she had had an idea. 'You say that you would like to remain in India, and work here.'

'Yes,' I said.

'Even if the only work we could offer you might be considered . . . well . . . unusual.'

'I ask only to be allowed to support myself, milady.'

I assumed that she had some kind of missionary work in mind.

'Then tell me,' Lady Hardinge said. 'What do you know of Jhansi?'

The Offer

'Milady!' Loveridge protested, but was silenced by a glance.

'I know almost nothing of Jhansi, milady,' I said, totally mystified. 'Save that it is a native principality.'

It was actually quite close to Cawnpore, but Mr Hammond had never contemplated visiting there.

'It is situated in what is known as the Bundelkhand,' Lady Hardinge said. 'That is the large area to the south-west of Oudh which was given to the Raj by the then peshwa, some forty years ago. When, I may say, the peshwa, as leader of the Maratha Confederacy, was a far more powerful figure than he is now. However, the Raj was quite content to leave some of the component states, and in particular Jhansi, as virtually self-governing, although garrisoned by British troops, and of course we maintain a political agent there to keep an eye on things. The present rajah's name is Gangadhar Rao. I understand that he and his family have always been good friends of the Raj. He is in his forties now, and a few years ago he was so unfortunate as to lose his wife.' She smiled. 'Putting him in the same position as yourself, in reverse.'

I stared at her in consternation. She could not be suggesting . . .

She wasn't. 'Sadly,' she went on, 'he was never blessed with a son, and of course he is very concerned about the succession. He therefore determined, last year, to marry again, and this he has done to a girl who, as rani, has been named Lakshmi Bai. Her personal name is Manikarnika; I believe she was so-called after a tributary of the Ganges, which as I am sure you know is their holy river. Like the rajah, she is of course a Maratha, and she comes from Benares. Her father is a Brahmin.'

I breathed a sigh of relief, but I was still mystified.

'However, the new rani is only about to celebrate her fourteenth birthday,' Lady Hardinge went on. 'I suppose that is not exceptionally young to be married, here in India, and the rajah appears to be a very sensible and thoughtful man. He wishes his bride to be the best-educated and most complete princess in the land, and to this end he wrote to Lord Ellenborough, asking him to recommend a suitable governess to reside in Jhansi for the next five years and to teach the rani English manners and deportment, as well as completing her education. It would appear that his lordship, no doubt concerned with the many other matters attending his unexpected departure, did not find the time to reply, nor to take any action, and so this request, along with a good many other matters has, as it were, been inherited by my husband.' She paused to regard me for several seconds, while I found my head spinning quite as much as it had done when first exposed to the tropical sun.

'With respect, milady,' Loveridge said.

'Thank you, Mr Loveridge. I do not think your presence is actually required any longer, and I know how busy you are.'

Loveridge gulped, then stood up, gave me a glare, bowed to Lady Hardinge and left the room.

'Of course he has a point,' her ladyship remarked. 'I am asking a great deal of you: that you should travel alone into the heart of a Hindu community and live there for some time. However, our agent there, a Colonel Sleeman, who I understand is a very good man, will see to your safety and general well-being, and as I have mentioned, there is a garrison of native troops under British officers, as well as a sizeable business community. And as I have indicated, the rajah gives every evidence of being a cultured and indeed civilized man. But . . .' another pause.

My brain was racing. One half of it was reminding me that I never wished to get close to any Indian again for as long as I lived, and here I was being asked to go and live with one. The other half was pointing out that if I wished to remain in India I would have to be close to Indians, and that this was a golden opportunity to survive the misfortunes fate had thus far piled upon me, to disappear from the awareness of all those who would do me down, and perhaps . . . but imagination could take me no further. As for the sizeable British community, I had not the least desire to be involved with it.

'The situation has posed Sir Henry quite a conundrum,' Lady Hardinge continued. 'I understand that the pay and conditions offered are very good, but of course whoever takes up the post will have to be unmarried or a widow and, shall I say, these are thin on the ground as most ladies who are so unfortunate return to England just as soon as they can. Additionally, few ladies of good breeding are willing to contemplate isolating themselves so far from European manners and society for such a long period of time.'

Another pause, while she studied my expression. 'As I said, my husband really has been unable to come to a conclusion in this matter,' she went on. 'He has discussed it with me and we had virtually determined that the position would have to be advertised in England, when . . . well . . . would you be prepared to consider the matter?'

Because of course if I, the widow of an unpopular missionary who was also guilty – even if at second-hand – of a criminal offence, were to wander off and never be heard of again, no one was going to lose any sleep, not even this essentially pleasant lady. But did I ever want to be heard of again? My sole ambition was to be able to live, in comfort if not in luxury, beyond the reach of either the police or hypocrisy.

'I should add that should you go to Jhansi as governess to the queen, you could be beyond the reach of British justice, save unless your life were in danger.'

As they say, man, or woman, proposes, and God disposes. But, no doubt fortunately, we are not able to foresee the future. 'I do not think I need to consider the matter, milady,' I said. 'I am most grateful for the opportunity you are giving me, and I accept.'

Once again she studied me for several seconds, making me apprehensive that she might be considering that she had made a mistake. Then she said, 'I still think you need to think about it, Mrs Hammond. You must be very clear in your mind what you are taking on. I don't know much about Gangadhar Rao, but he is definitely Hindu royalty, and will require to be treated as such. As I understand it, the rani is not of royal blood, but as I mentioned, her father is a Brahmin and is chief political adviser to the brother of the Peshwa of Bithur. The peshwa was recently deposed, as you may know, and has in fact taken up residence in Benares, but he remains a wealthy and powerful man, and Moropant Tambe, the rani's father, is a man of considerable substance. How you reconcile this with being the young lady's governess may present some problems.'

'I am sure I will be able to cope, milady.'

'I am pleased with your confidence. However, the point I need to make is this: no matter how you find the situation, if you take it on you must stick it out for the contracted five years. For you to go to Jhansi on our recommendation and with our blessing, so to speak, take one look at the place and the set-up, decide you do not like it and wish to leave again would not go down very well, either in Jhansi or here in Calcutta. Jhansi, as I am sure you know, is situated on the very edge of the Company's territories in the north-west, and with this situation in the Punjab getting worse every day, not to mention the situation in Afghanistan, it is absolutely essential that we remain on the best of terms with Gangadhar Rao.'

'I understand that, milady. I shall not let you down.'

'Thank you. There is also the matter of religion. You say you did not subscribe to your husband's beliefs. May I ask to which denomination you belong?'

'I was brought up in the Anglican faith, milady.'

'Of course. Gangadhar Rao and his court, and indeed his entire country, are Hindu. I think it would be most unwise for you to attempt any proselytization.'

'I would not dream of it, milady.'

'Except in so far as you may feel it necessary to introduce the rani to Christian principles of behaviour.'

'Of course, milady.'

'I still feel these are all points you should consider very carefully. I wish you to think about them for the next week. At the end of that time your decision, whichever way it is made, will be irrevocable.'

'With respect, milady, the ship on which I am supposed to sail leaves Calcutta the day after tomorrow.'

'I will cancel your passage. If you decide that you wish to leave after all, we will find you another ship.'

She was already certain that I would not.

'Thank you, milady. There is also, unfortunately, the matter of money. I have none.'

'Dear me,' she commented. That was clearly a situation in which she had never found herself, and which she could not truly appreciate. 'Well, your hotel will be at my charge. As for pin money . . .' she went behind the desk, sat down and wrote rapidly on a sheet of paper. 'Give this to Mr Loveridge, and he will advance you five hundred rupees.'

I could not believe my ears; I had never possessed so much money at any moment of my life.

'This should be considered an advance against your salary which, as I have said, will be considerable: Jhansi is a very wealthy country. Which of course means that the rajah is a very wealthy man.' She frowned at me, tapping her teeth with her pen. 'Are those all the clothes you possess?'

'I have another gown, milady.'

'Which is also black, I assume.'

'Yes, milady.'

'May I ask where they were made?'

'Indore.'

'Ah,' she said, assuming one of her quizzical expressions; but however little she might know of the town apart from its name, she certainly knew that it was provincial. 'I will lend you the services of my own seamstress, although I quite understand that you will be required to wear mourning for some months yet.'

I would have preferred to abandon my widow's weeds immediately, but I suspected the wife of the governor general might not appreciate that attitude, so I merely said, 'I cannot possibly pay for new clothes.'

'I am sure you will be able to, soon enough,' she said. 'I look forward to hearing from you,' indicating that the interview was at an end.

I clutched my precious piece of paper and returned along the gallery to the secretaries' office. At that moment I really was not sure whether I was standing on my head or my heels; certainly I felt like bursting into song. I had been saved from catastrophe and I was being given the opportunity to make my own way. I had no idea what I was going to, but I was certain that after the last six years it would be paradise. In fact, I was already there, as I stood before Mr Loveridge's desk and laid the order in front of him.

He gazed at it then raised his head to give me one of his glares. 'Be sure your sins will find you out, Mrs Hammond,' he remarked.

'What, are you in the preaching business also?' I asked.

He paid out the money and I returned to the hotel where Mrs Ross was waiting.

'I trust you had a satisfactory meeting with Lady Hardinge?' she sneered.

I had been looking forward to this moment. 'Very satisfactory,' I said.

'And what did you talk about?'

'Me, mainly.' I sat beside her. 'I am sorry to say that we are to part company.'

'What did you say? It is my business to escort you to England.'

'But I am no longer going to England,' I pointed out.

She stared at me with her mouth open.

'Lady Hardinge has decided it would be best if I stay here,' I told her.

'You mean she does not know the facts of the case. Well, I shall put that right.'

'You would be wasting your time. And may well receive a snub into the bargain.'

Another glare, but my manner was so confident she could not doubt that I was telling the truth.

'You are an evil and deceitful woman,' she declared.

'Whose sins will no doubt find her out,' I agreed. 'But not in your company, at least.'

My triumph was complete.

The next few days were the most relaxing of my adult life. I slept late, went for walks as I chose and retired early. Just to be able to keep entirely to myself was a treat.

I went down to the docks to see the departure of the ship bearing Mrs Ross and various other people with whom I would have had to share the discomforts and the intimacies of the voyage, all the time pinching myself to be sure I was not dreaming.

The next day, an Indian seamstress presented herself at the hotel, and informed me that she had come to make me some clothes. I was delighted, not only because it revealed that Lady Hardinge was a woman of her word, but also this woman was clearly an expert, unlike the rather haphazard methods I had seen applied in Indore. She took my measurements and informed me that she would have my new clothes ready in two days' time. I became quite impatient and felt like a scarecrow when going out from the hotel wearing my ill-fitting Indore garments.

This brief period, when I found myself with the time and the mental strength to review my life and my prospects, was of great value to me. For the first time I was in a position, both mentally and physically, to attempt to determine where I had gone wrong, because I had certainly done that in attempting to rob Lord Stapleton. I knew I had been very fortunate to escape being hanged . . . even if I could not help but feel that I had expiated that crime in the arms of Mr Hammond.

I have already indicated that the six years I spent as his wife were the most tiresome purgatory. Had I been older and more experienced in the ways of the world, and of men, I would have done better. But I went to his bed a virgin, with no more ideas on sexual relations than the happy and essentially innocent romances I had read in the pages of Jane Austen. Sexual matters had never been discussed in the vicarage; this was no doubt remiss of my mother, but I suspect she refused to accept that I was old enough to be interested in such things until it was too late. The deed itself had been painful, frightening and humiliating. And although the pain and the fear had in time subsided, the humiliation was constant, in that when my husband was in the mood I was handled like a side of beef, without the slightest regard for any feelings I might have.

I would not have been human had these not crept in from time to time, but on the occasion I first tried to reveal them, with the stupid idea that we might be able to share at least one aspect of our lives, I was told that I was wanton, had the instincts of a harlot, and was not fit to be the wife of any decent man, much less a man of God. Such a chilling judgement, delivered by a man who was not only my husband but twice my age, and *was* in addition a man of God, had left me devastated as I could not but believe that he must be right.

From that moment I think I ceased to *live*, as opposed to existing. I entirely suppressed any physical or emotional desires I might have. I envied Allia for not only possessing such things but actually glorying in them, but as she belonged to a culture so far removed from mine there seemed to be no way in which I could join her.

But now I could reconsider all those imposed points of view. Obviously I was an exile from my motherland for the foreseeable future. This made me very sad, but was quite beyond my control. Then I was a widow. This is actually one of the most desirable conditions in which a woman can find herself, where she has not loved her husband. Where she has actively disliked and on occasion hated him, it was very much like having the gates of purgatory sudden thrown open to allow one a glimpse of heaven. More importantly, I was now my own woman, able, and indeed required, to make decisions and adopt points of view. I had always enjoyed doing that, even if hitherto it had had to be a very private pleasure.

At the same time, I needed to be careful. Everyone with whom I had come into contact, including Lady Hardinge herself, had been taken aback by my apparent lack of grief at my bereavement. I actually did not give a fig for the opinions of anyone *save* Lady Hardinge, but I knew I could not risk antagonizing her. If these reflections create the impression that I was a cool and somewhat calculating young woman, I would merely say that circumstances had made me so . . . and that to my ability to be cool and calculating I certainly owe my survival.

But being a handsome, not to say beautiful widow, also had its problems. My experiences with Mr Hammond had left me quite certain that I had no desire to ever get close to any man again. One of the most attractive aspects of becoming governess to a young woman who was also a queen was that such a position seemed entirely to preclude male company, at least on an intimate basis. But at this moment I was entirely surrounded by men, and women, to be sure, but whereas to the women I was an obvious source of gossip, to the men I was a possible source of amusement and even gratification, my good looks being enhanced by the knowledge that I was a widow, undoubtedly used to the requirements of the marriage bed and even, perhaps, missing them. Thus when I sat in the hotel lounge drinking tea these gentlemen, for want of a better word, would approach me to pass the time of day, one or two even inviting me to walk with them in the evenings. These invitations I declined, but there was no way I could decline the printed card I received the day before I was due to give my decision, inviting me to dinner at the governor general's residence.

Not that I had any desire to decline. On the contrary, I was delighted. That very morning the seamstress had returned with two new dresses . . . and a ballgown. I had had no idea when I could possibly wear it. Although I had certainly wanted to. It was in black like all my other clothes, but was beautifully cut, very décolletage, exposing my shoulders and the tops of my breasts, with a delicious rustle of taffeta whenever I moved.

'Madam will turn heads,' the seamstress suggested.

She was obviously in the know, as the invitation arrived an hour later. She had also been instructed to assist me in every possible way as I had no maid of my own, and returned that evening to attend to my toilette. When I went downstairs, at a time when most of the hotel guests were assembling for supper, heads did indeed turn – every one of them. I smiled graciously as I passed them and went outside to the carriage that had been sent for me. I was extremely nervous, although I endeavoured not to show it, for this was the first such function I had ever attended; no one had ever invited Mr Hammond to dinner, and even if they had I doubt he would have accepted, as he did not hold with such frivolity. But I placed my faith in Lady Hardinge, and there she was to greet me and her other guests, as we swept up the stairs to Government House, together with her husband, a bluff-looking man who wore side whiskers.

'Mrs Hammond,' he said. 'I am so very pleased to meet you. I have heard so much about you.'

This I had to accept as a compliment, to which could be added his expression as he gazed down my décolletage, I having sunk into a curtsey before him.

Lady Hardinge squeezed both my hands and kissed me on the cheek. 'You look divine,' she whispered.

The party consisted of twenty people, evenly divided as to sexes. Most were married, and apparently members of the government, but one was the Hardinges' son, a subaltern in the army, a good-looking if somewhat gauche youth.

There was just one other single lady in the throng, a young woman named Deirdre Fullerton, who was the daughter of two of the other guests, and she was certainly very young; I learned that she was not yet twenty. Her face was handsome rather than pretty, but she already had a full figure, while her crowning glory was a mass of brilliant yellow hair, presently worn up, possibly for the first time, I imagined. To match the pair of us there were two other single gentlemen, apart from the Hardinge boy, both officers in the army, and very resplendent in their uniforms.

One of these men was of some importance, to me at least. 'Allow me to present Captain James Dickinson, Fourth Bengal Lancers,' Lady Hardinge said. 'I believe he is an old acquaintance of yours.'

I was utterly taken aback and decidedly embarrassed: this man knew more of me, physically, than anyone save my late husband. And if I had thought about him since my rescue, it had been a comforting reflection that I was unlikely ever to encounter him again. And here he was, smiling at me.

Unlike the other officers, who wore red shell jackets, Captain Dickinson wore blue with masses of gold braid. He looked even more splendid than I recalled: clean-shaven with regular features, as well as being tall and well built. All in all he was an extremely handsome man.

He kissed my glove. 'It is a great pleasure to see you looking so well, Mrs Hammond.'

I might have said the same.

'Captain Dickinson,' Lady Harding said, 'is one of the officers commanding the escort of the next caravan to Camporee, which leaves on Wednesday. He has orders to detach himself and a squadron of his regiment to proceed to Jhansi, should this be required.'

She gazed at me, intently.

'I am sure that all who travel with him will be most adequately protected, milady,' I agreed, roguishly.

She seemed to be pleased.

Captain Dickinson was my partner for dinner. I went in with my hand on his arm, and had no doubt that we were the handsomest couple in the room. I wondered how old he was? I knew that without purchase one seldom attained a captaincy before one's late twenties. His manners were impeccable, but at the same time he sought information.

'Do I gather this is your first visit to Calcutta?' he asked, crumbling bread.

'Yes, it is.'

'But you told me that you have spent some time in India?'

'More than five years,' I told him. 'But I landed at Madras, and my husband and I immediately went up-country.'

'And encountered tragedy,' he said, gravely.

'After five years, yes.'

'May I offer you my deepest sympathy?'

'I think that you have already done so. But thank you.'

'And now . . . I gather you may be considering a return to the north.'

'Yes.'

We gazed at each other as he considered how best to express his feelings without offending me, and I waited with some uncertainty as to how I should reply, feeling slightly flustered under the intensity of his stare.

'I shall deem it a great honour to escort you,' he said.

The gentleman seated on my left here felt that we had been

tête-à-têting for sufficiently long and engaged me in conversation, but I felt I had made a conquest.

It would have to rank as the very first of my life, although I wondered if the conquest had not actually been made on the road from Cawnpore?

I would have liked to discover just how much Captain Dickinson knew of my background, or that part of it I had outlined to Lady Hardinge, but I had no opportunity to find out that night as the conversation remained general throughout the rest of the meal and he naturally felt it his duty to pay some attention to the lady on his right. After the meal we ladies were escorted upstairs by Lady Hardinge and I entered another world I had not previously experienced, of luxurious bedrooms, soft scents and bowing, attentive maidservants. I had no opportunity for a conversation with her ladyship either, although she smiled at me from time to time, her obvious support for me doing much to protect me from the questions and suggestions of the other ladies, every one of whom clearly had her own idea as to what had happened to me. But with her ladyship constantly changing the subject they could not probe too far.

We returned downstairs to rejoin the men, drink port, and engage in party games, the most popular being Blind Man's Bluff. I had never participated in such a rout before. Equally, I had never drunk port before. In fact, as Mr Hammond had regarded strong drink as sinful, the last time any alcohol had passed my lips had been a glass of beer provided by my father on my wedding day. I am afraid I became quite inebriated, and found myself chasing both men and women, or being chased by them, with total lack of respect for propriety, so much so that it was not yet midnight when Lady Hardinge caught up with me.

'I have ordered your carriage,' she said, softly. 'I can see that you are very tired and should seek your bed.'

One of the menservants escorted me to the door. I had hoped that perhaps Captain Dickinson might hurry to my side to say goodnight, but he did not.

I awoke to a headache and a consuming sense of catastrophe. I had misbehaved, and no doubt lost the favour of Lady Hardinge.

I lay in a wallow of misery, from which I was aroused by one of the hotel maids, who informed me that my carriage was waiting.

'To go where?' I demanded.

'I do not know, Memsahib. But it is the same carriage as last night.'

I tumbled out of bed, washed my face and brushed my teeth, dressed as hastily as I could, crammed my hat on my head and hurried down the stairs, reminding myself that if it was Lady Hardinge's equipage, I was merely being summoned to my dismissal.

Her ladyship was as calm and cool as always. 'My dear Mrs Hammond,' she said. 'How well you look.'

I could not be sure whether or not this was sarcasm.

'I feel I should apologize, milady.'

'For what?'

'I drank too much. I am not used to strong liquor.'

'Nor should you be. But to overindulge once in a while does no harm.'

I could not restrain a sigh of relief.

'Now,' she said. 'Have you come to a decision?'

'My decision was made a week ago, milady.'

'Understanding that it is irrevocable for at least five years?'

'I understand that, milady.'

'And that such considerations as marriage are also impossible for those years?'

'Am I likely to meet anyone who would wish to marry me, milady?'

'I would say that you are. Captain Dickinson was most taken with you. He told me so, after you had left the party.'

'Oh.' I could feel myself flushing.

'And you and he will obviously see a great deal of each other over the next month or so. So I must warn you again, you are committed for five years.'

'I understand, milady.'

'Very good. Now, I have made up a list of subjects on which you may find it useful to touch with the rani. I have also compiled a selection of books for you to take with you, which you will no doubt find useful. They are in English, I'm afraid.'

'I read English, milady.'

'I did not doubt it. Unfortunately, the rani does not. Nor does she speak it, so far as I am aware. You will have to translate for her.'

'Yes, milady.'

'Well, then . . . there is one thing more. I have found you a servant.'

'A servant, milady?'

'Well, you cannot take your place at court, with all the social activities I am sure that will entail, without someone to look after your clothes and your toilette.' She rang her bell. 'Ask Mrs Marjoribanks to come in, will you.'

This name was pronounced Marchbanks, no doubt for convenience, and I was relieved to discover that the woman herself appeared similarly uncomplicated. In fact I was immediately taken with her: small and dark; except for her complexion and the fact that she was very thin, she reminded me of Allia.

Like me, she was wearing black.

'Mrs Marjoribanks's husband was a sergeant in the Third Foot,' Lady Hardinge explained. 'But he has recently died of a snakebite and, like you, she has no family to which she can return. I have explained to her what you are about and she has expressed her willingness to accompany you to Jhansi and remain there for as long as you do.'

'Well, then,' I said. 'We will be friends.' I extended my hand, and after an anxious glance at her ladyship, Mrs Marjoribanks took it.

I had spoken more in hope than expectation, for it seemed to me that to suppose two people, plucked from totally different backgrounds, could become friends instantly and remain so for any length of time was being very optimistic. As for five years . . .? There were also other matters.

'How do I pay her?' I asked Lady Hardinge when we were alone again.

'Out of your remuneration from the rajah. As I have said, I am assured this will be ample.'

'But you cannot quote an amount?'

I did not wish to appear mercenary, but Mr Hammond had hovered on the brink of penury throughout our life together, and indeed my principal memory *of* that life, apart from his unwanted sexual attentions and the ghastly ending of it, was attempting to make ends meet, often without success.

'No, I cannot,' Lady Hardinge said. 'But I am certain you do not have to worry. Like all Indian rulers, the Rajah of Jhansi is rich beyond our European ability to imagine. All you have to do is please him, and I am sure you will do that.'

I frowned. 'When you say please him . . .'

'Oh, I was not talking about *that*; Colonel Sleeman reports that Gangadhar Rao is absolutely infatuated with his young wife, who is apparently exceptionally beautiful. There are also rumours . . . well, we won't go into that.'

Why not, I wanted to ask, having no idea as to what she could be referring.

'I do assure you that you have absolutely nothing to worry about,' she said again. 'Either financially or . . . well, morally. All you need to remember, and accept, is that these people have a somewhat different concept of such things. They are not Christians, you see. But how you approach these matters will lie entirely in your control,' she added, meaningfully.

'And Mrs Marjoribanks?'

'She is your servant, required to obey you in all things.'

'Suppose she doesn't? I have never had a servant before, apart from an Indian girl.'

'Who always obeyed you?'

'Well, yes, she did.'

'And if she had not?'

'Well . . . I suppose my husband would have whipped her.'

'And now you have no husband. You will have to do the whipping yourself.'

I stared at her in consternation.

'You are supposed to be a lady,' Lady Hardinge said, severely. 'You will do best by behaving like one, at all times and in all circumstances. I am sure you understand this. I will wish you every good fortune. Do please write to me from time to time; I should be very happy to hear how you are getting on.'

This I did, but she never replied, and I was never to see her again.

Mrs Marjoribanks, whose name was Annie, was even more agitated about the future than I, even if it appeared that she had never been in domestic service before, and therefore had no idea of the powers I had been given over her – not that I had the slightest idea how to use those powers, or if I should ever have the courage to do so. Equally, like everyone else, she had her own ideas about what must have happened to me at the hands of the thugs, and certainly hoped to find out.

'I don't really know any Indian gentlemen,' she confessed as we packed up and made ready for our departure. 'We only had coolies around the encampment.'

'Well, I can't honestly say that I have met any Indian *gentlemen* either,' I said.

'But you have lived in the interior. Haven't you, Mum?'

She would clearly be intensely disappointed if it turned out that I hadn't.

'I have lived in various Indian cities,' I acknowledged. 'But our dealings were mainly with the class of people you describe as coolies. We were trying to convert them to Christianity.'

'Ooh!' she commented, apparently amazed at our temerity. 'Will you be converting this rajah?'

'Definitely not,' I told her.

'Will there be any other white people in this place Jhansi?'

'I am told there are quite a few.'

Well, I knew of at least one, this Colonel Sleeman, the political agent.

'To be alone, with all the darkies,' she said. 'It frightens me. Does it frighten you?'

'No,' I said, not altogether truthfully.

'But after what happened to you . . .' she gazed at me, eyes wide.

'Those were bandits. We are going to people who wish to welcome us as friends.'

'Yes, but after what they did to you . . .'

'I think you should know, Annie, that not one of those thugs laid a finger on me, or I would not be here now. However, they did murder my husband, which is not something I enjoy recalling. I would therefore be obliged if you would not refer to the matter again.'

'Yes, Mum,' she said, docilely enough.

That evening Captain Dickinson called, and we sat together on the hotel veranda. As I did not know what he was intending, I felt somewhat apprehensive. But, as always, he was the perfect gentleman.

'All ready?' he asked.

'Indeed.'

'And looking forward to it?'

'Yes, I am.'

'I am bound to say that I find you a most courageous woman, Mrs Hammond. When I consider what you have been through . . .'

I had by now formed a plan of campaign, as developed against Mrs Marjoribanks. And much as I liked Captain Dickinson, I knew the direct approach was the only way we could possibly spend the next month together and remain friends.

'What I have been through, Mr Dickinson,' I said, 'is the murder of my husband and eighteen other people, at least one of whom was my friend. I did not see any of these murders happen, but I looked upon the dead bodies shortly afterwards. That I was not amongst them was because I was absent from the camp when the thugs attacked. They did not find me, or I would be dead. It therefore follows that they did not manage to molest me in any way.'

'My dear Mrs Hammond,' he protested. 'I did not mean to pry.'

'I am sure you did not,' I lied. 'However, I do feel it is better we talk these things out now. It was an utterly horrible experience, even from a distance, and I would be most grateful if you would not refer to it again.'

'Of course I shall not,' he said. 'My only desire is to assist you in every way possible.'

'Then I am sure we shall have a most pleasant journey,' I said.

As we did, at least in so far as travel in India can ever be pleasant. As a matter of fact, for a while on the first few days we rode beside the railway that was being constructed out of Calcutta.

'The time will soon be here,' Mr Dickinson told me, 'when we shall be able to travel from Calcutta to Delhi in the most complete comfort and safety.'

'Will the Mughal not have something to say about that?' I asked.

'I imagine he will be the first passenger,' he laughed.

Our journey was to be as comfortable as possible. The monsoon being finished, the weather was fine. We were summoned before dawn, our people struck our tents, and we were away after a hasty breakfast. We proceeded at a leisurely pace until eleven o'clock, by which time it was very hot, so we halted and partook of a midday meal while our tents were again pitched, following which we had a restful afternoon and an early night before commencing our journey again the following morning.

We were well supplied with food, drink and medicine, and on the entire journey suffered only three cases of cholera, of whom only one died. If I may appear to speak of so grave a subject with unbecoming levity, it is because in India cholera, like malaria, is an endemic fact of life, or rather, death. What causes these dread diseases is not as yet known to medical science, although I have no doubt the heat has something to do with it. However, one simply has to accept that the possibility of contracting one or the other is ever present, and whether or not one survives is God's decision. I myself had had both in my first year in the subcontinent but had survived, in my case with fortune in that even my malaria was not of the tertiary type which can persist, with recurring attacks, throughout one's entire life. Mr Hammond naturally put my recovery from both illnesses down to God's good will; I was inclined to feel that my robust constitution had at least something to do with it.

We were a very military organization, with flankers out in front and to either side, yet for all that we were travelling through the most peaceful country imaginable. But the lancers had every hope that after gaining Cawnpore they would be sent on to join the army which was being assembled to go to war with the Sikhs.

They appeared to be looking forward to this.

'Depend upon it, Mrs Hammond,' said Colonel Follett, the officer commanding the squadron, 'it is very necessary for us to assert our authority, and most definitely in the Punjab, after that Afghanistan business, and the recent trouble in Gwalior. These people respect only force. Why, it is possible to say that those scoundrels who murdered your husband only acted as they did from a false impression that our power might be fading.'

I supposed he could be right. I rode every day with three of the officers, all captains, only taking shelter in the wagons when it rained, but this was a rare occurrence as the monsoon was still a few months away. Annie preferred to ride in the wagons all the time, as she was no horsewoman.

I was forced to wear the riding habit that had been cobbled up for me in Indore, but the men still seemed to find me attractive enough, and I also wore my broad-brimmed black hat, but I made a point of changing into one of my new gowns every evening before joining the gentlemen for supper.

Of course, when travelling every day over rough country it is never possible to look one's best, and it is quite impossible to achieve a proper toilette. Annie did the best she could, but I rapidly became aware that she had an admirer, a Sergeant Warren, who kept appearing outside our tent or at the back of our wagon with various insufficient excuses. He was one of a dozen English NCOs; the remainder of the squadron were all Indian, big men with even bigger moustaches, who gloried in their blue and gold uniforms, their long lances, and the swords and carbines with which they were also armed. They looked formidable, and had a formidable reputation also.

Keeping clean was our biggest problem. Obtaining water was not difficult; India is littered with rivers and streams and we had large numbers of bearers to fetch it for us. But privacy was at a premium. The officers did their best for us by having their people erect screens so that we could at least partially conceal ourselves from prying gazes, but we never dared risk taking anything off that was not absolutely necessary, while such moments were always confounded by Annie's overwhelming fear of snakes. It appeared that she had actually seen the attack on her husband, carried out by a large reptile called a cobra – which, quite remarkably, he had been attempting to train by means of a flute – and was inclined to jump out of her skin, and certainly out of her under-garments, at the slightest rustle from the bushes.

These rustles were usually caused by lizards, and in addition to them – and the odd snake – we passed the invariable variety of flora and fauna, and the invariable groups of people but these, having quickly established that we were a military party, kept their distance, while the only tigers we were aware of were a distant roar during the nights.

We had a great deal of time to think, or at least I did. As a girl I had been regarded by my parents as possessing too forceful a character, and I had to admit that it was my perhaps unfeminine approach to most problems that had led me to theft and thus the horrendous chain of events that had followed. Devastated by what then happened, I had determined to submerge myself entirely in being Mr Hammond's wife; by the time I had realized what a mistake *that* was it had been too late – I had been cast adrift in a totally foreign environment with only my husband to lean on.

But now I had been given a second chance. If I did not seize this one I did deserve to disappear without trace. But how to make sure of it? As Lady Hardinge had suggested I should, I reasoned that as I was being employed as a memsahib I had to become one in every way; that was surely what this Gangadhar Rao would expect. Therefore, whatever my fears or apprehensions, these must never be revealed. I must present a front of forceful confidence and certainty both of my abilities and of the immense power I represented – even if I didn't, actually. Politeness, certainly, and an acknowledgement that I was dealing with people of high birth and great wealth, but allied to a determination that in matters which were my province, the schoolroom and what was taught there, I was the mistress, even regarding the girl queen. Or perhaps especially.

I felt a surge of confidence. It is a considerable blessing that the future is hidden from us.

Naturally, given the growing chemistry between us, Mr Dickinson and I gravitated towards each other. Mr Dickinson had been more or less designated my escort by Lady Hardinge, and he rapidly assumed a proprietorial air towards me, rarely leaving my side. His manners were impeccable, but inevitably there came the evening, after we had been some two weeks on the road, when he held my hand.

It was after supper and, after an evening of flowing wine and compliments, Captain Dickinson had suggested that we take a stroll after the meal. The glances exchanged by the other officers had been knowledgeable, bringing to my mind the memory of Lady Hardinge's remarks. I had therefore anticipated this and did not attempt to resist him; it was a beautiful, balmy evening and together we had strolled away from the encampment to stand on the bank of a rushing stream. We were still within sight of the other members of our party but holding hands was not a military, or even a civil, offence. At the same time I was in a quandary as to how to proceed, or permit him to do so. Handsome as he was, pleasant as he was, owing him my life as I did and my undeniable attraction to him, I remained in a mental state of what can best be described as turmoil regarding the opposite sex, and besides, there was Lady Hardinge's warning that I could permit no dallying, or at any rate, no dallying that might lead to anything serious. On the other hand, I did not wish, and I did not think I could afford, to offend him, especially as he was the officer designated actually to take me into Jhansi.

'I would like you to know that I have never enjoyed an assignment more,' he said, tentatively.

'And I have never felt in safer hands,' I assured him, telling no lie.

'As you know,' he said, 'we anticipate that the squadron will be sent on to join the regiment, which is presently brigaded with the army on the boundaries of the Punjab, as it seems that it will be necessary to teach these Sikh fellows a lesson.'

'I do understand that,' I said, not altogether liking his choice of words – common enough in the army as they were. It seemed hard that 'these Sikh fellows' should need to be taught a lesson for endeavouring to preserve the integrity of their own territory. 'I will wish you every success.' Which *was* something of a lie.

'I would like to ask,' he went on, 'supposing I were able to obtain some leave when the campaign is over, would you object if I visited you in Jhansi?'

'I would have no objection at all. But you need to remember that I am in the employ of the rajah, and I imagine it will be necessary first of all to apply to him.'

'Hm,' he said thoughtfully. 'Still, when you return to Calcutta . . .'

'Which cannot be for at least five years.'

'Hm,' he said again, now looking thoroughly dashed. 'Still, I could write to you . . .?'

'I should like that.' I said. 'And I shall reply.'

He squeezed my hand and looked longingly into my eyes. But, although tempted to do so, I would give him no further encouragement. I could not, in my circumstances.

After five weeks on the road we reached Indore, where we were entertained by the Caldwells, both of whom were decidedly taken aback to find me once again in their midst, while Mrs Caldwell, at least, was horrified to hear of my destination.

'My dear Mrs Hammond,' she said. 'I am sure this is very unwise of you.'

'May I ask why?'

'Well . . .' she flushed and drank some tea.

We were alone, save for her maidservants, and I had recently enjoyed the luxury of a hot bath.

'Please go on,' I invited.

'Well,' she said again. 'I am sure Lady Hardinge put you in the picture.'

'She assured me that the rajah is a gentleman, and totally infatuated with his child bride.'

'Hm,' she commented. 'Hm.'

'If that is not the fact of the matter, I think I am entitled to know the truth of it,' I said, determined immediately to assume my new role of memsahib.

'I don't know that it is my place to tell you anything that Lady Hardinge has not.'

'Unless you are in possession of facts which might be unknown to her ladyship.'

'Hm,' she remarked again. 'I have heard a rumour that the rani is something of a hoyden.'

'I'm not sure I know what you mean.'

'She prefers boys' games to girls'.'

I was reassured; I had been the same.

'I am sure that is but a passing phase.'

'Let us hope so. As for the rajah . . .' another portentous pause.

I recalled that Lady Hardinge had also indulged in a portentous pause when apparently about to discuss the rajah's idiosyncrasies. 'You'll be telling me next that he prefers girls' games to boys',' I said, roguishly.

She turned as red as a beetroot.

'Good heavens!' I remarked. 'But . . . he has been married before.'

'It was his duty to do so. It is his duty to have an heir, for fear of the Doctrine of Lapse.'

'I'm afraid I do not know of what you are speaking.'

'It is a form introduced by Lord Wellesley, when he was

governor general, forty years ago. It lays down that in the case of any Indian ruler who dies without a legitimate heir, his principality becomes forfeit to the Company. It was by this means that the Company's rule was extended so far and so rapidly.'

'Good heavens!' I said again. 'That sounds rather high-handed.'

'It is. But the Company has always been rather high-handed. In any event, the government in England felt Lord Wellesley was going rather too far too fast. Since his recall, the doctrine has only been invoked where there has been a real risk of the principality in question descending into anarchy. Well, you can imagine the situation were the rajah to die, leaving a fourteen-year-old widow.'

'Yes,' I agreed, feeling distinctly confused. 'But if he . . . well . . .'

'It is his duty,' Mrs Caldwell said, primly.

I wondered what the rani thought of the situation.

I began to understand many of Lady Hardinge's hints and innuendoes, and could only wish that she had felt able to spell the situation out, as it were. But would it have made any difference to my decision? I did not think so. Homosexuality was not something with which I had come into contact during my brief life; I did not actually understand what it entailed, save a preference for male company by a male. That being so, my position was even more protected; my only fear had been that the rajah might find my unusual beauty – to an Indian – too much to resist. On the other hand, there might be emotional problems ahead regarding the young queen. Turning a tomboy into a young woman I did not regard as exceptionally difficult. Overcoming any feelings of rejection she might have regarding her husband might be much more of a problem. But Mrs Caldwell's revelations only made me the more anxious to get to grips with the situation.

The next day we continued on our way north to Cawnpore. We had now accumulated extra passengers, as it were, a Mr Orr and his wife and daughter. Unusually, Mr Orr belonged neither to the Company nor the army, but was on his way to Cawnpore to join his brother, who was in business there. They were a very pleasant Scottish couple, and their daughter, a girl named Lucy who was eight years old, was a charmer.

Our route required us to traverse the country where Mr Hammond had been murdered by the thugs, although we did not pass over the exact place. I endeavoured not to think about it, and besides, I felt safe at James's side.

I do not suppose many of the residents of Cawnpore were even aware that I was back and in any event I was only there for two days before my separate caravan hurried off, containing Annie and myself, half-a-dozen bearers and servants, and twenty troopers commanded by Captain Dickinson, Annie having bidden a tearful farewell to her sergeant. I wondered if he had also offered to call upon us when he returned from the war? The Orrs had already been welcomed by their family and I did not expect ever to see them again.

We now travelled somewhat south of west, riding towards the setting sun, and the territories of the great princes Scindhia and Holkar, upholders of Maratha power for more than a century. Jhansi was situated on the north-eastern side of these principalities, abutting on the east of the Company domains and on the north-west the principality of Gwalior, the home of the Scindhia, where recently there had apparently been some trouble, although I did not know the details.

All of these lands, although officially independent, were under the control of the Company, I suspect willy-nilly, and all contained garrisons of Company troops, which in the main consisted of regiments of sepoys commanded by British officers. Thus, as may be supposed, we travelled in the most perfect safety, as no band of brigands were going to attack twenty well-armed horsemen, especially when there were other forces in the vicinity.

It was difficult to be certain when we actually entered Jhansi territory, until we came upon a fort flying both the banner of the rajah and the Union Jack. Here we were greeted most warmly by the officer commanding, Lieutenant Nott, who, it appeared, was expecting us, having been informed by courier. He and Mr Dickinson put on quite a display of territoriality, Mr Dickinson being in possession, as it were, while Mr Nott felt that he was in the position of host. Mr Dickinson had seniority, but not by much, and I endeavoured to keep the peace between them by allowing them my smiles in equal proportion.

To be truthful, I was far more interested in the country which

was to be my home for the next five years, at least, and it also
kept my mind from thoughts of my impending separation from
Captain Dickinson. It was remarkably featureless, for although it
was, on the whole, several hundred feet higher than the valley
of the Ganges through which we had passed a few weeks earlier,
it contained no very high hills, much less mountains. But it was
incredibly lush, endless wheat fields broken up and irrigated by
several rushing streams.

'At least these people will never starve,' Mr Dickinson observed.

'There have been famines,' Mr Nott countered. 'In years
when the monsoon has been weak, and the rain insufficient.
But on the whole I would agree with you. They are a fortunate
people.'

Fortunate people, I reflected, are usually happy people. And
those we encountered on the road seemed content enough; the
men were stout and amiable, the women animated and eager,
and the children cheered us and ran beside the horses for as long
as they could. These were in the villages, but we had been only
two days on the road from the fort, waved on our way by Mr
Nott, when we saw the rooftops of Jhansi city, guarded on each
side by a sizeable fort, from each of which there floated lazily in
the breeze both the Union Jack and the yellow tiger on the green
background of the rajah. And soon enough we were in the narrow
streets of the town and looking up at the royal palace, a place of
ornate decorations and castellated walls dominated by a single
high tower, above which again there floated the Jhansi standard,
this time without the accompaniment of the Union Jack and in
front of which there was a large open park. There were a considerable number of red-tuniced sepoys and some officers to be seen,
who saluted us as we passed under an archway between two wings
of the palace and came to a halt in an inner courtyard, as directed
by splendidly dressed major-domos.

I now discovered myself to be quite nervous, whereas earlier
I had been all in haste to reach my destination. I had assumed
that I would be met by a British representative, hopefully this
Colonel Sleeman himself, but there was not a white face to be
seen and, although the people of Jhansi were in no way as dark-
skinned as those in the far south, they were definitely Indian.
And now I was entirely surrounded by them, both men and
women, the men dressed in flowing robes with daggers or tulwars

thrust through their sashes, the hilts studded with precious stones, and the women wrapped in saris, which I had always considered the most indecent of garments, the material being so sheer and scanty as to reveal the legs beneath. But these too gave every evidence of wealth, with gold bangles and ornaments everywhere, some even having been passed through their nostrils, while every one wore the mark of high caste upon her forehead.

To add to my dismay, my escort was now dismissed, somewhat peremptorily. 'There are barracks for your men and accommodation for yourself in the town, Captain Sahib,' said one of the major-domos in perfect English.

'Very good.' Mr Dickinson had dismounted and stood at my side. 'I will return as soon as I am settled.'

'That will not be possible,' the major-domo said. 'The memsahib will be in the women's apartments.'

'I will need to say goodbye,' Mr Dickinson pointed out.

'That will not be possible,' the major-domo said again.

Mr Dickinson appeared likely to explode with anger, so I rested my hand on his arm. 'We are not here to quarrel,' I said. 'I at least am required to conform to their customs in every way and as rapidly as possible. We shall say our goodbyes here and now, and I will express again my unending gratitude for your protection, and your friendship.'

He gazed at me with such longing that I feared he was about to do, or say, something rash, and my breath caught in my throat. But then he seized my hand to kiss it, bringing a stir of disapproval from the people around us. 'Till we meet again,' he said.

The Hoyden

I watched him mount and lead his men out of the courtyard. My boxes had already been unloaded from the wagon, as had Annie, who was looking extremely nervous.

'Memsahib will accompany me,' said the English-speaking major-domo.

'And my woman?'

'She will go directly to your quarters.' He gave instructions in

Marathi, a language Annie only barely understood. In any event, her anxiety obviously increased.

'What is to become of me, Mum?' she cried.

'You will go to our apartment,' I told her. 'I will be with you shortly.'

She was hurried off by two of the women, followed by several men with our boxes, while I followed the major-domo along a high-ceilinged and wide hallway, which had a marble floor, drapes on the walls depicting various Indian scenes, and contained a variety of potted plants. Several chandeliers hung above our heads, the candleholders being made of . . . brass? But they glinted too much for brass, and I realized they were gold.

At the far end of the hall, where it bifurcated into two further hallways, there was a seated statue of a quite beautiful woman, naked and sensual, gazing intently before herself.

'Is this a representation of Sita?' I asked, although the woman had only two arms.

'No, Memsahib, this is Lakshmi, the goddess of beauty, fortune and prosperity.'

'Lakshmi? But . . .'

'Yes, Memsahib, Her Highness has been named after the goddess, because she is the most beautiful woman in India.'

'I see,' I said, becoming quite anxious to meet this paragon.

But first it was necessary to meet her husband.

We marched along several of these large hallways, all a glitter of gold and silver on a scale that I, as suggested by Lady Hardinge, had never suspected to exist within a single house, even if it was a palace. We passed armed guards at regular intervals, each uniformed in the green and gold of Jhansi, and several servants; these were all male, and mostly young and handsome, who bowed to me most courteously. The overwhelming impression of the palace was one of quiet; the clicking of my heels on the wooden floor was both loud and slightly embarrassing. But eventually we debouched into a large room, reached by way of an ornate archway, in which my guide indicated that I should stop and wait.

I did this, disturbed by the clash of weapons, discordant in such a peaceful situation, and looked at several men dressed in historical costumes, two of whom were engaged in swordplay. I first thought I was beholding a duel and was correspondingly

alarmed, but then I realized that their exchanges were too styl-
ized, and that they were in fact play-acting, although urged on
with shouts from the spectators.

These were all men, save for one woman who was rather tall
and wore a yellow sari which was wrapped round not only her
body but also her head, effectively concealing her features. She
had her back to us when we entered, but was apparently signalled
our presence by one of the men facing us, for she clapped her
hands and the swordplay ceased.

Then she turned to face us.

My guide murmured, 'His Highness will receive you now,
Memsahib.'

I had no idea to whom he was referring, but as he obviously
required me to advance, I did so. He stayed at my side and bowed
before the woman. 'The Memsahib Hammond, Highness.' He
spoke in Marathi.

I gave a brief curtsey, anxious to discover who this lady was
and her connection to His Highness, and was totally taken aback
when she addressed me. 'How lovely,' he said. 'Welcome to Jhansi,
Mrs Hammond.'

My head jerked, and being off-balance because of the curtsey
I nearly fell over. Not only was the voice addressing me that of
a man, but the hand which was extended to hold my arm and
restore my balance was also that of a man. He now shrugged the
sari from his head to expose his face and reveal handsome features,
somewhat aquiline, with the firm mouth and chin giving every
evidence of strength of will which, combined with the muscular
if spare physique revealed by the transparent silk, was utterly in
opposition to the suggestion *of* that silk, or the rouge on his
cheeks.

The veiled hints of Lady Hardinge and Mrs Caldwell came
back to me. And perhaps he felt some explanation was required,
for he said, 'I am Gangadhar Rao, Rajah of Jhansi. We are
rehearsing a play. One I wrote myself. Do you enjoy plays, Mrs
Hammond?'

'Yes, indeed, Your Highness,' I said, not at all sure that I would
enjoy this one.

'Good,' he said. 'Good. And you speak our language. Excellent.
Perhaps you will act in one of my plays.'

I didn't know what to make of that, so I merely bowed.

'Come,' he said, and walked in front of me, apparently not in the least concerned at leaving his apartment dressed as a woman. I looked at my guide and received a nod, so I scurried behind the rajah.

'It is very good of you,' he said over his shoulder, 'to travel all this way and into a strange land to tutor my wife. I am most grateful.'

'I shall do my best, Highness,' I said.

'You are very young.'

'I was told that you needed a schoolteacher, which was my profession before my marriage.' I did not see that he could ever find out the truth.

'That I do. But I require something more. I know it is not proper in your culture, but I would like to ask your age.'

I drew a deep breath, but again, I did not see how he could ever learn the truth. 'I am twenty-eight years old, Your Highness.'

I now felt it was time to assert my position as a memsahib. In any event I was bursting with an anxious curiosity as to my situation and my immediate future, especially his veiled and somewhat sinister reference to 'something more'. And he seemed amiable enough; or did I feel I might, at this moment, have him at a disadvantage? 'It would be to my advantage, and yours, were I to know what you wish me to achieve.'

'Yes,' he said, thoughtfully.

We rounded a corner in the interminable hallways that made up the palace and I suddenly heard several shots, accompanied by high-pitchd screaming. Oh, Lord, I thought, am I to witness an execution within an hour of my arrival?

But the rajah merely remarked, 'My wife is very energetic,' and I realized that there was another sound, overlaying the shots and the shouts, that of drumming hooves.

I was led on to a small balcony, overlooking the rear of the palace. Here the ground fell away quite sharply, down to a wide expanse of close-cut grass, which I guessed was normally used as a polo field. But today it was in the possession of a single rider, although she was watched by several appreciative and, I suspect, anxious grooms, as well as a group of girls.

Mounted astride a large horse, wearing only a dhoti, long black hair flailing in the wind, a young girl galloped round and round the field, the reins held between her teeth, and a tulwar in each hand.

*   *   *

I nearly turned tail and ran. Obviously I could not do that, and in fact the rani made an entrancing if disturbing picture. Where exactly I was to begin turning her into a well brought-up young woman was another matter.

Her husband signalled one of the waiting attendants, who blew a loud blast on his whistle. This had the effect of making the rani look up. She saw us, waved her arm and then brought her mount, which for all its size she had been controlling entirely by her knees, to a halt. As it did so, she leapt from the saddle, landing lightly, and tossed her weapons to the guards; they already held the pistols she must have recently discarded.

'She will come up,' Gangadhar Rao said, turning to look at me. 'You are shocked.'

'I . . .' I knew I was flushing. 'I am surprised, Your Highness.'

'I wanted a wife with spirit,' the rajah explained. 'Perhaps . . .' he sighed. 'She is a diamond. To me, the most valuable diamond in the world. But all diamonds require a certain amount of polishing to be revealed in their best light. Would you not agree?'

'Yes, Your Highness.'

'This is your task.'

'Yes, Your Highness.' I drew a long breath, and tried again to establish my position. 'I will need to know where my authority begins and ends.'

'The rani understands that she has much to learn. In the schoolroom your authority is absolute.'

'If my instructions are disobeyed?'

He smiled; he had very white teeth. 'What would you do in an English school?'

'In England, a disobedient young child is beaten.'

'Well, then, you have that authority.' Another smile. 'You may need assistance.'

'And outside of the schoolroom?'

'Do you require authority there also?'

'If I am right in assuming that you wish the rani to be made into a young lady, by European standards.'

He appeared to consider before saying, 'Then you have it there also. But . . .' he held up his finger. 'I wish you to report to me every evening regarding what has taken place during the day.' Once again a quick smile. 'I am sure my wife will also do that. There is another point. Our customs are different to yours. I do not expect my wife to be required to change her customs, her beliefs, her background, only to be able to present herself with advantage in a European drawing room.'

'I understand, Your Highness. May I ask, is she to be taught English?'

'Incidentally. I do not consider that important, as I doubt she will ever speak it fluently. Here she is.'

I turned to watch the rani approaching, slightly out of breath. To my great relief she had wrapped herself in an upper garment; although this was muslin and essentially sheer it provided a certain decency to her appearance. Yet I have to admit that if ever there was a girl required to be presented in the nude, Lakshmi Bai was the one. Even in extreme déshabillé, by which I mean that her hair was undressed and hanging loose down her back – but what hair, thick and long and black as midnight – and her flesh was covered in a fine sweat, she was perfectly exquisite; hardly more than five feet tall and slender, but already very obviously a woman at both groin and breast, she had superbly carved features, perhaps a shade bold, dominated by red lips that seemed to glow and by black eyes that were even more brilliant. Her colouring was a nut brown, her complexion entirely lacking in blemish. She wore no jewellery save for a pair of gold bangles, one on each ankle.

Insensibly, I curtseyed. 'Your Highness.'

'This is the lady of whom I spoke, Manu,' her husband said. 'Mrs Hammond.'

'The schoolteacher,' the rani remarked with considerable contempt. Like everyone else, including the rajah himself, she showed not the slightest concern that her husband should be dressed as a woman.

'*Your* schoolteacher,' Gangadhar Rao pointed out. 'Your governess.'

We gazed at each other.

'I am to have a bath,' Lakshmi Bai said. 'Or is that under your instruction too, Mrs Hammond?'

'I am sure that is a good idea, Your Highness,' I agreed.

'Come to me, when the rajah is finished with you,' she said, and bowed to her husband. 'Highness.'

She walked away from us to join her ladies, who had waited at the end of the corridor.

My apprehensions were growing by the moment, as perhaps Gangadhar Rao could see.

'Come with me,' he invited.

I followed him along more corridors, beginning to wonder how Annie was getting on, or indeed, would get on in these distinctly unusual surroundings – far more unusual than I had even anticipated – until we arrived at another large room which appeared to be some kind of office: there were desks all over the place, and scribes who rose to bow to their master and look curiously at me.

'Be seated,' Gangadhar Rao invited, gesturing me to a divan and then sitting beside me. 'There are financial matters. I know these are important to Europeans.'

'I am a widow, Highness. With no portion.'

'I have been told this. But you are young and beautiful.'

'Your Highness is very kind.'

'And as I understand it, by your laws you may marry again.'

'Perhaps, Highness. In the course of time. But not while I am in your employ.'

'Still, it is a future to look forward to. No Hindu widow may marry again. Down to only a few years ago, she would have had to submit to suttee. Indeed, there are places where it is still the law, despite the endeavours of the British.' Like his wife, his tone was faintly contemptuous. 'You know this custom?'

'I have heard of it,' I said, carefully.

'The British seek to put a stop to the burning of widows,' he observed, perhaps regretfully. 'So they are left to dwindle into old age, at the mercy of their husband's relatives.'

'But not a queen, surely, Highness,' I ventured.

'Certainly not if she is also a mother,' he said, and sighed.

'Her Highness is very young,' I pointed out.

'And I am very old,' he agreed, gloomily.

'You do not appear old to me, Highness,' I said.

I had intended to cheer him up, but he seemed quite overcome as he stretched out his hand and stroked a finger down my cheek. I kept still with an effort, while thinking, Oh, Lord, what have I done?

He appeared to recall himself. 'Financial matters,' he said. 'You are to remain here for five years.' He paused for confirmation.

'Yes, Highness.'

'For the length of that time, you will live in the women's

apartments of the palace, next door to the rani. The entire cost of your living here will be borne by me.'

'I have a servant, Highness.'

'She is in your charge. During your stay with us, I will pay you ten thousand rupees a year for your private use.'

I gulped. Ten thousand rupees was roughly five hundred English pounds. As with Lady Hardinge's generosity, this was more money than I had ever possessed in my life – and hers had been a loan!

'Out of that you will also meet the needs of your servant.'

'Of course, Highness.'

'And at the end of the five years, if you have completed your task and turned my Manu into a lady, I will make you a present of a lac of rupees. You know what this is?'

I licked my lips. 'A lac is one hundred thousand rupees, Highness.' Five thousand pounds! I would be a wealthy woman. Well, perhaps not by his standards, but again, by any I had ever known.

'Does that please you?'

'I am overwhelmed, Highness.'

'That pleases me. Now, as regards the tutelage of my wife, if there is anything you require that is not readily available in the palace, you have but to ask.'

'Thank you. I have brought with me some books. I hope you will not object if I make use of them.'

'English books? Written by English authors?'

'Yes, Highness.'

'Dealing with what subjects?'

'History, economics, manners and literature.'

'English history, extolling the greatness of the British Empire? English economics, extolling the wealth of Great Britain? English manners? English literature, extolling the fame of William Shakespeare?'

I had to think very quickly. 'Well, Highness,' I said, 'you have brought me here to teach the rani English manners. A knowledge of English literature is an essential part of this. As for English history and economics, this is the world in which we live here in India, is it not?'

He studied me for several seconds, then smiled. 'Intelligent as well as beautiful. That is a rare combination. You may use your books, Mrs Hammond. There is one other matter. Your clothes.'

'I am in mourning for my husband, Highness.'

'I understand this. How long ago did he die?'

'Four months.'

'Then you have mourned long enough.'

'I have no other clothes, Highness, save black. You will have to bear with me while I employ a seamstress. Perhaps you could recommend one.'

'I would have you wear the sari.'

'Highness?' I knew I was flushing.

'I think it would greatly become you. And if you feel that you should continue to mourn your husband for a while longer you will wear white, which is our colour of mourning. I think this too will enhance your beauty, especially with regard to the colour of your hair.'

This was getting rather close to the knuckle. 'I have never worn a sari,' I ventured. 'I would not know how to begin.'

'Then the rani will show you. It would be good for her to have something to teach *you*.'

I swallowed, but I supposed that within the palace walls . . . 'Am I allowed to wear Western clothes when I leave the palace?'

'Do you wish to leave the palace?'

'Well . . .'

'There is no necessity. Anything you wish will be brought to you here.'

My God, I thought, I have after all entered a prison, voluntarily, for five years. But with a lac of rupees at the end of it!

Yet it was not my nature to surrender so abjectly. My experience with Mr Hammond had made me resolve that it should not happen again, and I remembered Lady Hardinge's mention of Colonel Sleeman.

'Lady Hardinge insisted that I should call upon Colonel Sleeman.'

'Ah, Lady Hardinge,' he remarked with more contempt. 'We must not risk offending Lady Hardinge.' The contempt had grown. 'But Colonel Sleeman will call upon you here in the palace. I will arrange it. Now, Kujula will show you to your apartment.' He flicked his fingers, and one of the major-domos came forward. 'You will dine with me tonight,' the rajah said, and smiled. 'Wearing a sari.'

★　　★　　★

I was escorted by Kujula to the women's quarters. These were in a separate part of the palace, but to my relief I could see no evidence of the presence of any eunuchs, as I had feared. The zenana was secluded, certainly, and there were armed guards on the great doors, but Kujula was allowed to enter and escort me along further corridors to my apartment. These corridors were only slightly less indicative of a careless wealth than the rest of the palace, and on our way we passed several women, some moving with stately grace beneath their saris, others wearing only dhotis and in a couple of instances stark naked as they chased each other to and fro with high-pitched screams of amusement. All stopped to stare at me and to bow with hands pressed together. I returned their bows, endeavouring not to be embarrassed – they certainly weren't – while wondering if they were members of the rajah's harem. As far as I knew, all rajahs had harems, although the evidence of my eyes had suggested that Gangadhar Rao might have little use for one.

After some ten minutes of this walking Kujula parted a pair of damask curtains and showed me into a most luxurious room, full of divans and with rich drapes on the walls. I did not manage to take in anything more at the moment because waiting for me was Annie, who virtually hurled herself into my arms.

'Oh, Mum!' she cried. 'Oh, Mum!'

I allowed her to hug me, while looking past her at a young Indian woman – I estimated she was about my own age – who stood behind her. She was of average height with handsome features, and wore a sari.

'This is your servant, Vima,' Kujula said.

'And my English servant?'

Annie clung to me even tighter.

'Two servants are better than one,' Kujula said. 'Now, Memsahib, I am your servant also. I will look after you in all things. Anything you wish, you have but to ask and I will provide it. Anything you do not wish, you have but to say, and I will remove it.'

Oddly, as I looked at his round face and huge moustache, I felt very reassured. 'Thank you, Kujula,' I said, even as I wondered just how far his duties went.

He bowed. 'I await your summons, Memsahib.'

He left the room.

'What a strange place,' Annie remarked in English, regaining some of her courage as she realized she was not immediately to be sent off. 'And the expense of it.' She gestured at the inner room, separated from us by an archway in which there was the usual curtain, presently open. 'Look at the legs, Mum.'

I went forward to do as she asked. The legs of the bed were shaped as a tiger's claws and shone . . . they were made of silver, as were most of the other metal objects in the room. I endeavoured not to reveal any great wonder and turned to Vima. 'Is it possible to have something to eat? And drink?' I had no means of telling the exact time, but it was certainly approaching noon; I was actually more thirsty than hungry.

'Food will be brought, Memsahib, as soon as you have bathed.'

'I'd rather eat first.'

She looked utterly confounded. 'You cannot eat until you have bathed, Memsahib.'

'I am quite prepared to wash my hands.'

'You must bathe,' she repeated, stubbornly. And then brightened. 'Her Highness is still in the bath. Why do you not bathe with her?'

I had no idea what to do. I did not feel like a bath until after I had eaten, and I certainly did not feel like sharing one, even with the rani. But Gangadhar Rao had specifically told me that he did not wish his local customs to be interfered with, and extreme cleanliness could not be considered a vice.

'Very well,' I said. 'I shall have a bath. But alone. In here. Is that possible?'

She did not comment on my request, but said, 'The bath is immediately beneath.'

'Very good. Well . . .'

I was again uncertain as to the exact procedure, and before I knew it Vima was removing my clothing, clearly very interested in the various buttons and bows, not to mention the layer after layer of undergarments she uncovered. Having got the message, Annie joined in and within a matter of seconds I had been stripped naked before I had a chance to protest. As I may have indicated, this was not a condition to which I was accustomed in view of Mr Hammond's distaste for nudity in any form. During the few days I had been my own mistress in Calcutta after the departure of Mrs Ross, I had allowed my thoughts to roam into previously forbidden directions, but even then I had not considered wandering about the place without clothes. Yet here I was, utterly exposed.

In all honesty, once I had recovered from the initial flush of embarrassment, I had to admit that it was in fact a most delightful feeling, and even more so to be rid of all the tight restrictions in which I had been confined for so much of my life.

I waited for Vima, who had definitely taken charge of the proceedings, to wrap me in a dressing robe, but to my consternation instead of doing this she proceeded to undress herself, a simple matter as she merely unwound her sari.

'Oh, Mum,' Annie remarked.

But she showed no inclination to follow fashion, and was ignored by Vima who, when she was as naked as I, all smooth but decidedly voluptuous brown flesh, went to an inner doorway and opened it. I went towards her, carefully avoiding looking at Annie but checking again as I reached the doorway, and heard both the sound of running water and voices.

'Memsahib?' Vima invited.

I drew a deep breath and stepped through to find myself standing at the top of a flight of steep stone steps, which led down some twenty feet to the edge of a cut in the rock on which the palace was built and through which there flowed what appeared to be a stream, the water bubbling along with some force. This underground cavern was lit by flaring sconces, and I could see, at various places along the stream, which stretched out of sight to either side, young women bathing themselves. I gave a brief consideration to how clean the water might be, but reflected that it was flowing too fast for any dirt to hang around, and it was also surprisingly cold; I gasped as I stepped into it, especially as it was deeper than I had expected and came up to my thighs. Indeed, I all but fell over, but was steadied by Vima, who held my arm. Her body actually touched mine, inducing a most peculiar reaction, but again before I could gather my thoughts she was encouraging me to kneel; when I was immersed up to my shoulders, she immediately fell to washing my hair, which had remained loose. This was done with some kind of shampoo which had been waiting in an earthenware container on the bank beside the stream; these containers were placed at regular intervals. In a few moments I was half-smothered in bubbles and foam, and being made to bend while she rinsed the hair and my head; having done those she turned her attention to my body, making me stand again to get at me the more easily.

As I remained quite unable to make up my mind how to deal with this situation I accepted her caresses, and they were certainly that, as her hands slid over my breasts and buttocks and up and down my legs, a most gentle and soothing business. I was in any event distracted by the amount of interest aroused in my neighbours by my very white skin and my hair, equally so very different in colouring from their own. But now I was even more distracted by the appearance of the rani walking down the side of the stream, as naked as everyone else save for her anklets, and even more exquisite to look at than when she had been partially clothed.

She stood above me. 'You are so big,' she said.

I wasn't sure that she had intended to pay me a compliment. Certainly my breasts were bigger and my thighs a trifle wider than any of the Indian women, but I had no idea whether or not voluptuousness was considered beauty in this society.

It was necessary to reply, and equally to achieve some kind of rapprochement with her. 'And you are so beautiful, Highness.'

'Yes,' she agreed, without arrogance; it was a simple statement of fact. 'But so are you. How shall I call you?'

'My name is Emma.'

'My name is Manikarnika, but my husband calls me Manu.' I understood that that privilege did not extend to me. 'Emma. Is that to do with the Christian religion?'

'I do not think so, Highness.'

'I am glad. I do not wish to be constantly reminded of your religion. I shall call you Angel. All religions have angels, do they not?'

It was not a point worth arguing over. 'Thank you, Highness.'

Vima was now indicating that I could leave the water and I stepped out on to the bank, but if I expected to be towelled I was mistaken; the water was left to dry on my flesh. Not that this was uncomfortable, as it was extremely warm in the middle of the day, and I was almost becoming used to being naked in the company of so many other people, certainly when none of my companions seemed to find it the least bit unusual.

'When do you wish to attend me?' Manu asked.

It was time to begin asserting myself. 'I wish to eat, now,' I said. 'I will attend you when I have finished.'

She shook her head. 'It is time to pray and then to rest. I will send for you when I wish you. When I wish to learn.'

Our first crisis. I could have wished it had taken place in more private, and less indecent surroundings.

'I will attend you when I have eaten, Highness,' I repeated. 'And as soon as you have finished your devotions. This will be in order that we may decide a timetable for your lessons. Starting tomorrow.'

Her frown was quite imperious. 'I will decide when I am to have . . . lessons.'

My turn to shake my head. 'That decision is mine, Highness. As instructed by your husband. You will have lessons every day, six days a week.' I doubted the Sabbath meant anything to her, but I felt I might well need a rest.

'Do you suppose I can be given orders by a slave?' she demanded.

'No, Highness. But I am not a slave.'

She glared at me. 'You were hired by my husband.'

'That is correct, Highness. I was hired for remuneration.'

Another glare, then she turned and marched away from me, followed by several of the women. The rest looked at each other, as if uncertain about what they had just witnessed.

'It is not good, to anger the rani,' Vima ventured.

'There must be an understanding between us,' I told her, firmly.

We returned to my apartment, where Annie was waiting, more anxiously than ever, as if perhaps she had not expected to see me again. I was able to put on my own dressing robe and Vima resumed her sari, an elaborate operation as she had to wind herself into the garment, but one which I watched with great interest in view of Gangadhar's instructions. We then sat down cross-legged on the floor to eat, the food being produced quickly. Needless to say it was a curry, a large plate of vegetables, spiced but not particularly hot, and served with an equally large bowl of rice.

'What do we eat it with?' Annie inquired. She was as hungry as I.

We both looked at Vima.

'With your permission, Memsahib,' Vima said. With the two forefingers of her right hand she scooped out a neat little parcel of rice, then with the same fingers and the parcel scooped out a portion of curry to go with it and conveyed it to her mouth, sucking her fingers clean of the sauce before chewing.

Annie and I looked at each other, and I attempted to follow Vima's example. I didn't do very well, and rice and curry fell everywhere, but enough reached my mouth and Annie's when she had a go, while Vima smiled indulgently.

'His Highness wishes me to wear the sari when I dine with him this evening,' I remarked.

'The sari will become you,' Vima agreed.

'I hope so. My problem is that I do not have one.'

'I will see to it,' Vima said. 'You will wear jewellery?'

'I have no jewellery, except for my wedding ring,' I pointed out.

'You wish jewellery?'

'You mean you have some to lend me?'

'I can obtain some for you.'

I frowned. 'From where?'

'From the rani. She has much jewellery.'

'Ah. I think we'll leave that for the time being.'

A brass bowl had been provided for me to rinse my hands and mouth, and then it was time to beard the lioness in her den. I considered the matter and decided I would do best in this first instance to be as formidably alien as possible. I therefore had Annie dress me in European clothes. Vima looked on with interest, and no doubt would have helped, but she was far more adept at taking clothes off than putting them on. Eventually, I was ready. I had Annie pin up my still damp hair into a bun on the nape of my neck, but left my head bare, as I had observed that this was unusual amongst Indian women, at least within the palace.

Then we set off along the usual interminable corridors. Gangadhar Rao had said my apartment would be next door to the rani's, but it still seemed some distance away. As usual, we passed several women on the way, and as before I was an object of great interest. But when we reached the doors to the rani's apartment we found our way barred by a formidable lady, quite old with a nose like a beak and eyes to match.

'Her Highness sleeps,' this dragon announced.

'Then we shall awaken her,' I suggested.

'That is not possible. She will send for you when she is ready to receive you.'

I glared at her, almost feeling like pushing past her. But Vima held my arm.

'You cannot go against the wishes of the rani,' she said.

Here was a fine start. Because, as the rani was making it plain that she was not really interested in anything I might be able to teach her, I was being employed simply *to* go against her wishes. But as everyone appeared to be terrified of her obvious temper, and she seemed to be able to use it at will, I could do nothing without the complete support of the rajah, and although he appeared to have given me carte blanche, he had not suggested how I should continue in such circumstances.

I returned to my apartment in a fine ill humour, which was not alleviated when Vima pointed out that it was the custom of everyone in the palace, and perhaps in all of Jhansi, to sleep during the heat of the midday sun. She suggested that I do the same. I took off my outer garments and lay down, as there did not seem to be anything else to do, but I was in far too much of a seethe to sleep, and merely tossed and turned and sweated, for it was certainly hot, until we were disturbed by one of the many young girls who surrounded the rani, informing me that Her Highness was now ready to receive me.

This annoyed me all over again, as Manu seemed determined to treat me as a servant, whereas Gangadhar Rao had indicated that I was virtually to be *in loco parentis* over his bride.

'You will tell Her Highness,' I said, 'that I am unable to attend her at this time. But I would be pleased if she would attend *me*, here.'

The girl looked at Vima in consternation, and Vima was herself beginning to look anxious. But she managed a shrug as if to indicate, this has nothing to do with me.

The girl pressed her hands together, bowed, and took her leave.

'Now,' I said. 'You promised to bring me a sari to wear.'

'Of course, Memsahib.' Vima hurried off in turn.

'Oh, Mum,' Annie said. 'Do you think there will be trouble?'

'I am sure of it,' I said. 'And I intend to make it.'

I was sounding more confident than I felt. For Gangadhar Rao to feel that I was being rude to his wife and send me back to Calcutta would be a disaster; I had no doubt that Lady Hardinge would ship me back to England, and prison, without hesitation. But I was following my instincts: that the rajah, whatever his true sexual inclinations, had been very taken with me, and more, that while there could be no doubt that he, like everyone else, was afraid of the young virago, he dearly wanted her to be, to coin an English phrase, taken down a peg, and he felt that I was the woman to do it. Thus any revealed weakness on my part would be regarded by him as a failure.

Yet I will confess I was very nervous over the following half an hour, but the rani never appeared, nor did any other messenger. And at the end of that time Vima returned, accompanied by several young women, each of whom carried a sari for my approval.

This was the first time I had had the chance to examine one of these garments as opposed to observing one worn, and I am bound to say they were quite magnificent, of the softest muslin and each in a different colour, blue and yellow and green and pink and crimson.

'I am required to wear white,' I pointed out.

'I have one here.' Vima extracted the white sari from the pile.

'Very good. You had better send the others back.'

'You do not like them, Memsahib?'

'I think they are all magnificent. But as I cannot wear them . . .'

'Your mourning period will soon end, and then you can wear them as you choose.'

'I doubt I can afford them all.'

'But they are all yours. They are a gift from the rajah.'

I did my best to conceal my delighted astonishment, and then it was a matter of putting the white sari on, which caused great amusement amongst my helpers. I was naturally concerned to discover that I would not be wearing undergarments. If I had observed this lack on the Indian women, I had assumed it would not apply to me. But I quickly understood that it would have to. The material being sheer, anything bulky beneath it such as drawers, much more so a petticoat, would be very obviously, and unattractively visible, while the garment, into which I had to turn time and again as it was wrapped about me, providing as it did layer over layer, concealed, or at least adequately disguised my privies, certainly between the waist and the knee. My breasts remained somewhat exposed, in my opinion, but then so were Vima's, or any of the other women's.

It occurred to me that within the space of twenty-four hours' exposure to Jhansi manners and morals I was losing my inhibitions much quicker than I could ever have imagined, but I reminded myself that it was part of my duty to adopt as many of their customs as possible. I imagined Mr Hammond turning in his grave, and even Lady Hardinge being at least censorious, the more so as it appeared that I was not to be given shoes but was to attend the rajah barefoot. Poor Annie was struck dumb.

But I had never felt more comfortable in my life, and I began to wish that I had some jewellery to add to my ensemble. Meanwhile, there was my hair to be attended to. This was gathered in a vast chignon on the back of my head – thanks to Vima's earlier ministrations it was absolutely clean – and there secured with a variety of brooches, decorated with semi-precious stones; these were also apparently a gift from Gangadhar Rao.

One fold of the sari being carried over the head, there was no necessity for a hat or any form of headdress, and in fact it was customary for the face to be half-concealed by this fold.

The afternoon was now drawing in and it was time for me to attend the rajah. Once again feeling extremely nervous, I left my apartment to be joined by Kujula, who escorted me along the corridors to Gangadhar Rao's private dining room. I had no idea who, or what, I was going to encounter, but to my great relief, apart from the excessive wealth displayed on every side, I found myself in quite normal surroundings, at least in this part of the palace. That is to say that while there was a perfect regiment of servants, all male and eager to anticipate my every move, there was no one else present other than the rajah, and he was dressed this evening as a man, in flowing robes, to be sure, and wearing several valuable rings, while round his neck there was a gold chain from which hung a pearl as large as a pigeon's egg but unmistakably masculine; even the rouge had been removed from his cheeks.

More importantly, the rani was not to be seen, and this I had feared more than anything.

The rajah stood up to greet me. 'Now are you revealed in your true beauty,' he remarked.

'Your Highness is very kind.'

He gestured me to the end of the room where several large embroidered cushions waited on the floor. I understood I was required to sit on one of these, and realized how impossible it would have been in a dress, as it was again necessary to be cross-legged; even in a sari it was difficult enough, and having got down I was not at all sure how I was going to get back up, except via my hands and knees.

Gangadhar Rao sat opposite me, also cross-legged. 'You have admirable feet.'

'Thank you,' I said again.

He was wearing slippers.

'And have you arranged matters with the rani?' he asked.

I had no doubt this was a trap. 'Sadly, no, Your Highness. The rani and I have not been able even to arrange a meeting.'

He gazed at me for several seconds, then flicked his fingers, and sherbets were brought. Mine went a long way to salving the dryness of my throat.

'I suppose it was too much to wish, that two young women, both beautiful, both spirited, would immediately be friends,' he mused.

I held my breath; was I about to be dismissed?

'Would it offend you,' he asked, 'if I stepped in to make the necessary arrangements?'

'I would appreciate it, if by doing so you will make my task easier, Your Highness.'

'Well, then, let us see. My wife likes to indulge in her martial exercises first thing in the morning.' He glanced at me. 'Perhaps you do not approve of this.'

'It is unusual in a woman, Highness.'

'Perhaps in Europe. Perhaps even here in Hindustan amongst, shall we say, the common folk. But Lakshmi Bai is a queen, and does well to understand and enjoy arms and the thought of battle. Not,' he added, 'that I anticipate her ever having to use such skills, protected as we are by the might and authority of the John Company, but her tastes and abilities earn her the respect of our people, and this is important.'

'I understand, Highness,' I said, not altogether truthfully, while I could not help but wonder if his reference to the John Company had contained an element of sarcasm – not that I had a thought for the Company, which had done so little to help me, except in its own peculiar fashion.

'The rani then has her bath,' Gangadhar Rao went on, 'following which it is time for her devotions, then to eat, and then to rest.

The heat begins to leave the day about the ninth hour, and I would say that is an ideal time for you to commence her lessons. You would be able to use all the time until the evening meal, which is generally an hour after sunset. So here, you see, you would have something like five hours. It would be very nice if you could have the evening meal together and perhaps spend some time after it in each other's company, getting to know one another.' He frowned at my expression. 'This possible arrangement does not please you?'

'I would have reservations, Highness.'

'Tell me.'

'Well, five hours non-stop is a long time to expect anyone to concentrate sufficiently to learn.'

'How would you order it?'

'In Europe, each lesson lasts about forty-five minutes, then the subject is changed.'

'Can you not do this here?'

'Yes, Highness. But after every two lessons, three at the most, there is usually a break.'

'For how long?'

'Not less than ten minutes.'

'I think you could practise that also. I do not see that there is a problem here. You spoke of another reservation?'

'Well . . .' I drew a deep breath. 'Your suggestions fill the rani's day from dawn until past dusk.'

'It is good to fill the day.'

'Certainly, Highness. But your proposed schedule leaves no time for your wife to spend with you.'

He gazed at me.

'I understand that you may feel it is not my place to interest myself in such matters, Highness,' I said. 'But a governess is required to oversee every aspect of her charge's life.'

'Not to the extent of interfering in her relations with her husband,' he pointed out. 'When I require the company of my wife, I will send for her, and you will release her from whatever task she is performing. Does that satisfy you?'

'My arrangements are yours, Highness,' I said diplomatically. He smiled. 'Then that is settled. Shall we eat?'

The Interview

We were not required to move, our food being brought on trays by young boys who knelt beside us, the trays being held absolutely steady. As earlier, there were no utensils, but other boys held trays with golden water bowls so that we could rinse our fingers between each mouthful.

'I am afraid I am not very good at this,' I confessed when the inevitable grains of rice began to sprinkle my cushion and the floor around it.

'You are doing very well,' he said. 'Would you like a spoon?'

'No, Highness. I must learn.'

'That is an admirable point of view. Is the food too spiced for you?'

It was lamb, and certainly hotter than my lunch, but I enjoyed the taste. 'I find it very pleasant,' I said.

'Excellent. Now tell me about yourself.'

'Me, Highness?'

'Everything about you. Where and when were you born?'

'I was born in Stapleton – that is a village in Hampshire, England – on the 14 December, 1825.'

'That is in the Christian calendar,' he observed. 'But as we are required to obey this calendar, that would make you . . . twenty-four years old.'

'Yes, Highness.'

'And this Hampshire is a . . .?'

'County, Highness. England is divided into counties.'

'Is it a powerful county? Has it an army?'

'Well, no, Highness. It is a part of England, and is ruled by the government in Whitehall.'

'And is not allowed an army of its own. You mean the British conquered it.'

'Ah . . .' I searched my memory for the details on Anglo-Saxon history. 'The counties were independent states once, but they conquered each other, gradually, creating larger and larger groups, until the whole country united as England, which became Great

Britain.' I decided not to go into such complications as the Norman Conquest.

'I think that is what the British are seeking here,' he remarked. 'And then, so I am told, you married an English reverend. How did this happen?'

I had no idea how much else he had been told, but I did not consider it my business to incriminate myself, as it were. 'Mr Hammond was a friend of my father's, and he asked for my hand. He was a missionary. Someone who taught the word of God to . . .' I dared not say it, to this man, in his house, 'those who might not have heard of it.'

'The English God. Are you a very religious person?'

'It is the missionary who needs to be very religious, Highness. Not necessarily his wife.'

He regarded me for several seconds, as was his custom when I said something that required consideration, while he chewed thoughtfully. Then he asked, 'Do you approve of missionary activities?'

It was again necessary to be careful. 'The Christian Church does.'

'Because they believe that it is necessary to save the soul of the heathen Hindu.'

'Ah . . .' I licked my lips.

'What do you suppose would be the reception accorded to a Brahmin teacher who went to England and started telling people that, as Christians, they are bound for everlasting hell and that their only hope is to renounce their religion and join his?'

'Well . . . I don't suppose he would be very popular.'

'Unless he was supported by a Hindu army, which had overrun most of the country.'

'I suppose so. But . . .'

'That is impossible for you to imagine ever happening. I am sure you are right. Tell me of your husband.'

'He was a most upright man.'

'Was he older than you?'

'He was approximately twice my age.'

'And did you love him?'

I took refuge in a lie. 'It was an arranged marriage, Highness.'

'Even in those circumstances, love is possible.'

Was his tone wistful?

'I was not so blessed, Highness.'

Another studying gaze, while our plates were removed and mangoes were brought. These essentially messy fruit were carefully sliced for us by the servants, so that as little of the juice as possible spilled on either us or the carpet.

'Have you any children?' the rajah asked.

'No, Highness.'

He gave one of his sighs. 'Neither have I.'

'But with a bride who is young, strong and beautiful . . .'

'All things are possible. And then your husband was murdered, some say by thugs.'

'He was strangled, Highness, as was the rest of our caravan.'

'But not you.'

'I was absent from the camp when they struck.'

'In the middle of the night?'

'I was answering a call of nature.'

'The English,' he remarked contemptuously, 'are never able to be straightforward. You mean you were having a pee.'

'Yes, Highness. I was having a pee.'

'And they did not look for you?'

'They did, but they did not find me.'

'Then you were fortunate. But so am I. Had they found you, you would not be here now.'

He waited for a reply, but I decided against making one.

'The British agent in Jhansi, Colonel Sleeman, will be interested to hear your story,' he said. 'It is he, it is claimed, who put an end to thuggism, several years ago.'

'Oh. But . . .'

'It appears that he might be mistaken? That is very possible.' The rajah looked quite pleased at that possibility. 'He is coming to see you, tomorrow.'

'Oh,' I said again.

'Do you not wish this? This morning you indicated that you were anxious to make his acquaintance.'

'Yes,' I said. 'I am. I was just surprised.'

'Well, he cannot harm you here.'

'Should he wish to harm me, Highness?' I could not believe that Lady Hardinge would have betrayed my confidence, but I did not know who else she might have mentioned my story to.

Her husband? That would have been natural. And he might have mentioned it to an aide . . .

'Who can tell? The British spend much of their time harming people, always, they will say, in the cause of civilization, their civilization, and Christianity.'

'Have they ever harmed you?'

'No. Because I have never attempted to oppose them. Indeed, I have to thank them for my present position. My father died young, and so when my grandfather died, there was a disputed succession to the throne of Jhansi. The British supported my claim against those of my uncles, so here I am.' A quick smile. 'And thus, here you are as well.'

'But you hate them,' I said without thinking, and bit my lip.

'The British, Mrs Hammond, are a fact of life. So are disease and death, drought and disaster. These things happen. There is no use cursing them; they must be accepted until they go away again. But I did not invite you here to talk politics. I wished to talk about you, and I find what you have told me very interesting. You have had, shall I say, an unsatisfactory life, thus far. We must try to improve this.'

'Highness?' I felt distinctly uneasy.

'You speak Marathi. Do you also read it?'

'Slowly.'

'These are books which need to be read slowly.' He snapped his fingers and one of the servants, obviously previously briefed, hurried forward with a silver tray, on which there were two large volumes. 'These are for you.'

'May I?'

'I have said, these are now yours.'

Cautiously, I picked up the first book and studied the name. 'The *Kama Sutra*.'

'It is a book on love. On relations between the sexes.'

I raised my eyes to look at him, and then made to open the book.

'No,' he said. 'Do not open it here. It is a book to be read in private.'

I laid it down again and picked up the second book. '*The Perfumed Garden*.'

'That too deals with love, in a more practical way.'

'And is it also to be read in private?'

'That is best, certainly. Unless it can be shared with someone with whom you intend to share your love.'

I swallowed, quite unable to determine what might be coming next, what I *wanted* to come next.

But he merely gave one of his smiles. 'Now I think we have talked long enough. I will inform the rani what arrangements we have made for her schooling.'

I returned to my apartment in a state of some confusion on several counts. Firstly there were the relations between the rajah and his wife and the possible implications of these for myself. Of course the concept of marriage between a man of over forty and a girl of thirteen – as I understood had been the rani's age when she had come to Jhansi – would have been quite unacceptable in Europe, and certainly in England; in fact, it would have been illegal. However, if such a marriage *were* to take place, consummation would have been required to wait on puberty . . . but I had the evidence of my own eyes that Lakshmi Bai had certainly reached that. On the other hand, every other observation I had been able to make indicated that she might still be a virgin, either because the rajah still revered the memory of his first wife, or he did not wish to get that close to his Manu until, as he had put it, she had been polished or, most likely of all and most critical, his homosexual instincts prevented him having any desire for her. In view of her beauty I found this difficult to accept. But if, as Lady Hardinge had told me, he had married her simply to make sure of the succession, it was an emotion he was going to have to overcome.

I could tell myself that I would have departed Jhansi with my lac of rupees long before the situation could become critical, but I was sure that my relations with the girl queen, which had begun so badly, could improve if I could also help with her matrimonial situation . . . which might indeed be mainly responsible for the temper everyone seemed to fear. Unfortunately the rajah had specifically forbidden me to interfere in his relations with his wife.

Then there was the matter of his relations with *me*. Mr Hammond had never wasted time flirting with me, and it was a business I knew very little about. But were this Calcutta, and Gangadhar Rao a British officer, I would have felt that his interest in me was more than just passing. Why, if he was homosexual? But was he? That he enjoyed writing plays and playing the female lead and surrounding himself with pretty boys was no proof of it, however suggestive it might be. He would certainly never have encountered a woman like me before, either in appearance or colouring or background. What would happen if . . . My surroundings were clearly having an effect on my mind – Lady Hardinge had assured me this would not happen.

Perhaps the books he had given me to read might provide a clue.

'Have you ever read books like these?' I asked Vima as I was unwound for bed.

'No, Memsahib. I have never read any books. I cannot read.'

There did not seem much point in continuing *that* conversation. And my instincts warned me that the two treatises were not to be shared with Annie, at least before I had had a chance to peruse them myself.

The two maids slept in the outer room. I retired to bed by myself with a single candle, sitting up to turn the pages of the *Kama Sutra*, and gave a little gasp at the first illustration which represented a man coupling with a woman, but in what a manner! The woman was on her knees, her head resting on her forearms. Her sari, if it was a sari, was gathered about her shoulders and she was naked from the waist down. The man knelt behind her, also naked from the waist down. His buttocks were clearly depicted in the coloured drawing, but at least his member was concealed. But that he was most indecently abusing the woman seemed obvious, save for the fact that her expression, her face being turned towards the artist, was one of the most utter delight.

I almost shut the book immediately, but curiosity got the better of me and I turned some more pages, past more engravings of shocking explicitly, to reach some text on Chapter 3, which was headed On Kissing. Glancing down the page I came to a paragraph which began:

In a case of a young girl there are three sorts of kisses, viz:
The nominal kiss.
The throbbing kiss.
The touching kiss.

There were several more varieties of the kiss, but I did not read them then; I was relieved that these did not appear to be very indecent. I thus opened the second book, *The Perfumed Garden,* flicked over a few pages, which included the usual erotic engravings, and arrived at a section which began:

I have now only to mention the various movements practised during coitus, and shall describe some of them.

FIRST MOVEMENT − Neza el dela (the bucket in the well). The man and woman join in close embrace after the introduction. Then he gives a push, and withdraws a little; the woman follows him with a push and also retires. So they continue their alternate movement, keeping a proper time. Placing foot against foot, and hand against hand, they keep up the motion of a bucket in a well.

My imagination really couldn't cope with this, and when I turned the pages there were several more ways recommended, all of them quite incomprehensible to a virtual virgin like myself, whose only experience of sex had been to lie on my back with my eyes shut while my husband arranged me to his satisfaction.

I hardly slept a wink that night. It was not merely the contents of the books that were disturbing, it was the concept that everyone in Jhansi, perhaps in all of India, who could read would have read these. Gangadhar Rao, certainly. Lakshmi Bai? I had no doubt she could read. Kujula? Surely not.

But what of the British? Mr Dickinson? I would never be able to look him in the face again. Lady Hardinge? I could not believe that.

Neither could I believe that Mr Hammond ever had. If he had, he would certainly have consigned the volumes to the flames.

A brief nap shortly before dawn did not really allay my agitation, the more so as after breakfast it was necessary to have an early bath, as Vima told me that the resident was coming to see me in the middle of the morning. Bathing meant again exposing myself to all the young women − I could no longer think of them as ladies − of the palace. At least I felt that by going to the bath early I would be spared an encounter with the rani, who would still be out galloping about the polo field and waving her swords. But in fact she came in early, having no doubt been informed of my own movements, and strode along the bank of the stream, wearing as usual her dhoti and gold bangles and nothing else, as I left the water.

'You are to come to me this afternoon,' she said without preamble.

'We are to meet this afternoon, Highness,' I said, 'so that you may commence your lessons.'

She gave me one of her glares. 'See that you are not late,' she said, and walked away again.

'I do not think Her Highness likes you,' Vima suggested.

'Few pupils like their teachers,' I pointed out. 'She will like me, in time.'

She looked sceptical, and I didn't blame her.

But for the moment I was more concerned with my coming meeting with this Colonel Sleeman. How to dress? But then, how to dress as governess? In the first instance, at least, I decided to be as European as possible, and put on one of my black dresses, together with my hat, beneath which Vima and Annie pinned up my hair. Then it was a case of sitting down and waiting, and resisting the temptation to read some more of my books, until at about eleven o'clock Kujula came to inform me that Colonel Sleeman had arrived. I followed him along various corridors to a reception room which had obviously been set aside for receiving Europeans: it actually had two chairs.

The colonel was on his feet to greet me. He was a thin man of medium height, which meant that he was no taller than I, with thinning sandy hair and strong features. But he looked genial enough at the moment and squeezed my hand.

'Mrs Hammond. I had the pleasure of taking supper with Captain Dickinson last night. He speaks highly of you.'

'The captain is most kind,' I remarked, sitting down. 'Is he still here?'

Sleeman did likewise. 'He left at dawn to rejoin his regiment. You know there is to be a campaign?'

'I had heard of it. The campaigns appear to be endless.'

'Yes,' he agreed, somewhat to my surprise. 'But then, Empire is an endless business. Now tell me, have you been made comfortable?'

'Most comfortable.'

'Good. Good. And you have met the rajah?'

'I dined with him last night.'

'Did you, by Jove.' It was his turn to be surprised. 'Have you also met the rani?'

'Yes.'

'And?'

'I start on my duties this afternoon.'

'I meant, what do you think of her?'

'I cannot possibly offer an opinion until I come to know her.' And why should I give you the benefit of that opinion anyway? I wondered.

He studied me for some seconds. 'Captain Dickinson brought me despatches from Calcutta, including one from Lady Hardinge.'

I waited.

'She has outlined to me something of your background,' he went on. 'Of your claim to have been attacked by thugs.'

'I did not claim anything, Colonel,' I said. 'My husband's caravan was attacked by some men he had allowed to travel with us, and he and all our people were strangled. I was told this is the thug method.'

'Indeed it is,' he agreed. 'I have some knowledge of these people.'

'I understand it was you who *claim* to have eradicated them.'

'I thought I had,' he said without rancour. 'I look forward to hearing the outcome of this affair. I am very sorry about what happened to your husband and am only glad that you managed to survive. However, I am sure the event will have taught you that it is a very risky business to trust an Indian.'

I glanced at the servants waiting by the door. But we were speaking English.

'Those men were bandits.'

'They were Indians,' he insisted. 'And I think you would find, if questioned in one of their bazaars, that the average Indian would regard them as patriots, engaged in ridding Hindustan of the hated feringee. This hatred of us permeates Indian society from the lowest to the highest.'

Of course he was right; I recalled my conversation with Gangadhar Rao. But I could not resist saying, 'Are they not correct in regarding the British as usurpers, and indeed robbers on a scale which makes those thugs or whatever look like amateurs?'

'That is a point of view. The fact is that we are here, and we intend to stay here, against all the odds, which are quite tremendous. To do this we need, all of us, to concentrate our minds, and to play our parts, in the maintenance of the Raj.'

'I am sure you are right, Colonel,' I said, agreeably. 'However, I do not feel I have anything to offer in that regard. I am here to tutor the queen in English ways. I am sure you approve of that.'

'You have placed your finger on the nub of the matter. You may hold the future of central India in your hand. How the rani develops may be of vital importance to us all.'

'A fourteen-year-old girl?'

'Who in a very short space of time will become a twenty-four-year-old woman, and in another very short space of time may become a thirty-four-year-old dowager. She is thirty years younger than her husband.'

'You are looking very far ahead,' I suggested.

'It is my business to do so.'

'I am sure you are right, Colonel, but I really cannot see that the attitude of a woman towards the Raj can have the slightest effect, for either good or bad.'

'I recommend you study Indian history, Mrs Hammond. Learn about women like Akkadevi, who commanded large Chalukya armies in the eleventh century, or Umadevi, who led the Hoysala forces a hundred years later. But you need go back no further than two or three years. Do you not remember that only two years ago we had to take strong action in Gwalior, just across the border from Jhansi?'

'I heard something about it.'

'Then let me remind you. Two years ago the Maharajah of Gwalior, Dowlut Rao Scindhia, died. He left no son, but it was agreed that a nephew, Jyajee Rao Scindhia, should succeed. As this boy was but eight years old, it was further agreed that the widowed Maharani, Tara Bai, a very young woman, should act as regent, with one of our own appointees as her chief minister. Within a couple of months the queen had quarrelled with our man, Mama Sahib, driven him from office, forcibly expelled our resident, and assumed total independence. It took an army and a campaign to reduce her to obedience.'

'You would not say that she was within her rights to wish to run her own affairs?'

'The affairs of Gwalior are our affairs,' he snapped. 'Before then there was the business in Kolapur, when again the widowed Maharani sought to take over the government. Another campaign and much bloodshed. And perhaps you are unaware that the Sikhs, against whom we are about to launch a campaign, are also being controlled and encouraged by a widowed rani. All the evidence indicates that Indian women, at least where they are of noble blood, are far more formidable than their menfolk. Now, this Manikarnika already has a built-in hostility to the Raj. Her father works for the brother of the Peshwa of Bithur.'

I nodded. 'Lady Hardinge gave me her background.'

'Then I assume she also told you that a few years ago we found it necessary to depose the peshwa for incompetence and dishonesty.'

'She didn't tell me why we, I mean the Company, had done this.'

'I should have thought that would have been obvious. However, the point is, the peshwa would not be human if he did not resent this, or did not pass on his resentment to his brother and his chief minister, and him to his children, and especially his daughter, who I understand is a somewhat strong-willed young woman, already deeply interested in military affairs.'

'Yes,' I said, thoughtfully.

'So you will understand that it is your duty to educate your charge into a proper frame of mind.'

My charge! He had clearly never met the rani. 'I understand that it is my duty to educate her,' I agreed.

He did not pick up my abbreviated response, or he preferred not to. 'In this regard,' he went on, 'the rajah's decision to seek an English governess is a bit of a godsend. But I must tell you, Mrs Hammond, that we have our suspicions regarding this gentleman as well. My predecessors assisted him to his throne, on the basis that he was the lesser of several evils, but I happen to know that he corresponded with the Maharani of Gwalior during her rebellion. It was decided not to take that matter any further, but I would be grateful if you, with your privileged position inside this palace, would keep me informed as to attitudes, and indeed, comings and goings, in the rajah's household.'

'Do I understand that you are asking me to be your spy?'

'That is rather an extreme way of putting it. You are here as an agent of the Company, and therefore, by definition, of the government of British India. Your duties in this regard are perfectly straightforward: they are to do everything in your power to maintain the Raj. And the best ways of doing that are firstly, by educating their leading people into an understanding of the inevitability of our position, and therefore theirs, and secondly, by obtaining and forwarding all possible knowledge of their opinions and therefore their intentions.'

Another pause, to gaze at me.

'Lady Hardinge mentioned nothing of this to me,' I pointed out.

'Well, when she gave you this appointment, she had only been in India a few weeks, and possibly did not herself yet understand the situation. Had she been here longer, well . . . I am sure she made a very good choice.'

I was becoming increasingly irritated by his arrogant assumption of superiority. 'You mean, had she been here longer she would have chosen someone else instead of me. The fact is, Colonel Sleeman, you have been quite misinformed. Lady Hardinge gave me, as you put it, this appointment simply because she could find no one else willing to take it on. And the only instructions she gave me were to do all in my power to maintain the good relations that she said existed between the Company and the Rajah of Jhansi. She certainly did not have spying on him in mind, nor did I.'

'Yes. Well, as I said, she was still finding her feet, shall we say. I am now expanding her instructions.'

'I am sorry, Colonel. I do not wish my instructions to be expanded.'

'My dear Mrs Hammond,' he said, in what he no doubt felt was a very reasonable and placatory tone of voice, 'your wishes do not enter into the matter. You are a servant of the Company. I am a servant of the Company, and in this regard, as I am its agent here in Jhansi, I am your superior. You are also a servant of Great Britain, as am I, and here again, as representative of the governor general and . . .' he permitted himself a smile, 'his lady, I am even more your superior. In this respect, I have given you certain instructions, which I expect to be carried out. I hope I have made myself clear. I would not like there to be any misunderstanding on this point.'

'You have made yourself admirably clear, Colonel,' I agreed. 'However, as to there being a misunderstanding between us, your entire premise is based on one.'

He frowned at me.

'In the first place, I am not, and never have been, a servant of the Company,' I told him. 'Neither was my husband. After his death the Company's only interest in me was to treat me as virtually a prisoner and inform me that I would be shipped back to England as soon as it could be arranged. I went to Lady Hardinge in search of employment as I did not wish to leave India. She suggested I take up this position, mainly because, as I have said, she could find no one else to do so and she did not wish to offend the rajah. There was no suggestion that I needed to become an employee of the Company. I now regard myself as an employee of the rajah, and I would consider it extremely disloyal for me to relay to you, or anyone else, any observations I may make on his attitudes, and even more, on any actions he may undertake.'

Sleeman snorted. 'Perhaps I should remind you, Mrs Hammond, that should circumstances ever arise in which the rajah, or his widow, considered it necessary to oppose the will of the Raj, and possessing foreknowledge of this, you did not inform an agent of the government, you could be considered guilty of treason.'

'Against the British Government?' I was by now thoroughly irritated. 'I owe no allegiance to that government, Colonel Sleeman.'

'My dear Mrs Hammond, one does not select one's allegiance as one might select a bolt of cloth in a shop. One is born to it, and retains it, throughout one's life.'

'Absolutely,' I said. 'However, I have equally been rejected by the British Government.'

'For what reason?'

'That is my business.'

'I'm afraid your business is my business.'

'I'm afraid I cannot agree with you.'

He gave me an imperious stare. 'You mean that you have been given this position under false pretences.'

'I am sorry to disappoint you, Colonel Sleeman. I was given this position *after* Lady Hardinge became fully aware of my situation.' Which was of course untrue, but I was determined not to become a Company spy, and I did not think Lady Hardinge would let me down.

'You are telling me that you refuse to assist the Raj?'

'If it means betraying my employer, yes. Even women can have a sense of honour, Colonel.'

The stare became a glare. 'You realize that I will have to report this point of view to my superiors?'

'I am sure that you will.'

'And that they may well classify you as an Indian sympathizer.'

'As that happens to be true, that is a risk I shall have to take.'

He studied me for some minutes longer. Then he said, 'I may also have to classify you as a very dangerous young woman.'

'You are entitled to your opinion,' I conceded.

'Well,' he said. 'I have never in all my life been so . . . well, confounded, madam.'

'I am sorry. We must all act as our conscience dictates.'

He stood up. 'You may very well come to regret this absurd stance you have taken.'

I bowed my head.

The Rajah

I understood that I had made a regrettable enemy, and one who could prove formidable. It was necessary to determine what harm he could do me, and this seemed obvious: he would recommend to the governor general that I be recalled and thus expelled from India, and in these circumstances I did not feel that I could rely even on the goodwill of Lady Hardinge. The only support I could hope for would be from Gangadhar Rao himself, and that would depend upon how much he had come to value my services before any communication could travel to Calcutta and a reply be received – I reckoned that gave me at least a month, possibly longer unless the mails travelled a good deal faster than the average caravan.

But there were other imponderables. Presumably the rajah would be pleased to know that I had turned down the demand that I spy on him, but that would not be sufficient if I did not prove a success with his Manu. It was quite a decision. Go to him now, and risk my relations with Manu later, or take on Manu first and hope to have accomplished something before the dread summons arrived from Calcutta?

It was not something I could discuss with anyone: to acquaint

Annie with the situation would be a disaster. So I wrestled with my problem and determined to risk Manu first.

Our lessons were due to begin that afternoon. The ninth hour of the day approximated our three o'clock so, having spent the day since Sleeman's angry departure resting and preparing myself as best I could, for I was both agitated by the morning's events and apprehensive of the possible afternoon's, at the appointed hour I had Kujula escort me to the schoolroom, as I did not know where it was. I dressed as earlier in European clothes, one of my black gowns, my hair pinned up, and wore my hat.

The schoolroom turned out to be one of the large, empty rooms that marked this palace; on one side great open windows looked out over the polo ground and the rolling hills beyond, and through which there drifted a very acceptable breeze, although even this was warm; on the other the high archway through which I had entered gave access to the hall along which I had come. To my dismay I realized there were no doors, nor even drapes, so I would be carrying out my duties exposed to the gaze of anyone who happened, or chose, to pass by. Kujula, indeed, did not leave me, but merely retired to the first corner of the corridor and stood there with his arms folded. But, as always, his presence, the suggestion that he might repel any curiosity seekers, was reassuring.

The room itself, as I have said, was largely empty, save for the rich drapes on the inner walls, constantly rustling in the breeze. But Gangadhar Rao had clearly studied Western methods, for in the centre of the vast expanse of floor there had been placed two tables, the wood richly carved, and before each, facing each other, was a chair. Significantly, on one of the tables there lay a three-foot length of thin cane. My heart pounded; it could only have been placed there by order of the rajah.

Kujula had brought my books, and these I had had him place on the table facing the archway, so that I might see anyone who approached. My pupil would have her back to the archway. But for the moment I was the only person in the room.

I sat behind my table and waited for some considerable time, feeling a growing mixture of anger and despair, before I heard the sound of chattering voices, and a few moments later several girls came round the corner by Kujula, who bowed before them.

I remained seated, hands clasped before me, and indeed the

gaggle stopped at the sight of me and for a moment looked quite startled. I imagine I presented a formidable figure in my black dress, with my hair severely knotted on the back of my head.

'You are late,' I remarked, as the rani advanced towards me, her companions close behind her. They were dressed in various stages of what had best be described as déshabillé, in that most of them wore dhotis and nothing else, although Manu had added a sort of tunic. Her hair was loose, as was that of her companions.

'We overslept,' she said.

'Well, please do not let it happen again,' I told her, determined to keep a sense of perspective and thus not lose my temper. 'Now kindly dismiss your attendants.'

'I am never without my women,' she announced.

'In here you will be. I have come to teach you, not the entire palace.'

We gazed at each other, while I prayed that she would not openly oppose me again, at least this early in our relationship. But this was clearly what she had come here to do.

'My women will remain,' she said. 'I have decided this.'

'And I have said they will not. If you will not send them away, if you disobey me, I will have to punish you. Would you have me do it in front of them?'

She tilted her chin. 'You, will punish me? I am the Rani of Jhansi.'

'And I have been instructed by the rajah.'

We glared at each other, and I picked up the cane.

'If you touch me with that,' Manu said, 'I will have you staked out on an ant hill.'

'I should warn you that your husband has given me full authority, Your Highness. Education can only be based upon discipline. I must have that if you are to be taught.'

I found I was holding my breath.

'I will hear that from the rajah's own lips,' Manu said and, turning, left the room, her gaggling girls following behind her. Kujula looked at me for instruction and I was tempted to tell him to stop the rani, but I had no certainty that he would obey me in such an irrevocable command, nor did I know what the reaction of Manu's girls might be. If they were to defend their mistress we would have a most unseemly fracas.

I had to put my faith in Gangadhar Rao's word, and so I followed them, Kujula following me, obviously very alarmed. We ranged through the corridors of the palace, Manu still out in front, silent but panting slightly, her features set and angry. Her girls were commencing to chatter again, looking over their shoulders at me. I assumed that my features were also set and angry – I certainly intended that they should be. And behind me came the unhappy Kujula.

As our procession passed other rooms, other women emerged to watch our progress, amongst them Vima and Annie, both looking terrified. In the main part of the palace the guards looked thunderstruck, and at the archway to the rajah's apartments a major-domo stood in front of us.

'His Highness cannot be disturbed, Your Highness,' he said.

'Get out of my way, lout,' Manu told him.

He obeyed, like everyone else, looking terrified.

Manu marched past him and we followed her. More major-domos, secretaries and guards appeared, but none had the courage to attempt to stop the rani, who clearly knew exactly where she was going. Thus we arrived before an inner archway, but this one was curtained, and guarded by two soldiers.

Here at last was opposition. 'His Highness rests, Your Highness,' one of the guards said. 'No one may enter.'

'I wish to speak with my husband,' the rani declared, loudly. 'I will speak with him.'

Everyone hesitated, then the curtain was jerked aside and the rajah appeared, closing the curtain behind himself. He wore a loose robe, and nothing else that I could see, and was definitely in a state of some arousal. I was totally taken aback: I had never actually seen a man's member before. And what a member – princely in every aspect. I wonder I did not faint.

The rajah also looked somewhat put out, which I suppose was natural. 'What is the meaning of this disturbance?' he demanded, looking at his wife.

'That woman has threatened to beat me,' Manu announced, half-turning and throwing out her arm to point at me, while I realized to my consternation that in all the kerfuffle I was still holding the cane.

Gangadhar Rao was also looking at me, and still looking at least irritated. 'I gave you instructions,' he said.

'Her Highness refused to accept them, Your Highness,' I said. 'And she was supported by these . . . ladies.'

The rajah looked from his wife to me. 'What is the cause of the trouble?'

'I requested Her Highness to dismiss her ladies before we commenced our lessons and she refused.'

'You do not wish my wife's women to be present?' he asked, apparently determined to get his facts exactly right.

'Learning is a business of concentrating, Your Highness. These girls are a distraction. They will not keep still, they will not keep quiet.'

I had no proof that they would behave like that in the school-room, but as it was their usual mode of conduct I felt I had a valid point.

So apparently did the rajah, who bent a gaze upon the girls that had them trembling; certainly they were quiet at the moment.

'I think Mrs Hammond is right,' Gangadhar Rao said.

'How may a queen not be attended?' Manu demanded.

'You would be attended, by Mrs Hammond,' Gangadhar pointed out.

'Ha!'

'Your girls can wait in an adjacent room.'

'Ha!'

'So, now, leave me,' the rajah commanded, clearly anxious to get back behind his curtain.

But I conceived that, at the moment, anyway, I was on a winning roll and this was a matter that had to be resolved now.

'There remains the matter of discipline, Your Highness.'

Gangadhar sighed. 'I have given you the necessary authority.'

'Her Highness does not know this. Or will not accept it. She has threatened me with execution if I touch her.'

'Execution?'

'She says she would have me staked out on an ant hill.'

Gangadhar turned to his wife. 'Did you really threaten that?'

'I was angry,' Manu said, sulkily.

'Nonetheless, it is a fascinating thought.'

I gulped. I could not yet tell when this man was joking and when he was not.

'You must promise not to think it again,' the rajah said.

'Then she must promise not to beat me.'

Gangadhar looked as if he might scratch his head.

But, whatever the risk, for me to surrender now would indeed reduce me to the level of a servant.

'I must have the right to discipline my pupil, Highness. We have agreed on this.'

'Yes,' he said, to my great relief.

'You cannot permit it,' Manu protested.

'When Mrs Hammond is acting in her capacity as your governess, you must look on her as your mother, entitled to do whatever she sees fit.'

'I shall not,' Manu declared. 'Shall not, shall not, shall not. I am the queen.'

Gangadhar looked at me. I did my best to stand still and keep my face impassive, although inside I was shaking like a leaf: this was definitely the crisis. But even in my distress I observed two things: firstly, that Gangadhar was now looking distinctly angry – the question was, with whom? My second observation was that he was, if anything, more aroused now than when he had been interrupted in . . . whatever he had been doing.

That I should be standing before such a man when he was virtually naked and in such a state, again should have left me faint with embarrassment, but somehow that did not really apply in these circumstances.

And now he had reached a decision.

'Leave the room,' the rajah said. 'Everyone.' He pointed at Manu and me. 'You stay.'

I stood still, quite uncertain as to what was to happen next, while the girls and the major-domos and the secretaries filed from the room, followed reluctantly by the guards.

'Everyone,' the rajah repeated, loudly.

From behind the curtain a young boy emerged. Like the rani's ladies he wore only a dhoti, and this had clearly been hastily assumed. He did not look at either Manu or myself as he sidled past us and scuttled for the door, but Manu certainly looked at *him*. Gangadhar as usual did not look the least embarrassed.

The outer curtain was drawn and the three of us were alone. Gangadhar now drew back the inner curtain to reveal a vast bed, somewhat tousled.

Manu gave a sharp little intake of breath. But surely, I thought, she must have known the bed was there.

'It is time,' Gangadhar said.

'No,' Manu said, and took a step backwards.

'I can do it, now,' he asserted. 'Suddenly I know this.'

'No,' Manu said again, taking another step backwards, so that she was virtually standing against me.

'Hold her,' the rajah commanded.

Not altogether sure what I was doing, I obeyed, grasping her arms from behind.

Her head turned, sharply, her hair flailing. 'Let me go,' she snapped.

'Bring her here,' Gangadhar commanded.

I thrust the rani into his arms.

'Now leave us,' Gangadhar ordered. 'But wait here,' he said to me, indicating some cushions on the far side of the room.

I seated myself, now subject to considerable emotions as I knew what was happening behind the inner curtain. But there was very little noise beyond the odd gasp, and after about half an hour Manu emerged, looking distinctly tousled; there was a trickle of blood on her thighs. Ganghadar was with her. 'Now remember,' he said, 'your lessons begin tomorrow. You will be on time, you will leave the other girls behind and you will regard Mrs Hammond as your mother. Do you understand this?'

'I understand that I must obey you, my lord,' Manu said in a low voice.

'Then give Mrs Hammond your hands and acknowledge her.'

Manu turned towards me and placed her hands in mine, raising her head at the same time to stare at me. 'I am your pupil, Mother,' she said. And then her lips continued to move, silently, but clearly forming the words, 'I hate you.'

Justice

My instincts warned me that I had achieved everything I could possibly expect in so short a period of time; my sole objective had to be to maintain the regard that Gangadhar Rao apparently had for me and never to overplay my hand. I therefore merely smiled at her and squeezed her hands in turn.

Gangadhar had been studying us, and he could see my face.

'Excellent,' he commented. 'Excellent. Now off you go, Manu.'

She walked to the archway. There she hesitated for a moment, as if she would have looked back, but instead she asked, 'Shall I send your people to you, my lord?'

'No. I will call them when I wish them.'

She bowed, still with her back to us, and crossed the outer room to disappear beyond that curtain. We heard voices, but no one dared enter.

However, I was anxious to leave. I had never been so exposed to a naked man before, much less a naked prince whose arousal showed no current signs of subsiding. I therefore inched towards the archway, anxious to take my leave as soon as possible.

'Where are you going?' he asked.

'I have my duties, Highness.'

'I have just established that you have no duties until tomorrow. And even then, you must always remember that you have no duty superior to that of pleasing me.'

I opened my mouth and then closed it again; this was getting very close to the nitty-gritty. But in my position he was simply stating the truth, to a point . . .

'You understand about me?'

What a question. I licked my lips. 'I think so, Highness.'

'And you condemn.'

'I prefer not to do so, Highness.'

'I have heard it said that in Great Britain people like myself are executed.'

'I believe there is a movement to change that law,' I ventured.

He smiled. 'Because so many noble Britishers share my tastes.'

'Because it is somewhat extreme for a quirk of nature.'

'A quirk of nature,' he said, thoughtfully. 'When Manu was first brought to me a year ago and our knots were tied she was thirteen years old. She seemed anxious to fulfil her duties. I remember that when *her* knot was being tied, she told her attendants to make it very tight. That was taken as an example of her determination to belong to me. But that night her spirit failed her, and she sought to fight me. And I . . .' he sighed. 'My spirit was always weak when it came to women. I knew what I had to do, but I could not do it. I do not know if she was relieved, or if she never forgave me. Thus it was I sought help. I encouraged her boyish behaviour. And I sought . . . what is it they say? An English nanny. But she was already too old for a nanny, so it had to be a governess. I do not know what I expected. I certainly did not hope. But you . . .'

He was beginning to twitch, and I understood that I was in great danger. My best course, as I saw it, was to temporize and wait for his homosexual nature to regain control over any temporary heterosexual lust.

'I am privileged to be of assistance to Your Highness,' I said.

'You are far more attractive than any of the other European women in Jhansi,' he remarked.

'Are there many, Highness?'

He waved his hand. 'A dozen or so. With their husbands and children. Would you care to meet them?'

'Not particularly,' I said. They would almost certainly be hostile to me, certainly after Sleeman had had a word with them.

'Then you need not,' he agreed. 'Undress.'

My head jerked. 'Highness?'

'I wish to look at you. I have never seen a naked European woman,' he added, ingenuously.

My brain was racing; here *was* a crisis. 'European women do not undress before any men other than their husbands,' I said, stretching a point.

'You have no husband.'

'That is my misfortune, Highness.' Stretching another point, 'It cannot be any other man's fortune.'

'You debate with spirit,' he remarked. 'But I am not any other man. I am the Rajah of Jhansi. I am both your employer and your master. You cannot refuse me.'

'Or you will have me staked out on an ant hill,' I said, unsure whether I was joking or not.

'It is one of the most painful ways to die,' he agreed, gravely. 'But I would never inflict it upon you, Mrs Hammond. Emma. Yet to attempt to remain here, lacking my favour, would be very difficult for you.'

I understood that I had protested for as long and as far as was possible. I undressed, slowly. It took some time, during which he never moved, but watched me with glowing eyes.

'So many clothes,' he commented. 'Are they not tiresome?'

'Extremely.'

'Then why do you wear them?'

'Because . . .' I realized I had no idea. 'Because every one else does, I suppose. It is the fashion.'

'It can be neither comfortable nor healthy,' he said. 'Now stand still.'

I had finished unlacing my boots, and was absolutely naked. Before a man. I realized that my introduction to this way of life, in the bath beneath the palace, had been a godsend, or I could never have done this.

I watched his hand come towards me, as if mesmerized, and waited for his touch as I might have done for an executioner's sword. When it came I shivered, but from what impulse I did not know; his hand was warm. He stroked my shoulder and my breast, my hip and my thigh and my buttocks.

'You are a goddess,' he said. 'Come to life.'

'But I have only two arms, Highness,' I said, attempting to lighten our mood.

He smiled, and moved his hand over my belly. I knew where he was going next, but there was no way I could stop him. His fingers sifted through my pubic hair and found the flesh beneath. 'This is your yoni. You know of this?'

'No, Highness.'

'The female reproductive part is called the yoni,' he explained. 'This . . .' he held his member, 'is the lingam. In Hindustan, these are objects of worship, as they should be, for together they are the fount of all life. Do you not agree?'

'Yes, Highness.' At that moment I would have agreed to anything.

'But it is not so in Europe. The Christian religion condemns such matters as obscene.'

'Yes, Highness.'

'And yet, there are so many Christians. I wonder how this does happen? Where the sexual habit is condemned?'

'I think because the sexual habit is ingrained in every human being,' I said, amazed at my boldness. 'And therefore will be indulged, regardless of the condemnation.'

'Well said,' he said again. 'I would have you throw away these absurd clothes, and wear only the sari or the dhoti.'

'I will need my European clothes whenever I leave the palace, Your Highness. Much more so when I leave Jhansi.'

'But we have agreed that you are not going to leave Jhansi,' he pointed out.

To my continuing surprise, he then allowed me to dress, and signified that I should leave. Relief was compounded by a sense of insult. But relief was the greater, even if I understood that my feet were firmly caught in the bog of the rajah's ambivalent personality.

Manu was icily polite to me after the rajah's command and proved a good and attentive pupil. Indeed she was a joy to teach, for she was exceptionally intelligent and had a retentive memory and, however much she might loathe her teacher, I could observe her growing interest in what she was being taught. With that I had to be content, and put my faith in time.

As to what was being said of me outside the palace, or outside of Jhansi, I had no idea. Gangadhar Rao did not tell me if he had received any communication from Calcutta, although he spent quite a lot of time in my company, having me tell him about Europe – to my great relief he did not make any more sexual advances. Colonel Sleeman did not visit me again, nor did any of the other European inhabitants of Jhansi. Apparently, as far as the Company was concerned, I had vanished off the face of the map. This suited me very well. I spent much of this first, and as it was to turn out, last, relatively peaceful period of my life in India learning about this society in which it then seemed likely I should be living for the rest of my life.

It was a fascinating subject, quite apart from the prevalent nudity or semi-nudity, which could logically be explained by the extreme heat, or the sexual orientation with which I was surrounded and which equally could be explained by the prevailing nudity, or more accurately, by the uninhibited attitude to life adopted by the Hindus themselves, and this included their religion.

This was necessary because I had been cut off, or as some would have it, had deliberately cut myself off from my own religious society. Actually, having felt thoroughly put off all religion by six years of marriage to Mr Hammond, who had warned me continually of the horrors of hell that undoubtedly awaited me for my criminal behaviour – all this while lying on my belly sawing away – I would have been in any event cut off even had I been an enthusiastic member of the European community. There was an Anglican vicar, and he came to call, but I was not in the mood to receive him, and once I had got over the strangeness of not celebrating Christmas or even having the date remarked upon, I was determined to practise my religion in private . . . while considering the alternatives.

I am bound to say from my experiences in the palace that I found the Hindu religion most attractive. This was at least partly because of its extreme tolerance. The Hindus took their religion very seriously; for example, anyone who mistreated a cow, or much worse killed one, these animals being held sacred, was damned for ever; tragically, the importance of this was lost on too many English administrators.

Over the centuries the Hindus had thrown up many distinguished teachers, of whom the Buddha is only the most famous, who had led the way in considering the true meaning of life and death. The Hindus took these things seriously, and in the main had rejected Buddhism in favour of their older beliefs, but it would never have occurred to them to inflict their beliefs upon anyone else. A man worshipped as he chose and it was, indeed, quite practical for someone to be both a Hindu and a member of another religion such as Christianity, supposing the Christians would have allowed it.

Not that they were basically a happy people. Indeed, they were profoundly pessimistic, because in their religion it was made evident that all mankind was in a decline from much happier times. One may say that this was an inevitable reaction to the repeated invasions the so fertile and so wealthy subcontinent had had to endure from successive waves of Mohammedans, followed by Portuguese, Dutch, French and English, but in fact it went back to the very beginning of time.

As I have mentioned, I saw little of the outside world in that I never left the palace. But the outside world often came to the palace, even if this was mainly the Indian world; for Gangadhar Rao's ambivalence was not confined to his private apartments. He enjoyed writing plays and acting in them even more, always taking the female lead; he undoubtedly enjoyed the companionship, and more, of his young men, but then, when in the mood, he equally certainly enjoyed the body of his girl bride, and when outside of his apartments he was a very vigorous, and masculine, ruler of his people.

For all his private pleasures, he took his duties and respon-
sibilities as the ruler of Jhansi very seriously. He held court on
three days a week, when he dispensed justice with total impar-
tiality and a good deal of severity. Hindu law was not in itself
as harsh as Muslim law, but it had lived too close to the often
horrific requirements of the sharia for too many centuries not
to have accepted some aspects of it. Larcenous hands were
regularly chopped off, the lash was decreed for social offences
and the death penalty was held in reserve for the more heinous
crimes. These misfortunes were usually far removed from the
women's quarters but we could not avoid some contact with
the realities of life, such as the day a woman staggered up to
the palace, blood pouring from her face. As I happened to be
outside at the time, I could not stop myself from rushing forward
to assist her if I could, and when I reached her I saw to my
horror that her nose had been cut off. Guards had arrived and
removed her, but I hurried to the rajah's presence to discover
what had happened and what might be done about it.

'Ah,' he said. 'Mootoo's wife. I'm afraid she was found to have
committed adultery by her husband.'

'And that gave him the right to cut off her nose?'

'He has the right to kill her. He was merciful.'

'But . . . you mean he will not be punished?'

'Of course he will not be punished. He was within his rights.'

I was shocked, but far more so a few weeks later when I
became personally involved in Jhansi justice.

Although, as I have indicated, we ladies had nothing to do with
the dispensation of justice, we could not help by chance occasionally encountering groups of criminals being brought into the palace
to stand trial. If I was not permitted to leave the grounds – none
of us were – we were allowed to walk within them as much as
we chose, and on one morning, before it got too hot, and while
the queen, having done her gallop and taken her bath, was at her
devotions, which she took very seriously, I was taking a walk,
accompanied by Vima and Annie. I did this most mornings, as I
felt that daily exercise was essential if I was to retain my health
and not grow fat, as did so many of the other ladies. Thus it was,
while walking, we paused to let a body of soldiers escorting half-
a-dozen handcuffed men pass on their way to the rajah's court.

I had merely intended to glance at these men as I always felt intensely sorry for them, whatever their crimes, but my attention was caught by the fact that one of them was looking at me. He hastily turned his head away when he caught my eye, but I was left quite speechless. For those features: the big nose and thrusting chin, and above all the glinting eyes and pressed lips, were burned on my brain. Without thinking I pointed in horror and even fear, for all that he was manacled and heavily guarded.

I recalled myself in a moment, dropped my arm, and turned away to collect my thoughts. But the havildar, or sergeant, in command of the soldiers had observed my action and now hurried across, bowing before me.

'You know these men, Memsahib?'

'Yes,' I said. 'No. I mean . . .'

'Which one, Memsahib?'

I bit my lip. But that man had belonged to the group of thugs that had murdered my husband and, perhaps more importantly, Allia. 'That one.' I pointed again.

The sergeant checked his list. 'He is called Zavildar Khan. You know this name?'

'No,' I said. 'I know the face.'

'He has harmed you?'

'He was one of the men who murdered my husband.'

'You are certain of this, Memsahib?'

'I could never forget his face.'

'Then you must give evidence of it to the rajah.'

'Oh, but . . .' I bit my lip. It had certainly not been part of my plan to appear in a Jhansi court. But there was nothing for it. Zavildar Khan was taken away with his fellow prisoners to answer the immediate charge against them, that of robbery, and I was informed by Kujula that the separate charge, that of murder, was to be heard the following day, when I would be required to attend and give evidence.

In an attempt to escape, at least partially, I hoped, the consequences of my denunciation, I requested an interview with the rajah, but was informed this could not be permitted until after the second trial. So I was stuck with it, and could only keep reminding myself that if Zavildar was sentenced to death that would have been his fate in any event had he, for instance, been captured by the British soldiers who had rescued me. But I did not doubt that I could apply for commutation – if I chose. I hadn't made up my mind yet.

Thus I was the more surprised to be informed, that afternoon, that Colonel Sleeman wished to see me on a most urgent matter.

Manu and I were in the middle of our lessons.

'Send him away,' she suggested.

'He says it is urgent,' I pointed out. 'It will not take long. You'll excuse me, Highness.'

'Ha!' she commented.

I hurried off. I had not expected ever to see the colonel again. He looked as spick and span as ever, but distinctly taken aback to find me wearing a sari rather than a dress.

'How nice of you to call,' I remarked.

'I would not have troubled you had the matter not been urgent.'

I gestured him to a chair and sat myself. 'The matter being?'

'This accusation you have made against a prisoner in custody.'

'Yes?' I was watchful.

'You have no doubt that this man was one of those who attacked your caravan?'

'None.'

'It happened very nearly a year ago.'

'His is not a face I shall ever forget. He was their leader.'

'Very well. May I suggest that you make out a formal deposition against him, and let me have it.'

'Is that necessary? He is to be tried tomorrow, before the rajah, when I shall give my evidence.'

'You will, of course, withdraw your accusation, and say that you were mistaken.'

'I was not mistaken.'

'Nevertheless, it would be best for you to say that you were. I am not suggesting that you allow this fellow to escape punishment for his crime. I am merely requesting that you permit that punishment to be carried out by us rather than by the rajah.'

'You will have to tell me why I should do this.'

'Well, you see, if he is sentenced by the rajah, he will have to die in a most unpleasant fashion. That is the law of this land. Whereas, if he is merely punished for theft, which will involve a flogging, and then released, we will be able to re-arrest him and take him to Calcutta for trial. I understand your reluctance to return there,' he hurried on as I would have spoken, 'but this can be overcome by means of your sworn deposition, which can be used in court.'

'The rajah would not release me, in any event,' I pointed out. 'But supposing I did as you ask, what would happen to Zavildar?'

'Why, he would be tried, convicted, and hanged.'

'And you would regard this as an entirely civilized procedure.'

'It is far more civilized than being impaled, I assure you, Mrs Hammond.'

'And would, of course, be a feather in the cap of the Raj, and your cap as well, for having been once again revealed as suppressing thuggism.'

He flushed. 'It would illustrate to all India that we uphold the rule of law.'

'And Gangadhar Rao does not?'

'Perhaps he does, in his own barbaric fashion. But what happens in a backwater like Jhansi is of no importance, and would certainly receive no publicity, outside of Jhansi. Whereas . . .'

'A show trial in Calcutta of the man who murdered an English missionary would be to the credit of every Englishman and Englishwoman in India.'

His gaze was frigid. 'Yes, Mrs Hammond,' he said. 'It would be to the credit of the Raj. And it would be the most merciful possible end to this affair. Or perhaps you are not interested in mercy, only in revenge?'

That was a shrewd thrust; revenge was certainly playing a big part in my thinking at that moment. But I had already realized that my desire for revenge, or at least the punishment of Zavildar, did not stretch as far as execution, and while I hoped that I could sort that out with Gangadhar Rao, there was no prospect of the Raj agreeing to any of my wishes in the matter. My mind was decided on the issue.

'I'm afraid I cannot accept any of your reasons, Colonel,' I said. 'In any event, it would certainly affront the rajah if I were to change my story now. He would know that I had done so as a result of pressure from you and he would therefore have to conclude that I was acting for the greater glory of the Raj rather than himself. That I cannot and will not do.'

He gazed at me for several seconds. Then he said, 'You intend to accuse this man of murder before the Jhansi court.'

'Yes,' I said.

Colonel Sleeman stood up. 'Then may God have mercy on your soul.'

So the next day, after another uncomfortable meeting with the colonel, I appeared before the rajah and his chief relatives and principal advisers, all of whom acted as judges. I was very nervous, and more so when I was brought face to face with Zavildar, but everyone was very kind, saving of course Zavildar himself, who stared at me throughout the proceedings; I will swear he never once blinked, except when the sentence of death was pronounced. Immediately after the proceedings I requested an interview with the rajah, and this was granted.

'You were very courageous,' Gangadhar Rao said. 'Very upright, when confronted with that thug.'

'Thank you, Highness,' I said. 'May I now make a request?'

'Certainly.'

'I would ask that Zavildar Khan's sentence be commuted to imprisonment.'

He frowned at me. 'Why is this?'

'I have no wish to take a human life.'

'This man murdered your husband.'

'I know that. So let him suffer, at hard labour, for the rest of his life. But his death would be on my conscience.'

'I cannot agree to your request.'

'Highness . . .'

'I cannot,' he repeated, 'because there is no provision in our law for the commutation of a sentence. Zavildar has been sentenced to death and he must die. Tomorrow morning.' He pointed. 'And as his accuser, you must be present.'

I swallowed. 'Highness . . .'

'That also is the law,' he said.

So there I was, dreadfully hoist by my own petard. I hardly slept that night feeling, I suspect, even more agitated than Zavildar himself. He was due to die for a crime he had committed, and of which he had to know he was guilty, and in any event, his way of life, throughout his life, had been such that he must have known for a long time that the odds were that he would end up in this situation. I was, for the first time and I fervently hoped the last, taking life, and while I could convince myself that Zavildar richly deserved to die, I could not convince myself that anyone, however heinous, deserved to die in so barbarous and painful a manner.

And that I should have to watch! But it was even worse than that. The execution was to take place on the open ground before the palace and a large crowd had assembled. Amongst them were a good number of women and, I saw to my consternation, more than one European, male and female. Gangadhar Rao and the male members of his court stood by themselves, surrounded by guards.

Equidistant from the spectators on every side and standing with me were not only Vima and Annie, but Manu and several of her women. The soldiers placed a large saddle on the ground, and it was to this that Zavildar was led when he emerged from the cell in which he had spent the night. He trembled as he walked but gave no other sign of distress. He wore only a dhoti, but on arriving before the saddle this was removed by one of the attendants, exposing him to the multitude. He was then made to kneel and lie on his belly, across the saddle, some care evidently being paid to his comfort. Two of the guards then knelt by his head, each holding one wrist very firmly and pressing it into the dust. Two others knelt by his legs, pulling them wide apart, and then grasping the ankles and pressing down on them in turn.

I found I was holding my breath, and fully intended to close my eyes, when to my horror I saw the executioner approaching me. He carried a stake of wood, perhaps three feet long, thin but clearly strong, and with a pointed end. This he held out to me.

I stared at it, quite uncertain what he wanted, or intended.

'It shall be as you desire, Memsahib,' he said.

I looked at Vima in confusion.

'He is asking, firstly, if you wish the stake to be greased,' she explained. 'If it is coated in grease, the entry is made easier. This is better for the victim,' she added, ingenuously.

'Yes,' I said. 'Yes. Oh, let it be greased.'

'Then he wishes to know if you require him to strike hard or soft.'

'What?' I felt close to fainting.

'It must be your decision, Memsahib,' she said. 'If he strikes hard, the stake will enter quickly, and death will be rapid. If he strikes soft, the stake will enter slowly, even if greased, and death may take up to an hour.'

I had to draw several deep breaths to stay on my feet. 'Strike hard,' I said. 'Strike as hard as you can.'

The executioner looked disappointed, but bowed and returned to the victim. The point of the stake was inserted; Zavildar gave a great gasp followed by a shriek as the first blow was delivered, but it was over in seconds.

Annie fainted.

And Gangadhar crossed the execution ground to stand before me. 'You did well,' he said. 'I am proud of you, Mrs Hammond.'

The Sickness

It can be imagined the effect that episode had on me. In the main it merely accentuated my position: the people of Jhansi regarded me with an increased respect and this, I felt, extended to the rani, even if she kept her feelings concealed, while the Europeans in the community, at least as reported by Annie who, with Vima, was allowed to visit the bazaars, regarded me as more of an outcast than ever.

I did not see how their opinions were going to affect me, in the short term at least. But I did resolve never again to attend a Jhansi court, a determination much easier to make than to keep.

We were also subject to visitations from neighbouring princes and princesses. One of these in particular aroused our interest, for it was Hazrat Mahal, the Begum of Oudh, a most important lady – because Oudh was a large and important state – and a startlingly beautiful one, roughly my own age, who possessed exquisite features and a full figure, as well as a tremendous person-ality, although hardly less compelling was her entourage, for she travelled with her personal bodyguard which consisted entirely of women, every one at once tall and handsome, dressed in bril-liant army uniforms, red tunics and white pantaloons, black shakos, polished muskets with bayonets on their hips and cartouches on their belts. Even Manu was quite overwhelmed by the begum's presence, the more so when she informed us that she was on her way to Bombay to take ship for England, where she was to be presented at court.

Obviously, at this stage of her life, the begum was a profound Anglophile, which was off-putting to Manu, who had been brought up to regard the British as usurping conquerors, like indeed the Muslims. But Hazrat's easy charm overcame all obstacles, even if her attitude to life caused a flutter in the Jhansi harem.

'I am told you have a problem, my dear,' she told Manu when she joined us after having paid her respects to the rajah. 'Your husband has no seed. Tell me, does he ever get it up?'

I had feared that Manu might take offence, but she merely giggled girlishly. 'Oh, yes, Highness.'

'But you have not become pregnant,' Hazrat pointed out.

Now Manu did look put out. 'Not as yet.'

'I,' Hazrat announced, 'have a son. If I were you, Lakshmi Bai, I would adopt.'

'Highness?'

'It is perfectly legal, and it is necessary to have an heir. I should think about that if I were you.'

'Her Highness is very young,' I suggested.

The begum glanced at me. We had been introduced, but I was not sure she actually registered who or what I was.

Now she surprised me. 'I remember you,' she said. 'You were in Lucknow.'

Which was, in fact, the capital of her state of Oudh.

'Why, yes, Highness,' I said, amazed that she should know of me; I had only ever beheld her from a distance.

'The wife of a missionary. Are *you* a mother?' she asked.

'Mrs Hammond is a widow,' Manu said.

It was the first time she had ever defended me – if indeed she was doing that.

'Without a son,' Hazrat said, disparagingly. 'Why have you not married again, Hammond?'

'Perhaps I have been too busy, Highness,' I suggested.

'Or perhaps you do not like men.'

I didn't know what to reply to that, so I looked at Manu, who waggled her eyebrows.

'One of the advantages of adopting,' Hazrat said, 'is that one no longer has to put up with men. Once they have their heir, one may allow them to pursue their own inclinations, providing one is allowed to do so oneself. Do you not agree?'

Manu was looking bewildered. As her inclinations were as yet limited, she had always been allowed to indulge them, even her martial hobbies.

Hazrat was regarding her speculatively, but clearly understood the rani had no idea what she was talking about. She turned to me. 'I would have you sleep with me, tonight,' she said.

I was speechless.

'You have no objections, Manu?' Hazrat asked.

Manu was also at least surprised. 'If it pleases you, Highness.'

'I am sure it will please me very much.'

I pulled myself together. 'I beg your pardon,' I said. 'With respect, Highnesses.'

They both looked at me.

'It will not be possible,' I said.

Hazrat looked down her nose.

I searched desperately for some defence. 'You would have to ask the rajah,' I explained.

Now she raised her exquisitely shaped eyebrows. 'You belong to him? Gangadhar?'

Obviously the rumours had reached Oudh.

I glanced at Manu, whose face was expressionless. But I felt I could sort Manu out afterwards. 'The rajah is my lord and master,' I said.

'An Englishwoman? That must please him greatly. You must have another name; what is it?'

'My name is Emma, Highness.'

'But I call her Angel,' Manu put in.

'Angel,' Hazrat mused. 'They're supernatural creatures, are they not?'

'They are part of the Christian belief, Highness.'

'Are you, then, a supernatural being?'

'Well, no, Highness. I . . .' Again I looked at Manu for support.

'The name was my choice,' Manu explained.

'I find that very interesting. I have never shared my bed with a supernatural being. It will be an experience.' She looked at Manu. 'You have no objections?' she asked again.

I also looked at the rani, as beseechingly as I could, but I knew I was lost.

'Well, then,' Hazrat said. 'I will speak with the rajah.' She summoned one of the waiting ladies. 'Take me to the rajah,' she commanded.

The woman looked at Manu, and received a nod. I waited for her to be out of earshot, then tried another appeal.

'Your Highness, you cannot send me to that woman.'

'She will not harm you.'

'I do not fear harm, Highness. But . . . two women . . .'

'What can two women do?' Manu inquired.

She obviously had no idea. But then, neither did I.

'It is not a part of our culture.'

Was it part of Hindu culture? I had no idea about that either. But then, from what I had seen there was nothing sexual that was *not* part of Hindu culture.

Anyway, Hazrat was a Muslim.

'What has culture to do with it?' Manu asked with devastating simplicity. 'The begum wishes to know more of you. That is a compliment. You should be honoured.'

I shuddered. 'What will happen to me?'

'Why, you will give the begum pleasure, and no doubt receive pleasure in return.'

'Have you ever . . .' I held my breath.

'No,' Manu said, somewhat wistfully. 'You must tell me of it. All of it.'

This was the first suggestion of intimacy between us. But I was too distraught to realize it. 'Can you not protect me?' Another first; I had never begged her for anything before.

'Protect you? I have said, you should be honoured. Anyway, she is a queen.'

'But so are you,' I almost wailed.

'She *rules*,' Manu said, darkly.

As it was now time for Manu's midday meal, which would be followed by her rest, I returned to my apartment. Vima had my meal ready, but I could eat nothing. I was in a state of near frantic apprehension. I felt as if I had been condemned to death, and awaited only the opening of my door to summon me to execution. Both Vima and Annie considered that I was sickening for

something, and wished to send for the court physician, but I sent
them off.

There was, of course, always the chance that Gangadhar Rao
might refuse the begum's request. But why should he? That Hazrat
might wish to take me to her bed was no more strange than he
should wish to do the same with a handsome young boy. And
although I even considered going to him and begging him not
to submit me to such an ordeal, I knew that was not practical in
a society so riddled with protocol. Hazrat Mahal was Queen of
Oudh, one of the most powerful states in India. More than that,
as Manu had grumbled, she had set aside her inept husband and
ruled, totally independent of the Raj. That she should choose to
visit Jhansi was an honour – he could not possibly risk antagonizing her in any way.

At four o'clock that afternoon I went to the schoolroom to
await Manu and found her already there. 'There will be no lessons
today,' she announced. 'I have received a directive from the rajah
that you are to dine with the begum in her apartment this evening
at seven. You must go and prepare yourself. Bathe and perfume
yourself.'

I did as the rani instructed, to the consternation of Vima and
Annie, as this was a complete break in my normal routine. I felt
some explanation was necessary, so I told them that I had been
invited to dine with the Begum of Oudh. Annie clapped her
hands.

'Is that not a great honour, ma'am?'

'I have been told that it is.'

Vima, however, was well up on backstairs gossip. 'You have
met the begum, Memsahib?'

'Yes. This morning.'

'She is very beautiful.'

I was bathed and perfumed, and my hair put up in a vast
chignon. I chose my red sari and as that seemed to be the role
I was required to play, added my gold bangles and was ready for
the fray . . . or as ready as I could compose myself.

At a quarter to seven Kujula escorted me along the interminable
corridors to the begum's apartment. At the door we were met by
two of the Amazons, who curtly sent him off, and in turn escorted
me along more exquisitely decorated corridors to an inner archway.
Here they parted the curtains, and I confronted the begum.

The room was large, and as usual studded with gold ornaments. There were of course no chairs or even divans, but several large silk cushions on the floor. On one of these sat Hazrat, and the splendours with which she was surrounded faded into insignificance. She was cross-legged . . . and naked, save for a sparkling bangle on her left forearm. This sight reduced me to a jelly. As I have mentioned, Mr Hammond had believed that nudity was a sin, and there had been no mirror around when I had had a bath, nor when I had been required to undress by Gangadhar Rao. While Manu and her girls, magnificent in their animal energy, had been just girls.

Hazrat's body was almost as beautiful as her face, which was shrouded in her released hair that descended on to her shoulders and beyond in a black mat, absolutely straight. Her breasts were full, her legs splendidly shaped.

She observed that I seemed to have been turned to stone. 'Do you find me unpleasing, Emma?' she asked.

I managed to speak. 'I find you breathtaking, Highness.'

'Release your hair.'

I obeyed, and felt it on my shoulders and down my back in turn.

'A crown of gold,' she commented. 'Now the sari.'

This immediate rush into what she wanted left me breathless again. I could not stop myself glancing at the two guards standing impassively before the curtain. This might be commonplace to them, but it certainly was not to me.

'Of course,' Hazrat said. 'You have the modesty of a memsahib.' She waved her hand, and the guards left. Hazrat then gazed at me. I drew a long breath, and unwrapped my sari, allowing it to fall to the cushions. Then I stood absolutely still, my hands at my side; as I had before Gangadhar. 'You are a very handsome woman,' Hazrat said. 'I am delighted to make your acquaintance. Sit.' She indicated the cushion opposite her, and I obeyed, sitting cross-legged as was she; it was a good deal easier, if more embarrassing, to do this when naked than when wearing a skirt and petticoat, or even a sari.

I was taken aback when she picked up a wand and lightly tapped a small brass gong. What new experience was I about to undergo?

'You know of me?' she asked.

'You are the Queen of Oudh, Highness. And a very great lady.'

'A very great lady,' she mused. 'At the age of ten I was walking the streets.'

I was not sure I had heard correctly. 'Highness?'

'I was a prostitute, Emma. My parents put me to work because they had no money.'

'But . . .' I was completely lost for words.

'Of course. Were I a Hindu I would still be there. But I am a follower of the Prophet, may Allah bless his name, and we do not have a caste system. My name then was Muhammadi Khanum, and I was born in Fauzabad, which is a city in Oudh. I was fortunate. I was a lovely child . . .'

'Who grew into a beautiful woman,' I muttered, involuntarily.

'Yes,' she agreed. 'As I say, I was fortunate. I attracted the attention of a courtier who made me his concubine. Then I was seen by Nawab Wajid Ali Shah. He took me into the royal harem, where I was fortunate enough to give birth to his son, Birgis Qadra. I was given the title Begum Hazrat Mahal, and became his number two wife. Now I rule the state.' This was a simple statement of fact, spoken without any suggestion of pride of achievement; she clearly considered it as the karma resulting from her beauty and personality. 'There you have the story of my life, thus far. Now I am to visit England; I am on my way to Bombay.'

'I have heard this, Highness.'

'Tell me of England. Is it as cold as they say?'

'Yes, Highness. Sometimes it is very cold. You will have to . . .' I hesitated.

'Wear more clothes? Like a memsahib? Like you, perhaps. But you no longer wear those clothes.'

'It is the wish of the rajah.'

'Who you regard as your master. He admires beauty. But you say he has not yet taken you to his bed.'

Her eyes drifted from my face for just a moment, and I heard movement behind me. I tensed myself, and found a naked young woman kneeling on either side me. Oh, my God, I thought. But two more were kneeling beside the begum. Now they placed golden plates before each of us, and from large bowls scooped out helpings of rice and a sweet-smelling curry. I waited, but they showed no sign of leaving, instead producing another tray on which were the customary gold bowls of water for us to rinse our fingers between mouthfuls.

'This is a northern dish,' Hazrat explained. 'Very tasty.' Delicately but expertly she rolled up a mouthful of rice and curry. 'We were speaking of the rajah.'

Having become proficient at Indian eating, I did the same. 'I came here under contract for five years, Highness, in order to groom the rani for her future role on a larger scale. For that period, yes, he is my master. But my contract also stipulated that I should at all times be treated as an English gentlewoman, and this the rajah has always done.'

'Except for requiring you to wear Indian dress.'

'The rajah hinted that he would appreciate it, and in fact I have found it a most comfortable garment.'

'The rani does not like you.'

'That is a cross all governesses have to bear, Highness. But she is prepared to learn, which is what matters.'

'You are a singularly self-possessed woman. As I told you, I once saw you from a distance in Lucknow, and was struck by your appearance. But your husband was not liked there. By anyone.'

I sighed. 'I'm afraid that is true, Highness.'

'Which is why you left so suddenly. To be murdered by thugs. Did you love him?'

I raised my head to look into her eyes. 'No. He was my husband.'

She smiled, a flash of white teeth. 'Did you enjoy sex with him?'

Again I met her gaze. 'No.'

'How many men have you had sex with?'

'I have only known my husband, Highness.'

'So you have never enjoyed sex with a man,' she mused, and drank some water; as she was a Muslim, there was no wine on offer. 'How many women have you known?'

'I have never known a woman, Highness. It is not in our culture.'

'So you said. I am to meet Queen Victoria. Tell me of her.'

'I know nothing of her, Highness.'

Hazrat raised her exquisite eyebrows. 'She is your queen.'

'And I am a humble governess.'

'But you know how old she is?'

A hasty calculation. As I remembered, Victoria had been born in 1819, but I had no idea of the date. 'She is thirty-one years old, Highness.'

'Ah,' Hazrat commented. I wondered how old she was. I had formed the impression, at our first meeting, that she was roughly my own age, and certainly I would not have supposed she was yet thirty. 'And is she a cruel ruler?'

'The Queen of England does not rule, Highness. She reigns.'

'I do not understand you. What is the difference?'

'The queen is the head of the state. But the actual ruling is done by her ministers.'

'Who are of course selected by her. We often have the same system here.'

'The queen does not select her ministers, Highness. They are elected by the people. The queen is required to approve their choice, but this is a formality.'

'And this is the most powerful nation in the world? I am sorry that I must leave tomorrow. I think you have much to teach me.' She washed her hands a last time, then dried them on a napkin provided by the girl at her elbow, uncoiled her legs, and stood up. 'Come,' she said.

Our conversation had lulled me into a sense of security, a feeling that, despite the bizarre surroundings, I had after all been invited here simply to talk. But now . . . my girl gave me a napkin, and I dried my hands. Then I stood up, a trifle uncertainly; I was trembling.

As Hazrat observed. 'You must not be afraid of me. I shall not bite you.' Another smile. 'Well, perhaps a little.'

The curtains over an inner archway were parted, and I held my breath again as I looked at the huge divan bed. To my relief at least the girls did not follow, but drew the curtains behind us. Hazrat advanced to the bed. 'Have you ever read the *Kama Sutra*?'

I drew a deep breath. 'Yes.' Even if, so far, only a part of it.

'It is a manual of love, between the sexes. But it can be applied, even more successfully, to the purest of loves.' She lay on the bed. 'Come, and lie with me.'

I had no choice but to obey, and so passed the forbidden – at least as I had been taught – portals into a world I had never suspected to exist. Mr Hammond's kisses, when he had troubled to kiss me at all, had been brutal and bruising, often leaving my mouth bleeding; Hazrat's were a gentle, intensely sensual brushing of the lips and tongue. Mr Hammond had handled my body like a sack of coal; Hazrat's touch was like the caress of a summer breeze. Mr Hammond had never been interested in what feelings I might have; Hazrat sought only to explore them and bring them to fruition. Mr Hammond had never permitted me to handle his body; he thought the concept obscene. Hazrat desired it, and for the first time in my life I beheld the glory of a woman in orgasm. And Mr Hammond had always sought me in the dark; here was the ultimate pleasure of glowing candles.

And yet, when we lay together exhausted, I found myself wondering if making love with, say, Mr Dickinson, might not be as deliciously rewarding.

We slept for over an hour, then Hazrat stirred. 'You have made me very happy,' she said. 'Now my women will return you to your apartment. But before you go, I have a present for you.' She drew the bangle from her arm. 'Take this, and remember me.'

I regarded it with consternation. 'But, Highness, are those not rubies and diamonds?'

'What else would you stud a bangle with?'

'To accept such a gift would make me a prostitute.'

'How can anyone prostitute herself to a queen? While as a queen, I have the power, and indeed, I have the obligation, to reward those who please me. I look forward to meeting you again when I return from England.'

The begum's caravan was on its way early the next morning, but before she departed she summoned me to her presence.

'You have given me much pleasure,' she said. 'Why are you not wearing your bangle?'

'I . . .' I actually could not yet bring myself to believe that I owned such thing, which in English pounds had to be worth something like seven thousand. '*I* was not sure it would be appropriate.'

'It is always appropriate. Wear it, always. Day and night.'

I could only bow, acutely aware that Manu was standing beside her.

'Did she really give you her bangle?' the rani asked as we watched the elephants undulating over the hills and out of sight.

'Would you like to have it, Highness?' I felt it was an offer I had to make.

'Certainly not. When the time is right, I will give gifts to you. I do not receive gifts from my servants. But you must have pleased her greatly. Did you learn much from her?'

'Her intention was to learn something from me, Highness,' I suggested.

She glanced at me. 'I am sure she did. Did you make love?'

'Highness?'

'The begum is reputed to make love to everybody,' Manu said and added, 'but she did not wish to make love with me.'

I was, as usual, on dangerous ground.

'I think she found me unusual, Highness.'

'Yes,' she agreed, again speculatively.

'Do you wish you were accompanying the begum, Highness? To England? To meet Queen Victoria?'

'Why should I wish to go to England?' Manu demanded. 'Why should I wish to meet Queen Victoria? She is but a queen. I also am a queen. Why does she not come to Hindustan, to meet me?'

I couldn't think of an answer to that.

Nor could I think of an answer to my own situation. I was not sure I wanted to. I felt that I should be shocked at what had happened, and even more at my acceptance of it. But I was not. Which was more shocking than anything else. I had been sucked into this culture, so unlike anything I had ever known, and had, however reluctantly, enjoyed it from the beginning. Now I was not sure that I wanted anything else.

Which does not mean I suddenly plunged into a world of debauchery. Quite the contrary. My night with Hazrat had been an unforgettable and intensely satisfying experience, as much emotionally as physically. All my life it seemed I had been starved of fulfilment in either sphere, and recently my secret desires had been encouraged by the erotic surroundings in which I now lived. Now suddenly I was sated, even if I understood that my feelings were not shared. To Hazrat I had been but a passing fancy, at once different and desirable, and able to convey some useful information. To me she had been an ethereal being, come to remind me of what I was, what I could become, what I might be able to possess, on a permanent basis. Even if this was a very remote possibility, as I could not stop myself dreaming of achieving such a rapport with a man rather than a woman, and there was no prospect of discovering that, at least in Jhansi.

Well, then, I asked myself, other women? But I knew that would never work. I had gone to Hazrat as a neophyte. There was no other woman of such superiority, in both rank and age and experience, in my acquaintance. While as for playing the seductress myself, the very thought terrified me. Annie? She was not the least attractive to me, and she would in any event be shocked. Vima? She was intensely attractive, and I did not doubt she would be willing. But she was one of the women of the palace, surrounded by her friends and even her cousins and sisters with whom she shared her every experience and her every thought. To have an affair with Vima would have been to sink into that seething morass. Hazrat had raised me up; I had no desire to fall down.

In November of 1850 Manu was fifteen. She had now been married for two years and had not yet become a mother. I had been her governess for a year, and was still unaware of her true feelings towards me. Gangadhar often invited me to dinner, ostensibly to discuss Manu's progress, which I considered to be excellent. Naturally it was in my interest to make this claim but he never disputed it. He seemed happy enough with her development, even if he became more and more concerned at her inability to successfully conceive – at least by him.

And then, what appeared almost as a miracle, a few days after her birthday I deduced that she was pregnant. I had a great deal of trouble convincing her that it was happening. She had only been menstruating for two years, and as she suffered little more than discomfort on each occasion, the sudden cessation of so natural a function did not seem such a vital matter. But when Ganghadar himself came to congratulate her, she had to concede that I was right.

Ganghadar was like a dog with two tails, and actually embraced me when I told him the news. Manu, needless to say, was a different matter. In the beginning she was consumed with both anxiety and irritation, the one for fear she might lose the child, the other at the necessity to give up her daily martial exercises to prevent that happening. Then, as her belly began to swell, she started to worry that she was losing her beauty for ever, and thus Ganghadar would never come to her again.

I did my best to reassure her, at the same time praying that I was right, and it was during this period that a true rapport between us was cemented. She still regarded me with suspicion as a hostile element foisted upon her by the hated Raj, but she could no longer deny that I was a source of comfort.

The birth itself was, as with all things physical where Manu was concerned, a simple matter, even if it terrified the wits out of me. This was because of the Hindu attitude to such things. It was unthinkable that even a doctor should look upon the naked body of his patient, much less a queen, even if it might be neces- sary for him to touch her. Thus the surgeon, Bhumaka, had to carry out his duties beneath an enveloping sheet, under which his head was not allowed to dip, so that in effect he was working entirely in the dark which, as far as I could see, brought him into far more intimate contact with the queen's reproductive organs than if he had merely been able to look and determine what needed to be done.

But despite all of this Manu, with her gift for making most things seem easy, gave birth to an apparently healthy baby boy.

The celebrations went on for days, the entire city being illumin- ated by fireworks and reverberating to the sounds of cannon fire and singing. Manu was at her sunniest, and Gangadhar Rao decreed and amnestied all prisoners awaiting execution in a state of sheer joy. All the palace officials and servants were given presents according to their ranks or place in the rajah's esteem. To my surprise I was promised a lac of rupees. 'But Highness,' I protested, 'I still have three years left on my contract.'

'This is a – how do you say it? An ex-gratia payment.'

As may be imagined, congratulations poured in from all over Hindustan, including Hazrat, now returned from England; as she made no effort to communicate with me, I had no idea whether or not her visit had been successful. Even Calcutta acknowledged the great event with, as we were soon to learn, the utmost hypocrisy, and Colonel Sleeman came to offer his congratulations in person. He was received by Gangadhar, not by me.

For that summer Jhansi bathed in a glow of security and then, after four blissful months, the boy prince sickened and died.

It was a terrible time. Manu refused to believe it had happened and hugged the babe to her breast, begging it to open its eyes. As in the Indian heat it was necessary to cremate the dead very rapidly, the little corpse had to be extracted from her arms. This task fell to me while the girls endeavored to prevent her from fighting; Bhumaka was present, but unable to touch her flesh. Gangadhar was also present, but seemed to be turned to stone.

I was happy for him to be there because Manu's fury was terrifying. 'You are a devil from the deepest pit of hell,' she shrieked. 'I will have your breasts cut off, and then stake you out on an ant hill.' But at last she subsided from sheer exhaustion. Bhumaka had prepared a sedative, and this she was persuaded to swallow before falling into a deep sleep.

'I am cursed,' Gangadhar said.

'There will be others,' I assured him.

'Never,' he said.

I sighed, but as it had taken more than a year to achieve this disaster, I had to accept that he was probably right. 'Perhaps,' I ventured, 'the answer may lie in adoption.'

He glanced at me. 'And admit to the world my inadequacy? We will give it a while yet. She is still very young.'

Perhaps that was the moment to clarify my own future but I let it pass; there were still three years to run on my contract, and the rajah at least did not seem to be blaming me for what had happened. And thus I was overtaken by events.

As may be imagined, the palace, and indeed all of Jhansi, was plunged into a gloom far more profound than the joy of four months earlier. The palace became a place of whispers, everyone wore white at all times, there was no music, and even the ritual and head-swinging boom of the brass drum used when the rajah was holding court was stilled.

This silence pervaded all of Jhansi, shrouding the city in a universal gloom. And of course the letters of condolence arrived by the sack load. Manu refused to read any of them, even those from people like Hazrat ul Mana, I did not blame her, as I felt they were all a mass of hypocrisy; that from Calcutta, delivered by Major Sleeman, the most hypocritical of all.

But the constant reminder of her personal catastrophe had a profound effect on Manu's already deeply depressed personality, despite my best attempts to lift her spirits, and it was only a few weeks later that she developed a cold. This in itself was not unusual. All the palace women, myself included, running around as we did virtually naked and with our feet always bare, were subject with some regularity to sniffles and coughs. But on this occasion Manu seemed to be extremely distressed and complained of a severe backache. She was certainly unable to attend the schoolroom. And so I went to her to discover the truth of the matter, hoping against hope that she might have conceived again.

Entering Manu's apartment was always a breathtaking business. She was like a magpie in her accumulation of bric-a-brac, and Gangadhar Rao was quite unable to refuse her any gift that might attract her fancy. Thus she lived in a world of low-slung silver chandeliers filled with scented candles, of plate-glass mirrors lining the walls, as well as a brazen throne on which she was wont to sit in thought, of ivory footstools and silver birdcages, their inmates setting up a perpetual twitter. Her beds, and there were several in various rooms, were made of silver, with satin sheets and velvet cushions and dozens of brightly coloured shawls scattered about, not to mention her tulwars, each with a silver haft encrusted with jewels, a collection of spears, her pearl-handled pistols and, naturally, statues of naked goddesses. Lakshmi herself predominated, although there was also Sita. Disturbing, however, was the statue of Durga, clutching her sword and riding a tiger, a constant reminder that perhaps Manu still saw herself as a warrior first and a queen second.

Yet in all this priceless accumulation, the queen remained the most priceless of all, even when she was clearly unwell. My initial reaction that she might be pregnant, especially when she suffered a fit of vomiting, was disappointed when one of her girls told me that she had just menstruated. But by now her skin was hot to the touch.

I was quite alarmed, my thoughts immediately turning to cholera, which for all the spices used on the food remained an ever-present risk. But there was no other evidence of the dread disease, and cholera seldom confines itself to one victim at a time.

Manu being unable to leave her bed, I went to see Gangadhar. 'I will send the physician,' he promised.

Bhumaka arrived an hour later, but by then Manu was covered in little red spots and was drinking quantities of water.

'What is happening to me, Angel?' she asked. 'Am I going to die?'

'No, no,' Bhumaka declared, peering at her throat and neck. 'Your Highness has an attack of the measles.'

'Oh.' She seemed relieved. 'I had measles, when I was a little girl.'

'Well, then, you see, Your Highness will soon be well again.'

I listened to the exchange in disbelief, beginning to recall my own experience and also the medical knowledge I had gleaned as a girl during my own sickness. And the next morning, as I had feared, Manu's spots had grown into large and distinct papules, yellow in colour and depressed in the centre. Once again, disturbing memories unsettled my mind. Manu herself felt much better this morning, and her fever seemed to have subsided, although her blisters were apparently itching. I had to catch her hands to stop her from scratching.

'Oh, really, Angel,' she complained. 'I cannot put up with this.'

Her girls were standing around, anxiously, but I dared not let them touch her. I bathed her face and arms myself, for it was here the blisters were most evident, then I tilted her head back to look up her nose. 'Whatever are you doing?' she inquired.

'Just checking,' I said, my heart sinking as I discovered the blisters inside her nostrils. 'Out,' I told the girls. 'Get out. All of you.'

'But who will look after me?' Manu asked.

'I will,' I promised, and having spotted Vima amid the other women, beckoned her. 'Go and fetch the rajah,' I told her.

'Me? Fetch the rajah?'

'Tell him that I request his presence, and that it is most urgent.'

She departed, most uncertainly. But Gangadhar himself arrived only a few minutes later, not looking terribly pleased. 'I am told Her Highness has measles,' he said.

'Unfortunately that is not the case, Highness.' I had met him at the door to the rani's bedchamber, and he could not see her clearly from where he stood.

'Then what is the matter with her?'

'Her Highness has smallpox, Highness.'

Gangadhar Rao made to step forward, and I checked him.

'Have you had the disease, Highness?'

He shook his head. 'I must be at my wife's side.'

'To do that is to risk death.'

'But . . . what is to be done?'

'This apartment must be quarantined. That is, no one must be allowed to enter.'

'You mean to let my wife die, alone?'

'I will tend to your wife, Highness. Our food and drink must be placed here, in the doorway. I will instruct the maids in whatever else I need. But they must not enter; otherwise the disease could spread throughout the palace. And should anyone else show symptoms of the disease, they too must be shut away.'

He stared at me. 'You will tend Manu? Will you not die yourself?'

'I will not die, Highness. I suffered this illness when I was a child, and recovered. That means I have a lifelong immunity.'

I could only pray that I, or rather the doctor who had attended me as a girl, was right.

Still he hesitated, his face twisting. 'But she will die.'

'It is in the lap of the gods, Highness. I will do everything possible for her.'

'You are a heroine, Emma. Save my wife's life and you may ask anything of me.'

He did not specify what might happen to me should the queen die. But this, as I had told him, was in the lap of the gods.

For the next week I was utterly alone with the rani. I fed her, bathed her, saw to her necessaries and attempted to soothe her spirit, which was often in a desperate state. In my anxiety I barely rested. Like everyone else, Bhumaka came to the door of the apartment to offer advice, but preferred not to enter. Annie often stood there, wringing her hands, no doubt worrying about what would happen to her should I succumb. Kujula stood there most of the time, looking utterly distressed. And Gangadhar came for a report every day. Happily there were only one or two other outbreaks in the palace, although there were several in the city itself.

Even Colonel Sleeman sent to ask if there was anything he could do to help the queen. It gave me some satisfaction to tell him, nothing.

Remembering everything the physician had told me so long ago, at the end of the week I knew that Manu would survive; he had said that if death was going to occur it generally took place within the first four days. Why she survived, apart from the fact that she was young and exceptionally strong and healthy, is as much a mystery to me as how she contracted the disease in the first place. But then it seems that no one knows the answer to these questions. The doctor had told me that most medical opinion held that smallpox, like cholera, was carried on the air, but I had to reflect that if that was the case, why had not everyone in the palace succumbed, as we were all breathing the same air?

My duties, onerous as these already were, became more so as Manu regained her strength. For the first few days she was so weak and debilitated that she was content to lie still and allow my ministrations, only asking me, time and again, 'Am I going to die?'

I always answered no, praying that I was right. When I began to be proved right, however, she became aware of the tremendous itch that was her entire body, for the little papules now covered almost every inch of her flesh, although most heavily gathered on her face and neck and arms. So desperate was she to scratch that I was forced to bind her wrists, which enraged her and brought forth a torrent of abuse.

'Do try to understand, Highness,' I said. 'Left to themselves, these blisters will eventually fade away. If you burst them, they are liable to leave blemishes or even pits on your skin. You must be patient.'

She understood my reasoning but was yet tormented, and the more so as, however careful we might be, the papules did from time to time burst and she could envisage her beauty disappearing. But as I had forecast, after ten days the blisters began to fade and by the end of a fortnight they were gone. So was the fever, and I could pronounce her to be over the illness.

'What is even more important, Highness,' I said, 'is that you can never again catch the disease.'

She squeezed my hands. 'You have saved my life, Angel.'

'You saved your own life, Highness, by the strength of your constitution.'

'I would not have done it had you not been here. You must never leave me, Angel. I would have you at my side, always.'

I did not feel that this was the right moment to remind her that my contract had only three years left to run. 'I thought you hated me, Highness.'

'I did. But now I love you. Can you love me in turn?'

'I always did, Highness,' I told her, not altogether untruthfully.

'And you will stay with me for ever?'

How to answer? However much I had grown to love Jhansi, and indeed the queen, I could not possibly contemplate spending the rest of my life here. But surely, in the course of time, the rani would tire of my company? 'I shall remain at your side for as long as you require me, Highness.'

'Then you shall call me Manu.'

The crisis was not yet over, at least emotionally.

'Does the rajah know I have survived?' Manu asked.

'I have informed him,' I said.

'And he has not come to me?'

I licked my lips. 'I have suggested that you remain in quarantine for another week, just to be safe.'

She gazed at me for several seconds. Then she said, 'Bring me a glass.'

'Time enough for that,' I suggested.

'I would have a glass,' she said. 'Now.'

I felt I had to obey. She had to look at herself at some time. And in fact, not all that much damage had been done. There was a deep pit above her left eye and several small ones on her cheeks; those on her arms and shoulders I felt were less important, as they would normally be covered by her sari, except of course when she was naked, as she now was . . . and would be, the next time she went to her husband's bed.

I held the mirror for her, and held my breath as she looked at herself, her face for the moment expressionless. Thus I was the more taken by surprise when she suddenly threw back her head and uttered the most anguished scream. Then, before I could think of anything to say, she rolled away from me, across the bed and off the far side, revealing that she had recovered more of her strength than I had supposed, and ran across the room to the table in the corner on which lay her swords and pistols.

My first reaction was that in her despair she sought my death, but when she turned the sword towards herself I understood her true intention. I hurled myself across the bed in turn, gained my feet on the farther side, and reached her as she presented the point to her stomach. I swept my hand sideways, striking her arm so hard that the sword clattered to the floor and she fell behind it, uttering a shriek. I kicked the weapon away, and when she reached after it, threw my arms round her to drag her backwards.

The sound of our conflict had drifted beyond the arch, and several people gathered there, at once curious and anxious, but afraid to enter.

'Go away!' I shouted at them. 'Go far away.'

To my surprise they obeyed, whispering to each other. I rose to my feet, still holding Manu tightly against me.

'Let me go,' she muttered.

'I will not let you go, in order that you may kill yourself,' I told her.

'What have I to live for?'

'You have everything to live for. What are a few marks on the face? You are still the most beautiful woman in Jhansi. Your body is still the most desirable in Jhansi. And you are still the Rani of Jhansi, with all your life to look forward to.'

She raised her head, tears dribbling down her cheeks. 'You seek to reassure me.'

'I am speaking the truth, Highness. Manu.'

She gazed at me for some seconds, then picked up the mirror again to peer at her face while we both heard the distant call, 'The rajah comes.'

'He must not see me,' Manu gasped.

'Of course he must see you,' I said. 'Only the rajah matters.'

'He will hate me. He will reject me.'

'He will love you more than ever,' I assured her, praying that I was right.

I was actually in a quandary. My instincts told me that I had to meet Gangadhar outside and warn him of the situation. But I was afraid to leave Manu alone for a moment, just in case she was overwhelmed by despair again. So I compromised, gave her a hug and said again, 'He will love you more than ever,' and went to the archway.

Gangadhar appeared a few minutes later, followed by a long gaggle of both men and women.

He paused at the sight of me. 'What has happened? They spoke of you and Manu, fighting.'

'I have to inform Your Highness that the rani is fully recovered from her illness.'

'That is marvellous news. But then . . .'

'The rani has had the smallpox, Highness.'

He frowned while he took in what I had said. 'Is she . . .?'

'Only slightly, Highness. But it is of considerable importance to so beautiful a woman.'

He drew a deep breath.

'Her Highness needs all the love of which you are capable, Highness.'

This time there was a quick glance, then another deep breath, then he went into the room.

I could do nothing more. I remained standing in the archway, joined now by the ladies and the guards, and watched the rajah slowly move across the floor to stand by the bed. Manu was kneeling in the very centre, her head bowed, her hair loose and masking her face. Nor would she move, even when he sat beside her. I could not hear what was being said, if anything, but I watched him put his hand under her chin to raise her head, and a moment later I saw him lower his own head to hers.

I drew the curtain and ushered the onlookers away. 'Her Highness is well again,' I told them.

The Crisis

In an unexpected fashion, the fact that Manu's complexion had been blemished brought her and Gangadhar closer together. I had always felt that he had been vaguely afraid of his child bride; now it seemed that he was less so as she had been proved to be human rather than a reincarnation of the goddess Lakshmi. For the next year the palace of Jhansi was a happy place.

I benefited as much as anyone from this royal glow. Manu wished me at her side always, except when she was actually closeted with her husband, and I took up permanent residence in her apartment. I could not of course take part in all of her activities, as it was quite beyond my capabilities, or in fact my desires, to gallop about the polo field with my reins between my teeth; in fact one of my aims was to get the rani to stop doing it as I worried for her safety. To please her, however, I learned to shoot with both musket and pistol, and endeavoured to be as interested as she when she wanted to talk about military matters, from the deployment of troops to the rumour that there was a man in America who had invented a pistol that would fire six times without reloading, although how this might be possible was beyond my powers of imagination.

But for the main part we talked, and laughed, and played. Her threats were entirely forgotten; indeed, they felt like a distant memory. She often returned to her desire that I should stay with her for ever, and as before, I temporized. I still had more than two years to run on my contract, and I felt confident that the overwhelming and almost irrational gratitude she felt towards me would fade. For the moment I was content to bathe in her friend-ship, shared by Gangadhar, and as a result the respect with which everyone in the palace treated me. And so I became caught up in the problem that was taxing all the rulers in India. Its name was the Earl of Dalhousie.

I have no means of knowing what instructions were given to Dalhousie before he left London to replace Sir Henry Hardinge, and certainly he came to an India that was as settled as at any time in its history, for all the ongoing rumblings of revolt in the Punjab. But he also came determined to make a name for himself. He was only thirty-six years old, which is very young to commence to rule a subcontinent containing many millions of people, certainly where one is entirely lacking in experience.

Almost the first thing the earl did on taking office was to re-invoke the Doctrine of Lapse and annex the state of Satara, claiming the lack of a male heir. Now Satara was situated a long way south of Jhansi; it was an enclave between Bombay itself and the dominions of the Nizam of Hyderabad. What happened down there could have very little effect upon the lives of us in the north. But it was the very idea that the pernicious doctrine could be resurrected that sent a shiver of apprehension and a ripple of unrest throughout all of the states.

'Who is this man who seeks to turn back the clock?' Gangadhar inquired. 'Do you know him, Emma?'

'No, Highness.'

I had never even heard of him until his arrival in Calcutta.

There the matter rested, but he returned to it. His first reaction after his and Manu's bereavement had been to reject out of hand my suggested solution of adoption. But now news arrived of a fresh annexation.

'This is a serious matter,' he grumbled, obviously thinking of his own situation. 'Now I am informed that Colonel Sleeman is leaving.'

Well, I certainly wasn't going to lose any sleep over that, but . . . 'You mean we are no longer to have a resident?'

'No, no. He is to be replaced by a Major Ellis. Do you know *him*?'

'No, Highness. But I am sure he will be an improvement.'

'Hm. Sleeman is being sent to Gwalior. What do you suppose that means?'

'I would say that Calcutta apprehends some possibility of trouble there.'

'Hm,' he said again. 'They have a succession.'

'They are like locusts, eating up the land,' Manu complained. 'Would it not be marvellous if another Shivaji could arise, and drive them into the sea?'

'Indeed,' I agreed, as I could not see it happening.

'Have you ever heard of the name Clive?' she asked.

'Everyone has heard of Clive.'

'And no doubt he was a great warrior. The beginning of the British conquest of India is generally regarded as dating from his victory at the Battle of Plassey, over the Bengalis of Suraj-uj-Dowlah, in 1757 by the English reckoning.'

I nodded.

'Do you know that there is a saying amongst our people that British rule would last for one hundred years from the date of that victory?'

'I have never heard that.'

'It is whispered in the bazaars. One hundred years. Do you realize that the hundred years will end in four years' time?'

Suddenly I felt quite anxious. 'There is no Shivaji, Manu.'

'One will arise. And then . . .'

'There would be enormous bloodshed,' I suggested.

She glanced at me, eyes flashing. 'Oh, yes,' she said. 'Oh, yes.' Then she smiled. 'But you need never worry, Angel. You are one of us, now.'

What she had said was profoundly disturbing. I had always known that while the Indians paid lip service to the Raj whenever they had to, they actually loathed their conquerors. But that they might have some ideas of overthrowing them was quite startling. I almost toyed with the idea of swallowing my principles and informing Colonel Sleeman before his departure. But then I reflected that it was the colonel's business to know all of this anyway, and equally that there was absolutely no chance of the Indians, subdivided as they were into rival princes and rival religions, ever uniting sufficiently to take on the Raj, save in the most exceptional circumstances, and I could not see such a situation being allowed to arise.

Besides, I had much to occupy myself nearer home, although in the first instance it was but a further example of British arrogance and Indian resentment. On a spring day in 1852 Manu, eyes gleaming, announced that the Prince Dondhu Pant was coming to pay us a visit.

'He and I were friends as children,' she told me. 'Although he is some years older than I. His father, who has recently died, was the last peshwa – the peshwas had been the hereditary chief ministers of the Maratha kingdom, an entirely meaningless title since the British conquest – and was Rajah of Bithur, for whose brother my father works. Now the rajah is dead, Nana Sahib – that is what they call him, you know, will become rajah.'

I wasn't at all sure about this, as I remembered that his father had been deposed by the British. But I looked forward to meeting an old playmate of the rani, and perhaps some of her family as well.

'Will your father accompany him?' I asked.

'Not at this time,' she said. But she was more excited at seeing her childhood friend again than regretful at not seeing her father.

★　★　★

Nana Sahib arrived a week later, riding a richly caparisoned elephant, and followed by a large number of the huge beasts. Cymbals clashed and flutes blew, and Gangadhar turned out the palace guard. The British garrison was less in evidence, as Nana was not a ruling prince, but many of the civilians lined the streets to watch the spectacle.

I cannot say I was taken with the prince, who was not a big man but had a large nose and shifty eyes. I liked him even less when he looked at me, for the eyes suddenly ceased being shifty and became extremely concentrated. This even while he was greeting Manu with every expression of joy.

'My dear sister,' he said. 'Your father sends you greetings.' Having embraced her he held her at arms' length. 'You have not been well.'

'I had the smallpox,' she said. 'Can you not see the marks?'

'But you survived the smallpox? That is a miracle.'

'It was thanks to the ministrations of my friend, Emma Hammond.' She beckoned me forward. 'Emma, let me present you to His Highness Dondhu Pant, Nana Sahib.'

'An Englishwoman,' Nana said, his tone suddenly angry.

He looked me up and down, to my embarrassment; I felt I was being stripped naked by his eyes, which was not difficult to do as I wore a sari. 'We must talk,' he suggested, getting a whole lot of meaning into the word talk. 'Your Highness,' he bowed to Gangadhar Rao.

'Welcome to Jhansi,' Gangadhar said. 'May all be well with you.'

'Nothing is well with me,' Nana said. 'Will you speak with me?'

Gangadhar gestured him towards his apartments. We women were not invited to join them, but that night Gangadhar sent for his wife and, when she returned, she woke me up to talk to me.

'He is very angry,' she said. 'Do you know what the British have done? He says on the express orders of Dalhousie himself?'

I waited.

'When they deposed Nana's father,' Manu said, 'they continued to pay him his pension as a rajah, eighty thousand English pounds a year. Now he is dead, they have ceased these payments to his son and heir.'

I could not help but feel the British might have a point, as

they could hardly be expected to continue disbursing such enormous sums of money to unentitled people for the rest of time
– but I was not about to say so.

'The prince wishes to fight them,' Manu said, her eyes gleaming.
'He says we will never have a better opportunity, with the war
in the Punjab dragging on, and now this business in Burma.'

Burma was where the Company was again embroiled, with
Dalhousie swearing that he had no intention of annexing any more
territory, but at the same time vowing to punish various insults
offered to British nationals by the Burmese, with the result that
an expeditionary force was on its way up the Irrawaddy. It was not
supposed they were going to come back empty-handed.

But that was not an adequate reason to take on the Raj!

Manu sighed. 'The rajah will not do it,' she said, sadly.

'The rajah is very wise,' I commented.

'Oh, you . . . you sympathize with the British. Because you
are one of them.'

'My sympathies are entirely with you,' I assured her. 'I have
no wish to see Jhansi destroyed.'

'Ha!' she commented.

Gangadhar Rao might not feel able to take up arms to assist Nana
Sahib, but he certainly entertained his guest on a lavish scale – if
at this time a rajah with nowhere to rule, Nana's pedigree as a
member of a ruling house was far stronger than Gangadhar's. So
we had an almost unending round of wild boar hunts and polo
matches and entertainments, great banquets to which all the upper
caste people of Jhansi were invited to consume vast quantities of
richly spiced food and watch troupes of performers.

I would have had to be blind as well as totally innocent not
to realize, at both these entertainments and on other occasions,
that Nana would far rather look at me than at any other
woman. I became quite apprehensive, but nonetheless was
totally surprised when one morning shortly before the prince
was due to depart I was summoned to the rajah's apartment,
together with Manu.

'I have had a request from Nana,' he said without preamble.

'We are to go to war,' Manu said, eagerly.

'No, no. I have talked him out of that absurd idea.'

Her face fell.

'I have persuaded him that the best, the only way, to handle this affair is for him to send an envoy to London to plead his case. I have heard from Lucknow that the begum was very well received by the queen and the government, and there is no reason why Nana's ambassador should not do as well.'

'The begum did not ask for a ruling of the governor general to be overturned,' I pointed out.

'This is the legal route, and will hopefully postpone any rash thoughts of fighting the Raj. Now, as I say, the reason I have summoned you here is that Nana has made a request.' He drew a deep breath. 'He has asked me to give you to him, Emma.'

I stared at him in total consternation. Fortunately, Manu had the same expression.

I tried to bring the subject down to earth, as it were. 'You mean, he wishes me to be governess to his children?'

'No, no. He wishes you for his harem.'

'That is quite out of the question,' Manu declared.

I could have kissed her. The very idea made me ill.

'I knew it would upset you,' Gangadhar said.

Did he *not* suppose it would upset me?

'But you must understand that Nana,' Gangadhar went on, 'if presently without visible power, is yet the last scion of a famous and powerful family, and were things to turn out badly between himself and the British, he could prove a formidable enemy. There are many in the Bundelkhand who would follow his lead.'

'He would never war upon us,' Manu declared. 'He and I played together as children.'

'That was a long time ago,' Gangadhar pointed out.

I could feel my entire being coagulating.

'He will be very angry if you do not go,' Gangadhar said, sombrely. 'He is in the mood to be angry about everything.'

'He cannot vent his anger while he is in Jhansi.'

'He leaves Jhansi tomorrow. It is his wish that Emma accompany him.'

'That is impossible,' Manu said again. 'Because . . . because she already belongs to another. Angel is betrothed.'

We both gazed at her in equal consternation.

'Who to?' the rajah asked. 'And why was I not informed?'

Not to mention myself!

'I will have the name within the hour,' Manu said. She squeezed my hand. 'I have had your marriage in mind for some time, but with so much else going on . . . I promise you, he will be young, and handsome, and . . .' she looked at her husband, 'wealthy.'

'Well,' Gangadhar said. 'She will remain here in the palace?'

'Of course. You will make him a captain of the guard. But . . .' she clapped her hands. 'He is already a captain of the guard. I know the very man: Abid Kala.'

I could only gulp.

I had never contemplated marrying again. I had certainly never contemplated marrying an Indian. I will not claim that the thought was abhorrent, but it was certainly worrying. Quite apart from differences of race and religion, it was now nearly three years since I had had relations with any man; I might as well have been a virgin. Additionally, I wasn't at all sure how I would react to an Indian's way of love-making in reality, as it were; I had of course by now read both the *Kama Sutra* and *The Perfumed Garden* from cover to cover – and more than once.

There was also the question of my contract, and thus my future. In two years I was supposed to leave the rajah's employment and in fact, as Manu was now seventeen years old and every inch a grown woman, and as educated as my teaching and her natural intelligence could make her, I had little more to contribute to her position. Now she wanted me as a friend, someone different to the sycophants with whom she was surrounded. But did I not have a life of my own to live? And if Gangadhar was as good as his word, and after nearly three years in his company I had the highest regard for his integrity towards me, I would begin that life as a wealthy woman.

But could I possibly suppose that could happen if I turned Manu into a liar before the eyes of all India? Because the news would spread: Nana, a man I had disliked on sight, would certainly see to that. Besides, an insidious but compelling reflection was that where did I have to go, where *could* I go if I left Jhansi? Even if I could be certain, and I could not be certain, that there was no longer a warrant out for my arrest in England, I knew there would be no welcome for me there. My parents had disowned me and I had no friends. I knew no other country but India and that would be barred to me.

There was also the perhaps unworthy thought that I would be

married to a man who would be regarded as my inferior within
the palace and thus who I should be able to control. Abid Kala
was also some years younger than I and was an extremely handsome man; he belonged to a family of soldiers and indeed his
elder brother, Risaldar Kala Khan, was colonel of the guard; they
were both, of course, kshattryas.

Abid was as surprised as I had been when he was summoned
to the rajah's apartment that very afternoon and informed that
he was to marry the memsahib. We looked at each other, and
I imagine he liked what he saw, for at twenty-seven I had just
about reached my apogee of beauty. His eyes glowed, and
glowed again when Gangadhar informed him that my dowry,
provided by the rajah himself, would be a lac of rupees. I may
be forgiven for wondering if this was the same lac that should
have been mine when I had completed my contract and as
there could be no doubt that the rajah was pleased with the
way Manu had turned out – delighted would be a more appropriate word – save in the matter of her inability to bear an
heir, and most fingers were being pointed in his direction at
that lack of fortune.

My fiancé and I were allowed no time together – I understood
that in normal circumstances I would not have seen him at all
before the knot was tied – because by now it was late and Nana
was returning, ostensibly to bid farewell to the rajah and rani
before he left early the following morning, but really to follow
up his claim to me.

'It is not possible, Your Highness,' Gangadhar explained.

'Not possible?'

'It is my desire to grant your every wish,' Gangadhar said.
'Except where it breaks the law. Mrs Hammond is betrothed, and
indeed, the wedding is set for tomorrow.'

'Betrothed?' Nana's face assumed a scowl, and he glanced at
his aide, a man called Tatia Tope, who commanded his own
bodyguard and was a very fierce-looking fellow, as if wondering
whether to take up arms on the instant. 'Why was I not informed
of this?'

'You did not ask,' Manu pointed out, pertly.

'I asked for her, this morning.'

'And in my anxiety to please you, I did not immediately inform
you of the situation,' Gangadhar explained. 'Instead I sent for my

lawyers, and indeed, summoned Mrs Hammond and her betrothed. But there is no legal way I can end a betrothal, save by the agreement of the couple themselves, and this they steadfastly refuse to accept. They are very much in love with each other.'

He was a consummate liar.

'The law,' Nana sneered. 'You are breaking the law by permitting this farce. Mrs Hammond is a widow. How may a widow marry again? A few years ago she would have been burned on her husband's pyre.'

I held my breath but Nana had no hope of out-arguing the rajah. 'You are speaking of Hindu law. Mrs Hammond is a Christian and an Englishwoman. In her religion, and under English law, widows are permitted to remarry.'

Nana still refused to accept defeat. 'Then where is this prospective husband?' he demanded.

'Why, standing next to his prospective bride.'

I was, as usual, immediately behind the royal couple and Abid was indeed standing beside me, more in his capacity as the rajah's bodyguard than as my fiancé, to be sure, but I gave him what I hoped was a loving smile.

'There is some subterfuge here,' Nana growled, accurately enough. But there was nothing he could do about it, save . . . 'When is this wedding to take place?' he asked.

'Why, as I have said, tomorrow morning.'

'Then with your permission, Gangadhar Rao, I will postpone my departure for a further twenty-four hours, that I may attend these nuptials.'

'Why, nothing would give me greater pleasure,' Gangadhar said.

'He does not trust us,' Manu said when we regained her apartment.

Which I supposed was reasonable enough.

'Are you afraid?' she asked.

'I am terrified.'

'Why? You were married before.'

'That was a long time ago. And it was not a happy business.'

'Your husband did not like the act?'

'He enjoyed the act too much. I did not enjoy it at all. At least, the manner in which he performed it.'

She sighed. 'I do not think my husband likes it at all. At least, not with me. But . . .' she brightened. 'Abid Kala will be a good husband. I know this. He will give you strong sons.'

That was something I had not actually considered. I became more nervous. And yet, filled with anticipatory excitement. Or perhaps anxiety would be a more accurate description of my emotions.

Annie was almost as excited as I, and certainly more anxious. 'Oh, Mum,' she said. 'Oh, Mum.'

'You have nothing to fear,' I assured her. 'You will continue as my maid. And Vima.'

'Oh, Mum! You'll be married to an Indian!'

'Why, yes,' I agreed, 'so I shall.'

She became even more excited when my wedding outfit was delivered, selected by Manu. My sari was a deep blood-red, made of brocade instead of silk, and a glitter of sequins. My headdress was a kind of shawl, which seemed to be composed entirely of small diamonds, rubies and sapphires. I would hate to be accused of being mercenary, but I could not help but wonder if this incalculably valuable garment now belonged to me, or if the rani would require it to be returned after the ceremony?

I was then required to visit Abid's family, who I had never met. Of course I did not wear my wedding dress for this occasion, which was quite low key. The Kalas were obviously disappointed at this, as traditionally a Hindu wedding is preceded by several days of huge feasting and entertainments. But like everyone else in Jhansi they were so used to obeying their rajah without question, and as I was known to be his favourite they were unfailingly pleasant, even if I was a little disturbed by the numbers of them, from babes at the breast to elderly grandmothers and great aunts, all studying my every move very carefully.

Manu was well aware of the ambivalence of my situation and she had Abid and I sent in to see her before the ceremony. We were both already dressed for the occasion, and if I say so myself, we made a splendid pair. My sari and headdress shone like the sun, and Abid was in full dress uniform of gold-coloured trousers, a green tunic adorned with gold braid and a gold-coloured shako; his tulwar hung at his side.

'I know you are going to be very happy,' the queen told us.

'But there are certain things you must bear in mind – you especially, Captain Kala.'

'I bow to your command, Highness.'

'Well, then, remember always that your wife continues to be my principal lady. Her duties require her to be at my side on all occasions, except when she shares your bed.'

'I understand, Highness.'

'Then go with the gods.'

And so the knots were tied and I was wed a second time. It was a strictly Hindu ceremony and none of the Europeans were invited. Presumably Colonel Sleeman would have had to be, for form's sake, but he had already left Jhansi. Nana and his followers were much in evidence.

And then it was done, and I was . . .? I didn't really know. Mrs Kala? I was certainly Abid's wife, and I was in a state of some agitation when we were left alone in our bedchamber, certainly after he had indicated that I should remove my sari; but then it was a night of firsts, so much so that I might have been a shivering virgin, as I was indeed trembling as he stood naked above me.

And then . . . I had never known masculine love-making, only sex-enduring. As I have mentioned, when he had cared to handle my body at all, my first husband had treated it like a sack of coal. And despite my reading of the *Kama Sutra* and *The Perfumed Garden*, and the fantasies I had since indulged in of myself and Mr Dickinson in particular, I had never expected personally to experience any of their recommendations. But Abid revealed not a trace of haste as he caressed me. When he began to make sure that I was ready to receive him I felt as if I was being whirled through space by an irresistible force, so much so that, when, always gently, he rolled me on to my face I merely anticipated some new caress, some unexpected source of pleasure. Well, I was right there; although when he raised my hips to have me on my knees I was suddenly alarmed, a moment later I was again in a world of sensations I had never suspected could exist.

Indeed, the first night of my second marriage, in such stark contrast to my first, was one of the happiest occasions of my life. To be allowed to explore a male body was as exciting and rewarding as anything I had ever known, while his virility – he was only twenty-six years old – was astonishing and might even have been alarming had I not been so determined to enjoy every minute of it. I felt like a young girl again, experiencing the joys of physical love for the first time; not that I, as a young girl, had ever experienced them at all.

I could only hope he shared my feelings; he certainly gave every evidence of it – we coupled five times on that first night. And yet, as the night progressed, I had found my mind drifting off to how wonderful it would be if the man in my arms, with whom I was sharing so much, could have been Captain Dickinson. Try as I might I could not shake off such unworthy thoughts, and at last I gave up the attempts and merely allowed myself to enjoy both the physical and the mental stimulation of what was happening to me. And so I entered a period of total bliss.

This extended beyond the mere business of copulation. Manu meant what she had said and my duties, both as her companion and as her governess, continued to be strenuous and time-consuming, but she also understood the values of domesticity, and I was given time off to visit Abid's parents, the first time I had left the palace compound without an escort since my arrival there four years previously. This was a nerve-racking occasion but they were absolutely charming, as were Abid's sisters, while even Risaldar, who usually presented an appearance of unbending severity, managed to laugh and joke.

Unfortunately, it is not possible to be happy in isolation. I was as happy as it was possible to be in the circumstances. Abid was happy. Abid's family appeared to be happy. But those around us, with whom we shared our lives, were less so.

This was not immediately apparent, as newlyweds are liable to be interested only in themselves. But I was surprised when I was informed that Major Ellis had arrived, had presented his credentials to the rajah and now wished an interview with me. I saw no reason to refuse him and so received him in the same chamber as that in which I had had my meeting with Sleeman, the difference being that I now wore a sari and was totally confident in my surroundings.

Major Ellis kissed my hand, taking in the many rings which I wore – all presents from Manu or the rajah – as well as the many bangles which adorned my arms and said, 'You are in every way worthy of your reputation, madam.'

I raised my eyebrows. 'Have I a reputation, Major?'

'Oh, indeed. You are famous for your beauty, and for the place you have taken in this community.'

Against my intentions, I found myself liking the man. He was tall and thin and somewhat cadaverous in appearance, but there was a twinkle in his eye.

'Do be seated,' I invited, and sat down myself, now in a position to watch his uncertain efforts to lower himself on to the cushions; fortunately, he was not wearing a sword. 'And no doubt you have spoken with Colonel Sleeman.'

He settled himself opposite me. 'Colonel Sleeman has made a full report on what he found here. This was his duty, you understand.'

'Yes. Then you will know that he tried to involve me in his "duty".'

He nodded.

'Is this also your intention?' I asked.

'I understand that would be impossible, and I would not presume. I merely wished to make your acquaintance, although not simply to satisfy myself that the tales of your beauty were not exaggerated. It is because I am sure we share similar objectives.'

'In which direction?'

'The keeping of the peace, throughout India, to be sure, but more especially here in Jhansi.'

'Do you see any evidence that the peace is about to be broken?'

'Indeed not. However, I am informed that His Highness received a visit from Nana Sahib a few months ago.'

'Nana attended my wedding.'

'You mean you knew him?'

'I have met him, certainly,' I said, carefully.

'I see. I presume, as he was here, he discussed his situation with the rajah?'

'I think you should ask the rajah that.'

'I have done so.'

'Then I can have nothing to add.'

He considered this, then he said, 'What did you make of Nana?'

'I did not, and do not, consider it my place to "make" anything of a prince, Major Ellis. I am not a princess.'

'I would say you are a singularly astute woman, Mrs Kala. I would merely like you to remember that we consider Nana to be a dangerous man, close association with whom can only mean trouble for Jhansi and all who live in it.'

'I am sure you said that to the rajah?'

'I am saying it to you. But I did not come here to quarrel with you. I merely wish to feel sure that your advice to the rajah will always be to keep out of trouble.'

'You flatter me, Major, in supposing that the rajah ever asks my advice.'

'If he does not he is a foolish man, and he did not strike me as being so. Now, Mrs Kala, I have a favour to ask you.'

'Another one?'

He smiled. 'This has nothing to do with politics. I have brought up with me several replacement officers and their wives. I know that you have kept yourself aloof from the European community here, but one of my companions is an old acquaintance of yours, and would dearly like to call, if that will be acceptable to you.'

'Ah . . .' The last person I wished to see at this moment was Captain Dickinson.

'She says you met but once, but she remembers you very well.'

'She?'

'Deirdre Wilson. She was Deirdre Fullerton when you knew her.'

'Good heavens! Yes, we met at a dinner party at Government House in Calcutta four years ago. By all means ask her to call on me, Major. I should be pleased to see her again.'

Deirdre Wilson was now twenty-three and had filled out a good deal, both in face and body; the somewhat sharp features I vaguely remembered were now rounded. She had become an attractive woman, and her hair was as glorious as ever, even when secured in a tight bun.

I wondered what she thought of the tall, sari-clad woman who greeted her at the palace gates. I supposed I had changed far less since Calcutta, save in dress and presence. Certainly she goggled at me for several seconds as I took her hand.

'How well you look,' I said. 'And now you are married, and . . .?'

'I have two children,' she said, getting her breath back from her journey.

'You must be very pleased. Are they with you in Jhansi?'

'Oh, yes,' she said.

I gestured her to a cushion, watching with sympathy her efforts to cope with her several skirts. 'And your husband . . .?'

'Is a captain in the thirty-fourth.'

Which I knew was a native regiment.

'I hope you are comfortable here?'

'Well, we are just settling in, really. But I am sure we will be very comfortable. It is a delightful place.'

'I find it so.'

'Well . . .' she looked embarrassed. 'We, my husband and I, would be very pleased if you would dine with us. When we have settled in.'

'Thank you for your kind invitation. But I do not think it will be possible.'

'Oh!' She looked disappointed. 'But . . .'

'I also have a husband,' I explained.

'Of course, he is invited as well.'

'I will discuss it with him,' I said.

Although I was sure her disappointment at my refusal was genuine, I wondered if the invitation had been a wish to secure a social cachet as I had never accepted any other invitations to dine in the European community, despite receiving several. One lady in particular, a Mrs Mutlow, had tried to lure me out of the palace on three occasions. She was, I gathered, a Eurasian – that is to say, of mixed Indian and European blood, but I did not hold it against her; my own children, supposing I ever had any, would be so described. But I did not have the slightest desire to be exposed to the gaze and the chatter of European ladies who would undoubtedly be fascinated at the concept of being married to an Indian.

In any event, before I could really consider the matter, or even discuss it with my husband, we were visited with crisis: Gangadhar Rao was thrown by his horse, and trampled, while playing polo.

As always, I was present to watch the match, together with Manu and all her other ladies; I had a double interest in the game as Abid was also playing. How the accident happened I cannot really say; there was a cluster of players and horses around the ball and when these separated the rajah was lying on the ground, his horse beside him. The horse scrambled to his feet, but in doing so trod on his rider, who gave a frightening shriek of pain.

Everyone dashed forward, excepting only Manu, who remained motionless in her seat as if paralysed, her face a mask of terror. Gangadhar was obviously in agony and was carried from the field straightaway to his apartment. Now at last Manu bestirred herself and walked beside him, holding his hand. Bhumaka was summoned and was present when the rajah was undressed. By now Gangadhar was spitting blood and had clearly suffered some internal injury, while he screamed again in agony when Bhumaka attempted to examine his chest and abdomen.

'What has happened?' Manu demanded. 'What has happened?'

'His Highness has broken a rib,' Bhumaka announced. 'At least one.'

'Will he be all right?'

'Oh, yes, Highness. Given time and rest.'

Manu breathed a sigh of relief.

Gangadhar was tightly bound up. He was in such pain that it was necessary to feed him hashish to dull his senses, but after a week he seemed to recover somewhat. Needless to say, all thoughts of accepting Deirdre Wilson's invitation had to be shelved; Manu was in a state of high agitation and needed me by her side constantly.

On the seventh day after the accident we were both called to the rajah's apartment. Gangadhar summoned a wan smile. 'There was a foolish thing.'

'Oh, my lord!' Manu knelt beside his bed to kiss his hand.

'I shall be well,' he assured her. 'I am feeling better already. But . . . I could have been killed.'

'Oh, my lord,' Manu said again.

'This has made me think,' Gangadhar said. 'It would appear that we are not to be blessed with an heir. Yet I must have one. I have therefore decided to adopt.'

Manu raised her head; here was the ultimate condemnation of a wife.

'This is essential,' Gangadhar went on. 'Not only for the succession, but how may a man die without a son to sacrifice to the gods in his honour? I have chosen Prince Damodar as my son.'

We looked at each other. The prince was a distant cousin of

the rajah, descended from that famous grandfather, to be sure, but his family had played no part in ruling the state, which was a possible reason for Gangadhar's choice. But he was only five years old!

'I know that he is very young,' Gangadhar conceded. 'But that is to the good. It will give us several years in which to train him to the position that will be his. This will be your duty, Emma. As you were governess to the rani, with such success, so will you be governess to the next Rajah of Jhansi, with equal success.'

I bowed my head. I did not doubt that I could do it, and again the prospect opened huge vistas of opportunity.

'And my role, Highness?' Manu asked.

'You will be the boy's mother, in every way,' Gangadhar said.

The wheels of adoption were set in motion immediately. The priests and teachers as well as all the prominent citizens of Jhansi were informed, as was Major Ellis. Somewhat to my surprise, he immediately asked for a meeting with me.

'I shall of course inform Calcutta,' he said. 'But may I inquire, as I am sure they will wish to know, what precipitated this step?'

'It is the rajah's decision, as he feels he may never have a legitimate heir of his own.'

'But . . . forgive me, is not the rani still very young?'

'The rani is seventeen years old.'

'Then surely she is entering her most . . . ah, fecund period?'

'She has now been married for four years, Major, only once conceiving, and then unsuccessfully; and as you may know, two years ago she was seriously ill.'

'Has she not made a complete recovery? And in any event, smallpox, unless it proves fatal, is not generally regarded as an inhibition to childbirth.'

'Still, four years . . .'

'Again, please forgive me, Mrs Kala, but . . . the rajah and rani *do* have conjugal relations?'

'Indeed they do. Or they did, until the rajah's accident.'

'You mean he is more seriously ill than is supposed? I understood that he was making a full recovery.'

'He is. But he has taken the decision to adopt. It is his right and his decision. What objections can you have?'

He considered for several seconds. Then he said, 'It is the

current policy of the governor general not to recognize adoptions as legal with regard to heirs.'

I frowned at him. 'Adoption is legal in Hindu law.'

'But not necessarily in British law. Do you know the stated reason Nana Sahib has not been allowed his father's pension? It is because Baji Rao was not his natural father. Donde Pant was adopted as a child. That is very nearly thirty years ago and has always been held valid, until now.'

'But that is outrageous,' I said, somewhat surprised to realize how much my feelings had changed on the issue.

'I am told Nana Sahib certainly finds it so.'

'But surely the government in England will overturn such a decision.'

'That I do not know. The case is still being heard. But I would not lay odds upon it. Now, it is possible to say that while that is the legal reason for the cancellation of the pension, the actual reason is Nana's long history of opposition to the Raj, his covert – using the very money paid to him in the form of his father's pension – support for the Rani of Gwalior during her opposition to our rule. However, British law, as you may be aware, rests to a very large extent upon precedent, rather than, shall I say, the Code Napoleon, where everything is written down. In those circumstances, it is possible to judge each case on its merits, and for a judge to say, well, you have broken this law, but as your guilt is affected by the circumstances of the event, you shall not be harshly punished, or perhaps not punished at all. But in Common Law, which has never been written down but has grown into a body of recognized crimes and penalties over the centuries, it is held to be unjust that a man should be punished for a crime and another man not punished for a similar crime merely because the circumstances were different. Having invoked the Doctrine of Lapse to deal with the situation in Satara, no doubt with very good reason, the governor general feels it his duty to continue to do so whenever the occasion arises.'

'It is also a very good way of enlarging the British dominions in India,' I suggested.

'It would be unworthy of me to suppose his motives were simply aggrandisement.'

'But not of me,' I pointed out.

'In any event,' the major said, 'I cannot believe such a pattern would be whole-heartedly supported by the British Government, if only because of the situation in Turkey.'

'What situation in Turkey?' I asked.

'Did you not know? The Russians are claiming the right to protect Christian churches and enclaves in the Turkish Empire, and more especially in Palestine. The Turks are refusing to accept this.'

'And the British are this time taking the side of the Russians?'

'Quite the reverse. The British, and the French, are supporting the Turks.'

'Two Christian countries are supporting a Muslim country against another Christian country?'

'Ah, well, you see, the Russian idea of Christianity is somewhat at odds with our own. But it is really a political matter. The Russians are talking about occupying Constantinople. This has long been a dream of theirs. Well, we can't allow that. Were a Russian fleet able to come out of the Black Sea at will it would entirely upset the balance of power in the Mediterranean.'

'Naturally,' I agreed. 'And how do the British propose to stop the Russians from occupying Constantinople? If that is what they wish to do.'

'A British squadron has been ordered into the Black Sea. It will pass the straits with Turkish permission.'

'That sounds uncommonly like an act of war.'

'Yes,' he said.

We gazed at each other.

'That is why I have suggested that it is unlikely the Raj will wish to become involved in any problems here,' he said. 'However, I must repeat my warning, that adoption must remain an uncertain business. There is also the point that if, happily, the rajah and rani do manage to produce an heir it might lead to endless complications later on.'

'That is extremely unlikely to happen, Major Ellis,' I said. 'And in any event, the adoption has already been publicized and cannot be changed now.'

'So be it.' He stood up. 'It is very good of you to give me so much of your time.'

I stood also. 'It was good of you to appraise me of the situation. Will you answer me a question?'

'If I can.'

'Supposing the worst were to happen and the rajah were to die, would you support the heir?'

'And his adoptive mother?'

'Well, she would have to be regent, were such a sad event to happen within the next few years.'

'A girl of seventeen?'

'A young woman of great talent, great powers of decision, and a superb education. There is also the point that Lakshmi Bai is no younger than Queen Victoria was when she succeeded her uncle, and not as regent.'

'That is indeed a valid point. And of course, Lakshmi Bai is your protégée.'

'I am happy to say that she is, yes.'

'And you consider her capable of ruling Jhansi. In the name of her adopted son, of course.'

'Yes, I do.'

'Then you may be sure, Mrs Kala, that should such an unhappy situation arise, I will recommend that the rani be allowed to continue her prerogatives.'

'Thank you, sir. That is all I can expect. As we both most fervently wish, the situation will hopefully never arise.'

Major Ellis's promise was indeed far more than I had hoped; I knew I would never have received such support from Sleeman.

I did not mention our conversation to either Gangadhar or Manu, who were both, in any event, fully bound up in the business of the adoption, which was accompanied by much religious ceremony and hours of prayer and meditation. I was just anxious to get my hands, metaphorically speaking, on the young prince, anticipating, correctly as it turned out, that I might be in for a difficult time. The prince might be only five years old but he was both wilful and disobedient, and imbued, no doubt by his parents, with the power that would one day be his.

The first time I had to discipline him, he turned on me and shouted, 'When I am rajah I will have you whipped.'

Fortunately, Manu was present. 'You will not be rajah for a very long time,' she told him. 'By which time you will have learned some sense. And in the meantime, if you do not do as Mrs Kala tells you, I will whip you myself.'

Indeed, she had to, on more than one occasion. Yet I believe she soon became genuinely fond of the boy, and his character indicated that he might well prove a successful ruler of Jhansi, given time.

But it did not appear that he was going to be given that much time; for in the autumn Gangadhar was taken ill. How much this was a result of his fall it was impossible to say, but he complained of violent stomach pains and often could not move because of the cramps.

Now seriously concerned about his health he began to dictate his will, and when it was done he summoned Major Ellis to the palace and had it read to him. Both Manu and I were present, as well as Damodar, although I doubt the boy understood what was going on.

The salient sentence read: *Should I not survive, I trust that in consideration of the fidelity I have evinced towards the British Government, favour may be shown to this child and that my widow during her lifetime may be considered the Regent of the State and mother of this child, and that she may not be molested in any way.*

Major Ellis listened to this and promised to do everything he could to have the rajah's wishes granted.

I wondered if I was the only person present who had noticed that the rajah had specifically said that Manu should be regent throughout her life, regardless of when Damodar attained manhood.

The will read, Gangadhar seemed to visibly decline. Bhumaka was in constant attendance but did not seem able to alleviate the pain. As for the cause . . . 'His Highness has angered the gods,' he muttered.

This upset Manu, who was well aware that not everyone approved of her husband's lifestyle.

I did my best to comfort her. 'That is the most complete nonsense,' I told her. 'Bhumaka is a quack. Can we not send for a proper doctor?'

'Where are we to find a doctor?' Manu wailed.

Well, Calcutta, certainly. But that was too far. Even Madras was a considerable distance. I snapped my fingers. 'Cawnpore! I know there was a doctor in Cawnpore.'

'Will a doctor come from Cawnpore to Jhansi?'

'Of course he will. I will have Major Ellis arrange it.'

I sent for the major, who came soon enough, although I gathered that he, and all the Europeans, were distracted by the news that Great Britain and France had declared war on Russia. Given the difficulties of the opposing sides actually coming to grips, situated as they were at opposite ends of Europe, no one knew what was going to happen or how it would affect India, again, given the historic Russian interest in Afghanistan.

But Ellis was eager to help. 'I had no idea the situation was so serious,' he said. 'I thought that the will was merely a formality. Of course we must have him properly examined.'

He sent off messengers the next day, but it was late in the year, November, and the monsoon was still with us; the rain teemed down and the roads were bad. Manu had to forego her morning gallops, but she would have done that anyway, as she spent most of her time at Gangadhar's bedside.

Bhumaka was now feeding the rajah great quantities of hashish to help him bear the pain, and he was hardly compos mentis most of the time. Manu's eighteenth birthday went uncelebrated, and we sat, or stood, around the bed, wringing our hands and all apart from myself wailing, as was the Hindu custom, until the morning, three days later, that Gangadhar Rao suddenly opened his eyes.

'Lakshmi Bai,' he said. 'Lakshmi Bai! Where is Lakshmi Bai?'

'I am here, Highness.' Manu knelt beside him.

'I give you Jhansi,' Gangadhar said.

'There is a doctor coming,' Manu said. 'From Cawnpore. He will soon be here.'

'I give you Jhansi, Lakshmi Bai,' Gangadhar said again. 'Guard it and our son, protect our people and obey the law.' Then he died.

The Doctrine

As was customary, Manu remained kneeling by her husband's body for some hours. In common with everyone else, I withdrew to the antechambers, carrying with me the new rajah. Here I was joined by my husband and Risaldar Khan.

'Will the rani rule?' Risaldar asked.

'Of course,' I said. 'Will you support her?'

'We will support her to the death,' he said, 'while she rules.'

I wasn't sure that I really liked that reply. But I said, 'thank you.'

'But you will stay in Jhansi?' Abid asked, anxiously, indicating that to the people at large I had been considered far more Gangadhar's woman than Manu's.

'Jhansi is my home,' I assured him. 'And you are my husband.'

When Manu emerged she immediately summoned me; we met in the schoolroom and stood at its great windows. Her eyes were dry, and in fact there was no evidence that she had wept at all. But then, Gangadhar had always been more of a father than a husband to her, and if she had had to allow him the use of her body this had never happened often enough, or enthusiastically enough, to arouse so tempestuous a spirit as that of Lakshmi Bai.

Now she looked out of the window at the town and temples. 'This is all mine,' she said. 'I will rule it well. But I will need help. Will you help me, Angel?'

'In every way that I can, Highness.'

'Manu,' she said. 'To you, I am Manu. What do you know of economics?'

'Very little, I am afraid.'

'The rajah would never discuss them with me,' Manu said. 'Did he never discuss them with you?'

'He never really discussed anything with me. Except you.'

'Did he love me, Angel?'

'I think he did.'

'And I never loved him,' she said, softly. 'But I belonged to him. Now all he possessed belongs to me. I will send for my father. He looked after the finances for the Rajah of Bithur. He will be my minister of finance. You will like my father, Angel.'

'I am sure of it,' I said, as confidently as I could.

'Now,' she said. 'Let us see to the funeral of the rajah.'

This took place the next day. Messages were sent to all the neighbouring rulers, but there was not sufficient time for them to attend. Yet the throng was immense, as all of Jhansi turned out, including the Europeans; I saw Deirdre Wilson and a man who presumably was her husband, but they were some distance away and there was no chance to speak. Major Ellis was also present, of course, and I indicated that we would like him to attend the palace after the cremation; my place was at Manu's elbow.

Dressed in mourning white saris, we proceeded to the banks of the river, into which the ashes would be scattered, and the pyre was set alight. The women wailed and gnashed their teeth, and Manu joined in, as custom demanded. This went on for some time, as the pyre burned for some time, and it was late in the day before we regained the palace. I was exhausted, I think emotionally as much as physically. My relations with Gangadhar Rao had been unusual and yet in many ways so very intimate, I felt that I had lost more than an employer – almost a lover. But Manu was keen to get down to business and summoned her secretaries: I wondered if she was reflecting that only a few years before she would herself have by now been dead, burned alive on the same pyre as had consumed her husband? She might hate the British, but she could at least thank them for outlawing suttee.

'I have many letters to write,' she told me and immediately began dictating, using the regal style. 'To Maropant Tambe. Lakshmi Bai, Rani of Jhansi, and your respectful and loving daughter, does earnestly beg and request you to join her in Jhansi as her minister of state . . .'

'To Hazrat Mahal, Begum of Oudh. Lakshmi Bai, Rani of Jhansi, sends greetings . . .'

'To Donde Pant, Rajah of Bithur, Lakshmi Bai, Rani of Jhansi, sends greetings . . .'

I wasn't at all sure that it was a good idea for Manu to open a correspondence with Nana while her position was not yet clarified, but he was an old friend, and in any event, Ellis, when he arrived, was entirely reassuring.

'I have forwarded the contents of the late rajah's will and his last requests,' he said. 'I have also been in touch with my superior, Major Malcolm, and he is agreeable to supporting me in having the rajah's wishes carried out.'

'Thank you, Major,' Manu said. 'I shall in no way disappoint your judgement.'

I accompanied the major outside when he left.

'Are you confident all will go well?' I asked.

'It should do. For the last fifty years Jhansi has been a loyal ally of the Raj, and has been well and efficiently governed, except for . . . well, there is no need to go into that. It is my opinion that to interfere with a system and a state that is operating so well would be very unwise.'

'But you yet fear that there may be such interference.'

He sighed. 'I have said there can be no reason for it. However, the decision rests of course with the governor general.'

'Well? He has never been to Jhansi.'

'Nor is he likely to. However . . . I am speaking in the most severe confidence, Mrs Kala.'

'I understand. And I appreciate your confidence.'

'Well, the fact is that the Earl of Dalhousie does not like India, or Indians. I have heard him say this, at a party at Government House.'

'But then, why is he here? How may one equitably govern or rule a country one does not like? Or people one does not like?'

Ellis shrugged. 'He is here because he comes from a distinguished family and is looking for advancement. I imagine there are several colonial governors who do not actually like the places or the people they are set to rule.'

'Are there any other colonies, if you choose to use that word, which quite compare with India?'

'Well, I suppose not. The best thing that can be said about the situation is that no governor is in place for more than a few years.'

And once I had thought that a handicap.

'Unfortunately,' I said, 'we happen to be here during his few years.'

'Well,' Ellis said, 'he has already been here more than three. His term of office must surely soon lapse and then, who knows. Again, I would be most grateful if you would keep this conversation to yourself, Mrs Kala.'

'I shall,' I promised.

And have done so, till now, when it no longer matters, all the calamities consequent upon the earl's attitude having occurred.

As I had long realized would be the case were the situation ever to arise, Manu threw herself into the business of ruling Jhansi with an energy that was frightening; one could almost feel that she had always known this position, this authority, this power would one day be hers. Now she seemed to stretch the human capacity to its limits. She rose at three in the morning, just before the first suggestion of dawn, did her exercises, had her bath, attended her devotions and then settled down to affairs of state, seated, as was the custom, on a high chair behind a drawn curtain so that she could not be seen by those she condemned, hearing petitions, passing judgements and making decisions, following which she reviewed her troops, drilling them and going amongst them, always surrounded by great enthusiasm.

During her mourning period she wore a white sari, but after that she changed her garb so as, it seemed, to represent both the male and female aspects of her personality: jodhpurs, a silk blouse with a low-cut bodice and a red silk cap with a puggree – known as a turban – wrapped around it. To this she added gold bangles and a variety of rings, mostly diamond and very feminine, but also a jewelled sword and two pistols thrust through her cummerbund, correspondingly masculine. Altogether she presented quite the most beautiful and compelling picture, the whole enhanced by the intense glow of her personality. Only after her rest did she appear to relax, but this was merely so that I could read to her.

To accommodate her day I had to restructure my own, and Damodar's lessons took place in the mornings to leave my evenings free. This actually suited me – I was not required to rise at three – as it was more in keeping with what I had been used to before coming to Jhansi. I was also delighted to watch the rani at work.

Marapant Tombe arrived to help his daughter within a week, and they spent long hours going over the financial records of the state. Marapant was a younger man than I had expected; like his daughter he was short and of an intense frame of mind. This in his case indicated pessimism, but perhaps he had a reason. Having spent most of his life working for the brother of a deposed rajah, he could hardly be blamed for supposing that his summons to power at his daughter's side would mean an instant upturn in his fortunes – I use the last word advisedly. However, a week in Jhansi auditing the books ended that supposition, so that the rani stormed into the schoolroom in the middle of one morning, when she should have been closeted with her ministers, dismissed Damodar with a wave of her hand – he was totally in awe of her – and threw herself into his chair.

'My father tells me there is no money,' she announced.

I was astonished. 'No money where?'

She waved her hand again. 'Anywhere. Actually, there *is* money, but none to spend. Debts,' she added, darkly.

'Debts? Whose debts?'

'The rajah's. It appears that whenever he wanted something, he just borrowed the money from people in Delhi. All those presents he gave me, bought with borrowed money!'

'Good lord!' When I looked around myself at the wealth in the palace I found that impossible to believe. 'You mean these money-lenders are dunning you?'

'They would not dare! But the debts are there. My father is afraid that if they become known they may upset the Raj. The Raj,' she repeated, angrily. 'A collection of upstart clerks.'

Who hold absolute power, I thought, remembering Ellis's veiled remarks. I had supposed his unspoken reservation had been because of the rajah's homosexuality, but it could easily have been referring to his lack of financial acumen.

'Can these debts not be paid off?' I asked.

'You are sounding just like my father.'

'Well . . .'

'Of course they can be paid off. But only by not spending the money on other things. I am the Rani of Jhansi. How may I not spend money?'

'Well . . . could you not sell some of the things in the palace? They must be worth a fortune.'

'How can I sell my family's heirlooms? My own possessions? I am the Rani of Jhansi. I would become the laughing stock of Hindustan.'

'Then what will you do?'

'My father says I must raise taxes and use the surplus money on repayments.'

'That seems very practical.'

'So, the first thing I do on succeeding to power is to raise taxes. That will not make me very popular.'

I could only say, 'You will always be very popular, Manu.'

She was not reassured, and went off muttering to herself. And certainly, immediately, nothing changed. The court was in any event in mourning for the dead rajah, so there were no polo matches or parades, and no decrees, whether regarding taxation or anything else. Nor would there be for several months, so we could all draw breath.

Manu, with her ebullient personality, soon recovered from her initial dismay at the state of her finances, and I could tell she was itching to get down to the serious business of government; but she had not been in power a month before she was confronted with, to her, a far more important problem than finance: an exhausted horseman rode in to tell us, between gasps, that the northern frontier had been invaded by a large band of Pathans, who were looting villages and burning crops.

'They have heard that we are ruled by a woman,' Tambe said.

Manu had listened to the news in silence. Now she seemed to rear like an angry tigress. 'Then they will learn the quality of that woman. Risaldar, summon my soldiers to arms. We march at dawn.'

'Do you mean the army or the guard, Highness.'

'I mean the army. The guard remains here. But everyone else is to march tomorrow . . . I wish these marauding brigands destroyed.'

'I will throw their heads at your feet,' Risaldar promised.

'I will throw their heads at my own feet,' Manu declared.

There was a moment of stunned silence. Then Risaldar ventured, 'Am I not to command?'

'You are commander of the army of Jhansi. I am the rani, and ruler of the state. Where I lead, you and your men will follow. You will obey my orders and my dispositions.'

Risaldar looked at me. But I was as thunderstruck as everyone else. 'Highness . . .'

'If you wish to discuss something with me, Mrs Kala, we shall do so in private. Haste, Risaldar.' She left the room.

'This is madness,' Risaldar said. 'How may a young girl command an army into battle?'

'Thanks to her studies,' I told him, 'the rani probably knows as much about military tactics as any man in India.'

Including the British, I thought. But I still felt it necessary to try to dissuade her from this adventure. 'Do you have to do it?' I asked, when we were alone. 'Isn't a situation like this the reason for having a British garrison in Jhansi?'

'Oh, Emma,' she said, laying out her weapons, 'you know how

the British operate. Captain Wilson will have to communicate with Calcutta before he can take the field; there are no British lives at stake here. And during the weeks that will elapse my people will be having their homes burned and themselves murdered. *My* people, Emma. I cannot remain here and allow that to happen.'

'But if you were to be killed, or even wounded . . .'

She rested her hand on my arm. 'I am not going to be killed or wounded. Those people are undisciplined robbers. I will command a disciplined fighting force. And I know how to conduct a campaign. Trust me.'

Actually I did; it was the fear of some unexpected incident, or perhaps a lucky shot, that frightened me.

The night was one of ceaseless activity, and at dawn Damodar, Abid – left in command at home – and I stood on one of the palace turrets to watch the army march out. They made a magnificent sight, Manu at their head, with Risaldar at her shoulder, then three hundred of her cavalry, followed by her six hundred infantry. A further hundred cavalry remained at the rear guarding the supply and medical wagons. All wore the green and gold uniforms, and the banners fluttered above their heads. Damodar clapped his hands and jumped up and down, and Abid hugged me.

Needless to say, the event brought Ellis hot foot to the palace. 'Would you like to tell me what is going on?' he inquired.

'I am sure you have heard of the trouble in the north. The rani is going to sort it out.'

'Intending to fight a battle?'

'If need be.'

'How can an eighteen-year-old girl command an army in a battle?'

'Forgive me,' I said, 'but was not Joan of Arc aged sixteen when she commanded the French army against the English at Orleans in 1429?'

'She did not command. She was a figurehead. The French army was commanded by professional soldiers.'

'Not every historian would agree with that evaluation.'

'In any event, are you presuming to compare Joan of Arc with Lakshmi Bai?'

He had now entirely aroused my temper. 'No, Major. I would never presume to compare an emotionally unstable girl, driven by her "voices", appearing at a low ebb in their fortunes to an essentially hysterical people, with a mature young woman, groomed and educated to rule, acting in her sworn duty as the leader of her people, taking whatever action she considers necessary to protect those people from harm.'

He stared at me. 'By God, what they say of you is true. You have entirely renounced your birthright and become an Indian yourself.'

'Sadly, Major, I am unable to do that. But if you mean that my sympathies are entirely with a civilization far older and more cultured than Christianity, which is now being systematically looted in the name of the inferior civilization that you represent, simply so that a lot of nabobs can grow enormously rich, you would be right.'

He left the room.

Brave words. And largely empty ones, unless something very dramatic were to happen, and that could involve a tragedy on an unimaginable scale. Meanwhile, I and all of Jhansi could do nothing but wait until, after a fortnight's activity, the army returned in triumph, bringing with them the grizzly trophies of their victory, amongst them several heads, which I with difficulty dissuaded Manu from mounting on the palace walls.

She was a bubble of enthusiastic triumph. 'We fought them in two battles,' she said. 'And beat them each time. They have gone scuttling back across the border, abandoning their loot. They will not trouble us again.'

I embraced her, as delighted as she was with her success, while Damodar gazed at his adoptive mother with wide eyes.

Manu's energy, stirred by the excitement of campaigning – something she had always dreamed of doing – now knew no bounds. She spent most of her time stalking the corridors of the palace, inspecting everything, talking with everyone. But she remained Manu, whatever her financial problems. One of her first acts was to order two of the new pistols, known as revolvers because of the revolving chamber which held six bullets and made them just about the most lethal sidearm ever invented. They came with an immense stock of bullets, and firing them became her greatest pleasure. Needless to say, she insisted that I join her in this potentially lethal sport.

I continued with my teaching duties, finding the young rajah just as quick-witted and intelligent as his adoptive mother. To my great relief and enjoyment, however, Manu did not insist that I remain within the palace, and so for the first time, save for the occasion of the rajah's funeral and my clandestine visit to the Kala family, I was able to go into the city and even visit the bazaars. This was a considerable adventure for me, leaving as it were the protective cocoon that had been erected around me, and wearing the sari which I still felt left me virtually naked.

Of course I did not go alone, but was always accompanied by Annie — who resolutely stuck to European dress, making her clothes herself — as well as Vima and Kujula, who acted both as bodyguard and as carrier for whatever purchases I might make. I did offer to have my salary reduced to aid the national finances, but Manu would not hear of it.

To my great relief, I encountered no hostility on these walks — quite the contrary. Everyone seemed to know who I was and was anxious to greet me, whether as the queen's friend or her governess, or as the late rajah's protégée; many attempted to press presents upon me and few wanted to take payment for my purchases. It was a most gratifying experience.

Less so were my inevitable meetings with Europeans. One of the first I encountered was Mrs Mutlow, who gave a monumental sniff.

'Are you allowed out now, Mrs Kala?' she asked. 'Or are you now the ruler of Jhansi?'

I could only ignore the wretched woman, and soon after had the far more agreeable experience of again encountering Deirdre Wilson, who was accompanied by her two children, both still quite small, and their ayahs, as well as a female servant.

'Mrs Kala!' she exclaimed. 'How very nice to see you.'

I couldn't be sure of the truth of that, for while she was wearing the tight-laced and all-concealing dress and petticoats and corset and stockings and boots and hat regarded as *de rigueur* by English women in the tropics, I was in a sari and my feet were bare save for a pair of shaped leather slabs secured to my big toe by a thong; these were simply to protect my soles from any sharp stones I might tread on.

'And you, Mrs Wilson,' I replied. 'I must apologize for not having taken up your kind invitation, but I'm sure you understand that what with the rajah's death . . .'

'Of course I understand,' Deirdre said. 'I did send a message of condolence to Her Highness.'

'I'm sure she will reply whenever she is able,' I said. 'But there have been so many, and she has been so very busy . . .'

'Grasping the reins of government,' Deirdre said. 'I entirely understand. But our invitation remains. We should be so pleased to entertain you.'

'Well . . .' I hesitated.

'I realize it cannot be a formal party while you are in mourning,' she said. 'But perhaps . . . you could come home with us now, and have a cup of tea. It is very hot.'

It wasn't actually, as in Jhansi January could be quite cool, but it was an invitation I felt I could accept. This was because, while I genuinely liked Deirdre, and was perhaps in the mood for a friend of similar background to myself, as I have said the one thing I feared about socializing was being exposed to the questions and implied criticism of a pre-selected group. But our meeting had been entirely by chance; there was no way she could have anticipated it and prepared for it. So I accepted.

The Wilsons lived in the cantonments, situated just outside of the city, only a short walk from the bazaar, which was itself outside the wall. This was the first time I had actually visited a British military establishment; it consisted of neat rows of barracks for the soldiers, and bungalows – single-storied little houses – for the married officers and their families, making a quadrangle around a large open space on which several bodies of troops were drilling, and even squadrons of cavalry galloping to and fro, raising a good deal of dust. Bugle calls rang out, the red tunics and steel bayonets gleamed in the sun, and above all the various regimental flags, dominated by the Union Jack, fluttered in the breeze.

'I'm afraid this rather tiresome business goes on all day,' Deirdre explained. 'And the bugle calls continue until Last Post, at half-past ten. As I say, very tiresome. But one gets used to it.'

I was escorted up a flight of wide steps to a veranda, beyond which jalousied doors gave access to a comfortably furnished lounge. Deirdre's servants took charge of Vima and Kujula, while Annie merely looked awkward.

'May she remain?' I asked.

'Of course,' Deirdre agreed, and escorted us into the house.

I felt that I was stepping back in time. It was not merely the chintzes and the stuffed furniture; there were pictures on the walls mainly of English scenes and there was a case full of books.

'I'm afraid it is not a palace,' Deirdre remarked.

'It is a home,' I suggested and glanced at Annie, who I could tell was as overcome by this remembrance of things past as myself.

'Do sit down.' Deirdre rang the bell and ordered tea. 'But that palace,' she said. 'I have never seen anything like that.'

'And you only saw a few rooms,' I said. 'Would you like to see some more?'

'Oh!' she cried. 'Do you think I could?'

'Certainly. You must come and have tea with me, and I will give you a guided tour.'

'Oh,' she said again, and could not resist a look at my bare and dusty toes. 'You have . . . well . . .'

'Gone native,' I suggested.

'No, no, I didn't mean that.' She gazed at me with huge eyes, knowing that was just what she had meant. 'Don't you . . . well, Mr Wilson forbids me, or the children, to go about without shoes. He says we could be, well . . .'

'There are insects which like to burrow into the flesh,' I agreed. 'But as long as one inspects one's feet every day, they are easily seen and removed with a needle.'

Deirdre gave a little shiver.

'And the pleasure, the freedom of going without shoes is unbelievable, until you try it.'

The two Wilson children had followed us into the room, and were sitting side by side on a settee, facing me. Now the girl asked, 'Do you wear anything under your sari, Mrs Kala?'

'Mary!' her mother admonished.

I smiled. 'No, I do not. But you see, the sari, once it is on, is several layers of cloth, so I am just as modestly dressed as you are.'

Which was not altogether true.

'I do apologize,' Deirdre said.

'I am not in the least bothered,' I said. 'Let them ask me whatever they like.'

'Well,' she said doubtfully, perhaps knowing only too well what they would like.

'Were you really captured by thugs?' asked the boy, Harry.

'No,' I said. 'If I had been captured, I would have been killed. Everyone else in my caravan was killed.'

'You speak of it so calmly,' Deirdre murmured.

'It was a long time ago,' I reminded her.

'And you executed the thug leader with your own hands,' Harry said.

'Harry!'

'That is not quite true,' I said. 'I had him arrested, and he was executed.'

'Oh, but, they say . . .'

'Harry!' his mother snapped again, and rang her bell. An ayah promptly appeared; no doubt she had been listening beyond the door. 'I think it is time the children had a nap,' Deirdre announced, in tones that left me in no doubt that within her own home, at least, she was fully in control.

'You come,' the ayah said, and the children obediently stood up.

'I hope you will visit us again, Mrs Kala,' Harry said.

'I'm sure I shall,' I said, and waited for them to leave the room. 'You mustn't be hard on them,' I told Deirdre. 'They are very well behaved. I had no idea so much was known about me.'

'My dear, everyone talks about you.' She flushed. 'Well . . .'

'They do not have much else to talk about. I am not offended. When you come to the palace you must bring the children with you; I'm sure they'll find it interesting. But surely there are more important things in life than me. What does your husband make of this business in Turkey?'

'Oh!' She threw up her hands. 'I don't even want to think about it. They are speaking of sending an army to the Balkans! Can you imagine?'

Actually, I couldn't, except that I couldn't see that the Balkans would be much different to India from a campaigning point of view. 'Mr Wilson won't have to go, will he?'

'Oh, I hope not. I don't think so. He is totally committed to the Indian army. He would like to stay here in Jhansi.' Another of her nervous flushes. 'So would I. I so like the place. And the people are so nice. So . . . so contented.'

'So well governed,' I suggested.

'Oh, yes. You're very happy here, aren't you?'

'Certainly I am. I also like the people.'

'And the rani is your close friend.'

'She is my friend, yes.'

'And now that you're married . . .' she hesitated, waiting. I knew that she was desperate to ask what it was like to be married to an Indian, but dared not. And I was not about to tell her.

'Well,' she said, when she realized I was not going to enlighten her. 'Do you remember that Mr Dickinson?'

'Yes,' I said.

'He was quite smitten with you.'

'That also was a long time ago.' I began to feel somewhat unnerved.

'Do you know, I met him just before we left Calcutta.'

'Did you? I had no idea he was still in India.'

'Oh, yes. He's a major, now. He told me he would probably be coming up here.'

'To Jhansi?'

'Yes.'

'Whatever for?' I was quite disturbed. I had no wish to meet James again as a Hindu housewife.

'It seems a squadron of the lancers is to be quartered here for a while, and he is to command it.'

'Good heavens,' I remarked. 'I suppose he is married by now.'

'No he is not. Did you never hear from him?'

'Was there any reason to?'

'Well, I would have supposed . . . he sends you his warmest regards.'

'After five years? Does he not know I am married?'

'I'm not sure. I . . . . Oh, here's Mr Wilson.' She seemed relieved.

So was I. I looked at the clock on the table. 'Good heavens! Is that the time? I really must be away. Annie, will you fetch Vima and Kujula?'

She scurried off, and I stood up as the captain entered the room. He was a good-looking man in a nondescript fashion, but wore his uniform well, although he was carrying what looked like a musket.

Hastily he removed his cap on discovering me, while he looked at his wife for an explanation.

'Mrs Kala very kindly came home for tea,' Deirdre explained.

'I was just leaving,' I said.

'But it is a great pleasure to make your acquaintance, Mrs Kala.' He shook my hand. 'Charles Wilson.'

'My pleasure, Captain.' I could not stop myself from looking at the gun, which he still carried.

'Ah,' he said, enthusiastically. 'This came this morning. It's an Enfield three-five-seven.'

'I beg your pardon.'

'It's a brand-new design. A rifled musket. Do you know about rifles, Mrs Kala?'

He was bubbling with enthusiasm.

'I'm afraid very little.'

'Ah. Well, you see, the problem has always been efficiency. You could say that a musket is the most inefficient firearm imaginable with its short range and poor accuracy; one has the certainty that the next shower of rain will render the powder useless. The concept of the rifled bullet was intended to overcome some of those drawbacks, but the other difficulties remain. The principal one is the length of time it takes to reload after your shot. And this takes long enough with the normal musket using the normal powder charge. Ramming a grooved rifle bullet home is infinitely more difficult. Now a Frenchman, Claude-Etienne Minie, has come up with the idea of a self-contained charge. Here.'

He produced one from his pocket, and I politely inspected it.

'It is made of paper.'

'Indeed. That is called a cartridge, and contains both the bullet and the powder charge. Thus, you see, there is no risk from the weather soaking the touchhole and the powder. It is all contained in the cartridge.'

'It looks too big for the barrel.'

'Well, the whole idea is that it should be a very tight fit. But it is well greased, you see, and is forced down with the ramrod. Once that is done and it is in place, it expands again to fill the entire barrel, so there is no escape of gases. And then, why, you have a weapon which is not only accurate at about twice the range of a musket, but is virtually impervious to the weather. Mark my words, Mrs Kala, it will revolutionize warfare.'

'Does warfare need to be revolutionized, Captain? I would have supposed it is quite horrible enough as it is.'

He gave me an old-fashioned look. 'There will always be wars, Mrs Kala. It is in the nature of man. And that being so, the object must always be to win a war, by the quickest and least costly method. This rifle will do that for the side possessing it.'

'Unless the other side possesses it too.'

He smiled. 'That is hardly likely to happen here in India, Mrs Kala. For which we must all be thankful.'

I didn't suppose I could argue with that. In any event I was more concerned at the possibility of Mr Dickinson turning up in Jhansi, apparently unmarried . . . but after very nearly five years since last we had seen each other. It was not possible for him still to be carrying a torch.

On the other hand, according to Deirdre, he had requested the posting. And sent me his warmest regards! If he did *not* know I was married . . .?

But did it matter what he remembered, or sought? I *was* a married woman, as he would discover the moment he arrived. When I thought that, I realized that it was usual to insert the word 'happily' before married, and I had not done so, even in my thoughts; the euphoria of the first days had long vanished, as Abid was apparently disappointed at my failure to conceive and I was realizing that we had absolutely nothing in common save for sex. But I certainly was not *unhappily* married, as had been the case with Mr Hammond. Abid was handsome and virile, unfailingly polite and deeply respectful. I understood this was because I was an intimate of the rani, but then, had I not been an intimate of the rani, we would not have been married in the first place.

Yet the fact remained, in Hindu law a husband's rights were absolute. Well, to a large extent they were in England. The saving grace in Europe, from a woman's point of view, was public opinion. It might be possible in some countries for a husband to kill his wife if he discovered she was having an affair, and certainly if he caught her in flagrante delicto, and get away with justifiable homicide. And in normal circumstances he would have no difficulty in obtaining a divorce. But in no circumstances would English or Continental public opinion, or their legal systems, accept that he had the right to mutilate her, and in such a fashion that no other man would ever look at her. Every time I thought of Mootoo my blood ran cold.

But what *was* I thinking? I had no intention of getting too close to Major Dickinson. Or of allowing him to get too close to me. That would be absolute madness. Quite apart from Abid's reactions, it could mean forfeiting the patronage of the rani.

My emotions were all a result, I told myself, of that visit to the Wilsons, of that glimpse of the past on which I had so resolutely turned my back . . . but to which I still aspired to return? I suppose I did, deep in my heart, but only in the company of a man who I could love with all my heart, and who would respond with all of his — and I had never met such a man.

Never had I felt so unsettled, so uncertain of the future, and thus I sought the comfort of Manu's reassuring confidence.

'How did your exploration of the city go?' she asked.

'It was very enjoyable. I took tea with Captain and Mrs Wilson.'

'Ah, yes. You told me that you knew Mrs Wilson in Calcutta.'

'Briefly, yes.'

'And is she happy here in Jhansi?'

'Very happy. She would like to spend the rest of her life here.'

'How very complimentary,' Manu said. 'But the British arrangements being what they are, her husband will probably soon be moved on. What do you think of the situation with Turkey? Or perhaps I should say, what do the Wilsons think?'

'That there will be a war.'

'Between England and Russia? That will be a great occasion. Who do they think will win?'

'Oh, the British.'

'How can they be so confident? Is not Russia several times the size of Great Britain? And does it not have several times the population?'

'That is true,' I agreed. 'But superiority in population, even by many times, does not guarantee victory.' I bit my lip.

Manu smiled. 'Or the British would never have conquered so much of Hindustan? You may yet be proved wrong.'

'Anyway,' I hurried on, grateful that she had not taken offence. 'The British are not alone. The French will help them.'

'The French,' she said, thoughtfully. 'The British beat the French too, here in Hindustan. My Maratha ancestors employed French officers to lead their armies, but they were defeated.'

I didn't wish to become involved in *that* aspect of history. 'The British will also have the advantage of better weapons,' I said. 'Not to mention the fleet.'

'The fleet,' she commented. 'Ships. How may a ship fight a battle?'

I realized with some surprise that the rani had never seen the sea, or, indeed, any large body of water, apart from the Ganges.

'Ships can stop armies being moved to where *they* can fight a battle,' I pointed out. 'Did you know that the British are about to start using a new rifle?'

'What new rifle?'

'It is called an Enfield, and will be more accurate, and at a greater range, than any existing weapon. And more easily loaded.'

She frowned. Now I had really caught her interest. 'How do you know this?'

'Captain Wilson showed me one, yesterday morning. A shipment of them has arrived for use by the garrison.'

'And you say you have seen one? I should like that.'

'Well, I have invited Mrs Wilson and her children to visit me here, if that is acceptable to you. I could extend the invitation to the captain as well, and ask him to bring one of the rifles to show you.'

'I should like that very much.'

'Will you re-arm your own guard with these guns?'

'Ha,' she commented. 'Even if I could, where would I find the money?'

'I am sure things will improve,' I said. 'But may I ask, is Risaldar Khan still in command of the army?'

She looked at me.

'I mean,' I explained, 'did you actually command your people in the battle with the Pathans?'

'I rode at their head,' she declared, proudly. 'I killed one of them with my revolver. Risaldar Khan was at my shoulder, obeying my orders.'

'He was content to do this?'

'Of course. Risaldar Khan will follow me anywhere. As will your husband. Will he not?'

It was my turn to say, 'Of course,' while I reflected on my conversation with the brothers immediately after Gangadhar's death. But the conversation was leading in the direction I wished. 'I wonder, have you given no thought to marrying again?'

'It is not possible for a widow to remarry. It is against the law.

Hindu law,' she added. 'Besides, I am the Rani of Jhansi. I could only marry beneath me, and that too is not possible.'

'Well, then,' I ventured, almost holding my breath. 'As you say, Manu, you are Rani of Jhansi. You are all-powerful.' At least within the palace. 'Have you never thought of sharing your bed?'

Now I did hold my breath, as she did not immediately reply.

'I mean, have you not considered taking a lover?'

'I will not break my marriage vows.'

'Surely they no longer apply now that you are a widow.'

'My vows apply throughout my life.'

'Oh. But you had no objection when I married again. It was your decision that I should do so.'

'You are not Hindu,' she pointed out. 'In your religion it is permissible. Besides, I could see how afraid you were of going to Donde Pant.'

I shuddered. 'I know he is a friend of yours, Manu, but I think he is a man who ill uses women.'

To my surprise, she nodded. 'I believe you may be right. But he is still a man who promises much for Hindustan.'

Promises much disaster for Hindustan, I thought, but decided it would be unwise to say it.

'May I ask you a question?'

'Of course.'

'Is divorce possible in Hindustan?'

'I do not know if it is in Hindustan. It is not possible in Jhansi.' Her eyes narrowed. 'You wish to leave your husband? Does he ill-treat you? Does he not treat you with proper respect?'

'Of course I do not wish to leave my husband!' I cried, rattled. 'And of course he treats me with proper respect. I am just inter-ested in the law. It is the law in Jhansi that divorce is illegal. Is that right?'

'Divorce is illegal in Jhansi because I will not recognize it,' the rani said. 'If one of the feringees wishes to divorce, let he, or she, go to Calcutta. Now remember, I would like to see this new rifle.'

So there it was. I reminded myself that it was not my intention to run off from my husband, or to indulge in an affair, but the rani's views on the matter were so rigid I doubted I could even let myself meet Mr Dickinson, which would mean once again cutting myself off from European society, as I did not doubt that should I accept an invitation from Deirdre to a meal after his arrival he would certainly be present, while to have Abid with me, as I would certainly have to do if it were a dinner invitation, would be positively dangerous.

I endeavoured to make my feelings clear to Deirdre when she brought her family up to the palace for a visit. Getting her alone was not difficult, as the children were in raptures over their surroundings and Manu, who received them herself, was equally in rhapsodies over the new rifle. Her knowledge of firearms quite surprised Captain Wilson, and the two were quickly into an animated discussion.

'Is there news of the arrival of the lancers?' I asked Deirdre.

'I believe they will be here around the middle of March,' she replied. 'With the next caravan from Calcutta. They will be its escort.'

'Ah,' I said. 'I have been thinking.'

'I know, my dear,' she said. 'I shall arrange a meeting just as soon as possible.'

'That is what I have been thinking about,' I told her. 'I do not wish a meeting.'

Her eyebrows arched, as they had a habit of doing. 'I don't understand. You do not wish to meet Major Dickinson? Again?'

'Yes,' I said. 'I do not wish to meet him, again.'

'Oh,' she said. 'Well . . . then we must see that you do not.'

'Thank you,' I said.

But I could tell that she was not convinced, and was considering that I was no doubt taking this attitude out of form rather than belief.

'I am going to shoot this gun,' Manu announced. 'Come along. You shall watch me.'

I looked at Captain Wilson, who waggled his eyebrows. But there was no gainsaying the rani. She set off down the stairs to the polo field, accumulating several of her people on the way, followed by the Wilsons and me. The children were off somewhere with Annie.

We reached the open space.

'Set up a target,' Manu told Abid, who with his brother had also now joined us.

Abid signalled two of his men and they hurried off with a target.

'At what range, Highness?' Risaldar asked.

'Captain?' Manu turned to Wilson.

'Well . . . the rifle is effective to four hundred yards, Your Highness. But we are talking of a marksman.'

'And you do not think I am a marksman?'

'No, no, Your Highness. But you have never used this gun before.'

'One gun is much like another, if the sights are true,' Manu pointed out. 'Four hundred yards,' she shouted.

Abid hesitated, as if unsure he had heard properly, but like everyone else he was not going to argue with his queen. The target was placed.

'Now show me how to load it,' Manu said.

'Well,' Wilson said, 'you have first to bite off the head of the cartridge, like so.' He demonstrated. 'Then you force it down the barrel with your ramrod . . .'

'Wait.' Manu said. 'I must do everything. Have you another cartridge?'

'Yes,' Wilson said. 'But . . .'

'Give it to me,' Manu commanded. 'Do you not suppose my teeth are strong enough?' She gave him one of her dazzling smiles. 'I have excellent teeth, Captain.'

With surprising reluctance Wilson handed her the cartridge, and seemed to be holding his breath as she placed it between her teeth, which were indeed very fine and white, and bit. Then she spat out the cap. 'Ugh,' she commented. 'That is a strange taste. Now . . .' she forced the cartridge into the barrel, and rammed it home. She then held the gun to her shoulder and sighted along it for some seconds, before being apparently satisfied.

'Ah . . . don't you think your people should stand aside?' Wilson ventured. For Abid and his two soldiers were standing immediately beside the target.

'I am going to hit the target, Captain, not them,' Manu pointed out, and squeezed the trigger. The puff of smoke rose into the air, and the watching courtiers broke into applause.

'I like this gun,' Manu commented.

Wilson went forward to peer at the rondels. 'Good heavens!' he commented. 'A bull.'

'You mean I placed my shot in the very centre of the target,'

Manu pointed out, disapprovingly. 'Which is where I intended to place it.'

'I do beg your pardon, Your Highness,' Wilson said. 'It is an English expression, and just slipped out.'

'I am sure,' she said. 'I would like to discuss these rifles with you, Captain Wilson. Now let us take tea.'

At the conclusion of the meal I accompanied the Wilsons on to the forecourt.

'Will you allow her to equip her army with the Minie rifles?' I asked. 'It would make her very happy.'

'She is a warlike young lady, isn't she,' he agreed. 'I'll have to refer the matter to Calcutta, but I don't think it would be a very good idea.'

'How can it possibly harm you? Her army is only a few hundred strong.'

'I was thinking of the other implications. There are quite a few, but principally the religious element. Concerning the cartridges, you see.'

'There is a religious element in a cartridge?'

'Well, yes. You see, it is greased. Well, it has to be, for it to be forced down the barrel.'

'I saw that.'

'And to get it into the barrel at all, the head needs to be bitten off.'

'I saw that too.'

'And your queen did not like the taste.'

'So she said.'

'Well, you see, the grease used on the cartridge is mainly cow fat.'

I stared at him in consternation. 'You allowed the rani's lips to touch the fat of a cow?'

'Well, she would bite it herself.'

'Don't you realize that as a Hindu she is now defiled?'

'Oh, come now, Mrs Kala, you must agree that is the most arrant superstitious nonsense.'

'Not to a Hindu, any more than the eucharist is to a Christian.'

He looked down his nose. 'That is very close to blasphemy.'

'As you committed blasphemy by allowing the rani to bite that cartridge.'

'Surely, if she never finds out . . .' Deirdre interposed, anxious to keep the peace.

'Do you intend to issue this rifle and those cartridges to the entire sepoy army?'

'That is the intention, yes,' Wilson said, his tone stiff.

'And you really think you can keep the composition of the grease a secret?'

'I do not think that will be necessary,' he said. 'The sepoys are professional soldiers, not hysterical women.'

'Charles!' his wife protested.

'I am sorry,' he said. 'But there it is. If the rani does not choose to use the Minie cartridges, that is entirely up to her. The army will do, as it has always done, what is required of it. Come along, children.'

They had been gazing at us with wide eyes. Now they hurried behind their father.

Deirdre hesitated. 'I am most terribly sorry,' she said.

'So am I.'

'Will you . . .' she bit her lip.

'No,' I said. 'No point would be served at this moment. You had better go with your husband.'

So there was the end of another potential friendship. I meant what I said, that I could see no purpose in telling Manu what had happened at the moment. If she went ahead with her ambition to re-equip her army with the new rifle, then she would have to be told. But hopefully she would learn the facts from another source before that happened. Whatever my attitude to the demands of the various agents, I still wished to keep the peace, certainly between the rani and her British overlords. If that were possible.

Like everyone, a few weeks later I stood on the palace balcony to watch the entry of the lancers into Jhansi. There weren't very many of them, only a squadron, but they made a splendid sight with their blue and gold uniforms and turbans and their glittering lance heads. From a distance it was impossible to identify the officers riding at their head, but obviously the one in the centre would be Mr Dickinson. I could at least reflect with some relief that after my quarrel with the Wilsons I was unlikely to have to meet him for a while.

The lancers made their way round the city to the cantonments and the spectators went about their business. I was rising from my afternoon rest, a few hours later, when I received a summons to attend the rani in the court room, to my surprise, where I found that she had taken her seat upon the throne, behind her curtain, and that her leading counsellors, including her father, were also present.

'Come to me,' she commanded, and I went to her chair. Seated beside her, on a smaller and lower chair, was Damodar Rao, for the first time. He was clearly in total awe of the proceedings.

'We are to receive an official visit from the resident,' she said in a low voice. 'He has received despatches from Calcutta, which will certainly include a directive from the governor general. I wish you here so that you may advise me on any point of language that may arise.'

I bowed, while my heart raced; suppose Ellis was accompanied by Mr Dickinson? But there was nothing for it. I took my place beside Maropant Tambe, on what might be termed the public side of the curtain.

Major Ellis arrived a few minutes later. He was accompanied by two secretaries, but not, I was relieved to see, by Dickinson.

He advanced into the centre of the room, and bowed. He had, of course, attended the rani on a state occasion before, and knew the drill. Yet I could see that he was nervous: it was a cool afternoon, but his jacket was stained with sweat.

He addressed the curtain. 'His Excellency, the Earl of Dalhousie, Governor General of India, sends greetings to Lakshmi Bai, widow of the late Rajah of Jhansi.'

We waited. I found I was holding my breath.

Ellis continued, 'His Excellency has instructed me to convey to Your Highness the sincere condolences and sympathy of himself and his government for the sad and premature death of the rajah.' He cleared his throat. 'His Excellency wishes me to inform you that he has received and studied the various documents forwarded by Major Ellis to Calcutta, including the late rajah's Last Will and Testament, which includes his request that the future government of Jhansi be vested in his wife and appointed heiress, as regent for his adopted son, Damodar Rao.'

Now I suspected that everyone in the room was holding his, or her, breath.

Another clearance of the throat. 'His Excellency has directed me to inform you, Your Highness, regretfully, that it is not considered to be in the best interests of either the Company or Jhansi that this request be granted.' He raised his head to look anxiously at the curtain, as if expecting to see Manu burst through it, perhaps waving her sword and firing her pistols – at him. But there was no sound from beyond the brocade. Or anywhere else in the large room.

Ellis drew a deep breath. 'As of now, therefore, while you will continue to be the Rani of Jhansi, the government of the state of Jhansi will be taken over and administered by the agents of the Company. However, His Excellency has graciously determined that you will be permitted to continue to reside in this palace, that you will retain the title of Highness, and that in place of the state revenues you will be granted, by the Company, a pension of five thousand rupees per month every year for the rest of your life.'

He paused, and waited, as did we all, for some response from beyond the curtain. Then we heard a dull thud, and a shriek from Damodar Rao.

The Prisoner

At the sound of the falling body I threw protocol to the winds, gathered my sari and dashed behind the screen. Manu had indeed fainted and fallen from her chair, watched by her adopted son, who was standing above her and wringing his hands.

I knelt beside the queen and raised her shoulders, making sure that she had not hurt herself in her fall, but I could see no serious bruises, and she was breathing evenly.

'Your Highness,' I said. 'Your Highness.'

We were joined by Maropant Tambe. 'Is she . . .?'

'She will be all right,' I said. 'Physically, at any rate. I will carry her to her apartment.'

I lifted her in my arms; to me she was as light as a feather. Then I carried her round the screen.

The waiting men all seemed struck dumb. Only Ellis had his wits about him. 'Is she all right?'

'We shall have to see,' I said.

'What do you wish me to do?'

'I think your best course would be to wait. Her Highness may wish to speak with you later. Vima,' I called, 'give the major some refreshment, and then attend me.'

I carried the rani along the corridors, surrounded now by anxious courtiers, all babbling questions. I dismissed them all, save for two of Manu's favourite maids, Mandar and Kashi. These I had help me undress the rani – as I was determined to continue considering her – and put her to bed. By now her eyelids were fluttering, and then her eyes opened and she stared at me, almost as if I were a stranger.

'They wish to take away my Jhansi,' she muttered. 'My Jhansi!' she shouted. 'I will never give up my Jhansi! Never!'

'I am sure we will be able to sort something out,' I said, inanely to be sure, but endeavouring to get her through the initial crisis. 'I shall order you some food and drink.'

'I do not wish food or drink,' she declared. 'I shall never eat or drink again.'

I could see no point in pressing the matter at the moment. 'Then you must rest,' I said. 'There is much to be done, when you feel better.'

'Much to be done?' she demanded. 'What is to be done? I no longer have the power to do anything.'

'Rest,' I said, firmly. 'We will discuss the matter after you have rested. Stay with Her Highness,' I told the girls, and went outside to face the anxious throng. 'Her Highness is resting, and is not to be disturbed,' I announced, although from their questions I got the impression that they were less worried about the rani's health than about their own futures. But with the aid of Kujula I managed to get rid of them, and be alone with Maropant Tambe.

'This is terrible,' he said.

'It was always possible,' I reminded him. 'Given the character of the governor general.'

'But you say my daughter will recover.'

'There is nothing at all the matter with the rani, Your Excellency, physically. As to her state of mind, well, I am afraid this will but confirm her hatred of the British. You know of this?'

'Of course Manikarnika hates the British,' he said. 'I hate the British. Does not everyone hate the British?' He stared at me, accusingly.

'I have never considered the matter,' I said. Although of course I had. I had always endeavoured not to hate anybody, but I had to admit that there were large numbers of the British I actively disliked; in fact, just about every one of them I had ever met, with the exceptions of Lady Hardinge, Mr Dickinson, Deirdre . . . and Major Ellis. Who had so sadly let us down!

'Still,' Maropant Tambe said, 'they are here, and we must do the best we can with them. Five thousand rupees a month! That is not very much. Perhaps we can get them to increase it. And there is the matter of the rajah's debts. We must get the Company to take over those. You must speak with Ellis.'

'Me?' I did intend to speak with Ellis, but not on financial matters.

'He is your friend.'

'He was my friend.'

'You must be friends with him again. You must make him understand our situation.'

'I think the major is very well acquainted with our situation,' I said. 'But I will ask him for more details.'

The major was waiting in the reception room, as I had requested.

'Please believe me when I say I am most terribly sorry about this,' he said when we were seated.

'How did it happen? Did you not recommend that the rajah's wishes be agreed?'

'I did.'

'And were you not supported by Major Malcolm's recommendation?'

'There is a slight mystery here. I am informed that no supporting recommendation has been received from Major Malcolm. In fact, somewhat the reverse.'

'You mean he betrayed us.'

'I wouldn't care to put it like that, Mrs Kala. I think it more likely that Major Malcolm came into possession of information which led him to change his mind about the rani's suitability to rule.'

'What information? Has she not proved, during the past three months, that she is in every way fit to rule?'

'I think that may be root of the problem. Rushing off with her army to fight the Pathans without referring, or even informing, the Company . . .'

'She was defending her country. And her people.'

'I understand that is how she saw the situation. But the Company necessarily has doubts as to when next she may act unilaterally and arbitrarily . . .'

'Thanks to your report.'

'I reported the facts, as my duty calls upon me to do. I had not anticipated so extreme a reaction. But the governor general appears to feel that her attitude, combined with her dislike of British rule, could well affect the lives and safety of everyone in Jhansi.'

'You mean every Englishman or woman. The rani's dislike of British rule is well known,' I conceded, 'but she would never let it interfere with the well-being of her subjects.'

'Perhaps, in herself, she would not. But . . . there is a saying that one should judge a man, or in this case, a woman, by the company she keeps.'

My head came up. 'I think you need to explain that remark, Major.'

He flushed. 'Oh, I am afraid that you are involved, Mrs Kala. Colonel Sleeman's report on your attitude is on file in Calcutta, and I suspect has been studied by the governor general, or certainly his advisers. And you are regarded as having a considerable influence over the rani.'

'Surely you mean the ex-rani,' I said, coldly. 'Do you really suppose I have, or have ever had, the slightest part to play in any decisions taken by Lakshmi Bai, or by her husband?'

'Sadly, my opinions don't seem to count for much in Calcutta. However, I would not like you to suppose that the government's attitude is based on you alone. More important, if you'll forgive me, is the rani's known friendship with Nana Sahib and with the Begum of Oudh.'

'And these friendships are regarded as dangerous to the Raj? My dear Major, the rani corresponds with the begum simply because they are both women in positions of power, or were, at any rate. What can possibly be dangerous about the begum? Has she not been to England to be received by Queen Victoria herself?'

'That is true. But it appears that the queen had no idea in what she was involving herself, attempting to be gracious to a foreign lady of distinction. Our reports indicate that the begum is a woman of the most atrocious morals.'

'I find it difficult to accept that a woman's morals, even those of a queen, can possibly be considered a danger to the Raj.'

'I doubt they are. They are but a symptom of the utter misgovernment which obtains in Oudh, and that, I can tell you, is a continuing source of concern in Calcutta. Oudh is, you should remember, one of the largest of the princely states, and should there be trouble there it would be a very serious matter.'

I smiled. 'And you cannot interfere, as the begum's husband is alive and ruling.'

'He is as dissolute as his wife,' the major grumbled, 'and is quite incapable of ruling. The various zemindars have set themselves up virtually as independent princes, and in their own territories do exactly as they please, regardless of what might be said in Lucknow. The country is in a state of anarchy.'

'Still, it is their concern. And I cannot believe anything that is happening in Oudh could have the slightest bearing on what happens here in Jhansi. The rani is not in the habit of taking advice from anybody, much less another woman.'

'But she may well be prepared to take the advice of another man, in the absence of her husband.'

'I doubt even that. You are thinking of Nana? Surely he is totally bound up in his lawsuit? Or does the mere fact that he is conducting a suit against your government make him a villain?'

'It makes him a potential enemy.'

'Without a state. And without a pension. Unless he wins his suit.'

'My information is that he is unlikely to do so. Which will only increase his animosity towards us.'

'I would have said he has good reason to feel he has been hard done by,' I said, surprised again to find myself defending a man I so disliked. 'However, as regards his relations with the rani, they were friends as children – I would say his relationship was something like that of an elder and admired brother – but since then they have drifted apart.'

'He visited her here just over a year ago.'

'He visited Jhansi. But that was to see Gangadhar Rao, not

the rani. I will be frank, and tell you that he hoped to enlist the rajah's help in changing your government's mind regarding the payment of his pension, even by force, if necessary. But Gangadhar, with his usual good sense, and I may say loyalty to the Raj, turned him down, and there the matter rested.' Obviously I was not going to tell the British agent that had Manu been in power then, she might well have fallen in with Nana's plans. 'Nana left in some annoyance.' Again, I was not going to tell him that the annoyance had been his failure to obtain possession of me. 'Since then, the only communication between the rani and Nana was her letter informing him of her husband's death and his reply.'

'I have no doubt everything you have said is true, Mrs Kala, but the relationship between Nana and the rani, even if it has dwindled since they were children, has been recorded in Calcutta and is held to be a dangerous association. I'm afraid nothing is going to change that now. The young lady will do best to accept her altered situation, and endeavour to live the rest of her life in peace and tranquillity. How is she, by the way?'

'At the moment, neither peaceful nor tranquil.'

'I am sure she will get over it. She needs to bear in mind the government's generosity in the matter of her pension.'

'Generosity?' I cried. 'A woman used to having millions to spend has been told that she now has sixty thousand rupees a year and is required to regard that as generosity?'

'She needs to remember Nana, in this case. He has been refused a pension at all. In any event, her expenses are going to be drastically reduced. She will no longer have to pay her army, for one thing.'

'She still has her husband's debts. Or will the Company assume those also?'

'Ah . . . no. I am sorry, but they will not take over the rajah's debts. She will have to come to some arrangements with her creditors. I have no doubt this can be done. If she requires a guarantee as to her income, I will be happy to supply it.'

I sighed. 'Well, then, there is nothing more to be said. I thank you for your time, Major.'

He remained seated, looking at once embarrassed and apprehensive. 'I would like you to know that I am deeply sorry that things have come to this pass. In confidence, I do not approve of the governor general's action, but I am a servant of the Company and must carry out its instructions. However, if there is anything I can do to alleviate the situation . . .'

'You have just said there is not.'

'I personally, no. But . . . it might pay the rani to appeal against the governor general's decision.'

'Appeal? To the House of Lords, you mean? That doesn't seem to be doing Nana much good.'

'The two cases are very different. Nana has lost his pension for a variety of reasons. The governor general's decision may be disputed. But it must remain a matter for his decision and the legalities are all on his side, the point being that the original agreement for the pension specifically stated that it was to be for the lifetime of Baji Rao only. Many people, including Nana, considered this was merely form, and the pension *would* be continued, but there is no legal basis for this, especially as Nana is an adopted son. I may also point out that while the gentleman is ranting and raving about eighty thousand pounds a year, he did inherit all of Baji Rao's personal estate, which is counted in millions, and with which no one has attempted to interfere.

'But the rani's position is different, as it takes us back to this adoption business, only in her case it comes down to interpretation of the law. The governor general has invoked the Doctrine of Lapse, on the basis that adoption, at least as regards inheritances, is not recognized by British law in Hindustan. However, it is recognized in Hindu law, and was so recognized long before the British set foot upon the subcontinent. And Jhansi is, of course, a Hindu country. It is therefore arguable, in law, that the governor general has no right to act outside of Hindu law. I know that he has already done this, in the case of Satara a few years ago. There were some doubts as to its legality then, but no one took it up. I think the rani would have a very good case if she were to challenge it now. Especially as the doctrine was virtually nullified forty years ago, and has never been used in the interim period. There is also the important point that once the appeal is launched and accepted, the situation reverts to the status quo ante. That is, the rani continues to be ruler of Jhansi until it is decided one way or the other.'

I could have kissed him. Instead, I clapped my hands. 'But that is tremendous. The rani will be delighted.'

'I don't think you want to consider the matter done,' he pointed out. 'There are some caveats.'

'Tell me.'

'Well, in the first place, once the appeal is made Her Highness will forego the state pension offered. On the other hand, she will of course again have access to the state revenue.'

'I hardly regard that as a caveat, Major.'

'Agreed. The other point is more serious. The governor general has been granted, at least tacitly, the right to overturn Hindu law where he regards it as inimitable to the public peace, or to Christian principals. I am thinking now of things like suttee. This had been Hindu custom, and had thus virtually attained the status of a law, for centuries. Lord Bentinck considered it barbarous and un-Christian, and outlawed it wherever the Company had the power to do so. This action has been universally acclaimed in England.'

'I do not see how something like suttee, which I agree is a barbarous practice, can be compared with a disinheritance.'

'It is that matter of precedents which I told you about. In the case of suttee, the governor general argued that it was both un-Christian and harmful to the public peace. And as I have said, this was accepted and indeed acclaimed. Of course Lord Dalhousie cannot claim the rani, as Rani of Jhansi, would be un-Christian, in a moral sense, although she is not a Christian in a real sense, but he could and will, I have no doubt, claim that her presence as ruler of Jhansi might well not be in the public interest.'

'The public interest in this case being the interest of the John Company,' I said, bitterly.

'I'm afraid so.'

'Then you have raised my hopes for nothing.'

'I should hope not. I have attempted to point out the pros and cons of the situation. I still think that the rani, properly represented, has a very good case, and one that is certainly worth putting forward.'

'And who do you have in mind to represent her? Yourself?'

'Good lord, no. For one thing, I'd lose my job. And for another, I am not a lawyer. I do know a lawyer in Calcutta, however, a very good man named John Lang, who might well be prepared to take up the case. He is already not very happy with the way the Company conducts its affairs. Do you suppose the rani would be prepared to see him?'

'I will certainly try to convince her.'

'This needs to be done as rapidly as possible.'

'Yes,' I said. 'Do send for Mr Lang, and leave the rani to me.'

Persuading the rani to go to law over her deposition was a difficult business. I had first to persuade her to resume living, and for a few days was extremely worried; she refused all sustenance for three days after her first interview with Major Ellis. But once she had regained sufficient composure to resume eating she began also to resume her interest in her surroundings. And, with her customary energy, threw herself into the business of making economies.

But my news restored her ebullience. 'Does this mean I can retain my army?' she asked Ellis.

'In theory, yes. But I do not recommend it.'

'Then who will defend the state?'

'Leave that to the garrison, at least for the time being. The point is that it was your use of your army that first, shall I say, interested Calcutta in your affairs.'

'As reported by you.' She waved her hand. 'Oh, I understand. You were doing your duty.'

'There is also the matter of your finances. Leaving the army in abeyance, for the time being, will be a great saving.'

'Ha! Very well, Major . . . We will appeal. Bring on your lawyer.'

I naturally felt, in the circumstances, that it would have been absurd for me to continue to insist on receiving what was, should the appeal be denied, now nearly a fifth of her annual income, even if she was determined that I should continue to be governess to Damodar Rao. In fact, in the five years I had lived in Jhansi I had spent very little of my salary, and thus had a good deal put by. I therefore rejected any further payment and asked only for my board and lodging. Sadly, this caused a crisis with Annie, who was not prepared to work for nothing. Thus I had to let her go, as I would still have Vima, and any other of Manu's women that I might need.

I gave Annie a good recommendation and assumed she would

take herself to Calcutta or Bombay and there seek employment. To my consternation she stayed in Jhansi, finding a position with the family of an English entrepreneur named Halliwell who had set up an emporium for European goods in the town. I could not stop her doing this in view of the rani's loss of power, but I shuddered to think what tales she might be telling of life inside the palace, and of my part in it.

And then I reflected that in the eyes of the European community I was damned anyway.

My refusal to accept any further salary brought me closer to Manu than ever, and now Major Ellis informed me that Mr Lang was on his way.

Manu clapped her hands at the news. 'We shall show that foul creature in Calcutta,' she declared.

I hastened to point out that this was a matter of law and might well take some time; Nana's case had not yet received a judgement.

'Still, we will be showing them that we are not to be trampled on,' she insisted.

The most important aspect of the rani's new situation had to do with her army, which had suddenly ceased to exist, at least in the eyes of the British. But the forced retirement of a thousand men was a distressing business. She held a last review and bade them a tearful farewell, after which they marched off. They were not now unemployed, unless they wished to be, as most of them were offered places as sepoys, but they were uneasy about the changed conditions and discipline under which they would now have to serve. Only a nucleus of a hundred men remained as palace guards, together with a few horses and half-a-dozen elephants.

'You will remain in command of my people,' Manu told Risaldar Khan.

But he was as unhappy as anyone and came to see me, accompanied by his brother.

'Once I led a thousand men,' he declared, waving his arms. 'Now I lead a hundred. Soon there will be none.'

'The rani will always require her guard,' I said, as reassuringly as I could.

'And what of our weapons?' he demanded. 'They are old and

antiquated. What of this new musket we have heard about? We were to be armed with this. Now we are told that is no longer possible.'

'It may be possible, in the course of time,' I assured him.

He went off in a very ill temper.

'Do you feel the same?' I asked my husband.

'We have been betrayed by the British.'

I could not argue this point, as it but echoed the rani's own feelings and indeed mine. In any event, it all became rather meaningless to me, for the following week I realized that I was pregnant.

It was a considerable shock. I had been married to Mr Hammond for six years without conceiving. Abid was certainly a far more vigorous and enthusiastic lover, but after two years I had supposed I was barren.

It was Vima, glowing in her new position as my principal lady, who first realized the situation. 'Memsahib is blessed,' she remarked.

I felt obliged to inform Manu immediately, not at all sure how she, never having a child who survived, would react. But she appeared delighted.

'I am so happy for you, Angel,' she said. 'Your son will be a playmate for Damodar.'

Relieved as I was at her reaction, I still felt very uncertain in myself. I do not suppose the age of nearly thirty, which is what I would be when the babe was born, was very great to be a mother, nor did I suppose that the dangers of childbirth would be any greater in Jhansi than say in Calcutta, although I was certainly apprehensive as to the methods that might be used by the Indians as opposed to the Europeans, but the concept of becoming a mother caused me to consider quite seriously my own future.

In the first place, the babe, whether a boy or a girl, would be half-caste, a Eurasian like Mrs Mutlow. This obviously would not present any difficulties as long as I lived in Jhansi . . . but was I going to live in Jhansi for the rest of my life? I had always secretly temporized about this. It seemed a *fait accompli*. I was an important part of the rani's entourage, I was committed to the education of her son, and I was married to one of her officers. Above all, I had sworn to remain at her side for as long as she needed me. This all added up to as permanent a situation as could be imagined. And yet I still dreamed of circumstances arising which would permit me to return to England. It did not look likely that I would have my lac of rupees, and I did not even know if my sentence still existed, but it had remained a vague dream, and I certainly had sufficient funds to live comfortably anywhere.

But I had never, given the circumstances of my life, considered returning home with a child, especially one who would be half-Indian.

So, did I wipe away that dream? It seemed that I would have to. And a lot of other things as well. Mr Dickinson took his time about settling in to his duties as commander of the cavalry branch of the garrison. I could not doubt that he had been brought up to date with my present situation, and attitude, by the Wilsons. At the beginning of April, however, he formally requested a meeting with me in the palace. Neither he nor the Wilsons were at that time aware of my condition, nor did I enlighten them in my reply; I merely wrote that, regretfully, such a meeting was impossible at this time, and left them to suppose that I was merely sharing my mistress's pique.

A week later it was time to forget about him again as Mr Lang arrived, being brought up to the palace by Major Ellis. The lawyer had a most impressive presence, his head all jaw and side whiskers, his eyes a piercing blue. I could tell that Manu was equally impressed, as we both were by his approach to the subject; as he spoke very little Marathi I was required to act as interpreter.

'We undoubtedly have a case that can be argued at law,' he told us. 'As for the outcome, these things are never certain, but we must do our best and put our trust in the British sense of justice.'

This brought a snort from the rani, and he felt obliged to make a point.

'However,' he went on, 'our case, while it may be legally strong, which presupposes that personalities should not enter into it, can yet, as can all cases, be affected *by* personalities, and seemingly unconnected events. So that while I would hope to prove that you have an incontestable *legal* right to succeed your husband as ruler of Jhansi, the eventual decision will undoubtedly be affected by an understanding on the part of their lordships that you are also the person most fitted for such rule. In this respect, the record of your husband and his grandfather, of unfailing loyalty to the Raj and hence to the Crown, will be of great value. Your own behaviour since the doctrine was invoked by the governor general, your dignity and forbearance in what everyone will accept has been a trying time, will be of no less importance. However, the matter of your going to war without even informing the resident or the commander of the garrison of your intention, will almost certainly be raised.'

'Am I not supposed to defend my country? Anyway, it was not a war. It was an incident.'

'With which the rani dealt both quickly and efficiently,' I put in.

'But yet without the permission of the Raj.'

'I am, or was, at that time the Rani of Jhansi,' Manu reminded him. 'I did not need to ask permission to defend my people.'

'Jhansi is a protectorate of the Raj. This was agreed long ago by your late husband's father. Under the terms of that protectorate, it is illegal for Jhansi to go to war without the permission of the Raj.'

'So I was obliged to apply to Major Ellis for support, but he would not have been able to order the garrison into the field without permission from Calcutta. We would have been talking about months, during which my country and my people would have been ravaged by those brigands. I could not permit that.'

Lang nodded. 'That is a very valid point, which I shall certainly put forward. However, it is inevitable that the resolution of this case will take some considerable time. I am speaking here of one, perhaps two years. Throughout that time there can be no doubt that the authorities in Calcutta will be watching and noting Your Highness's every movement, seeking any action which they might produce to their own advantage as against yours. Until there is a resolution, therefore, I must beg you to be most circumspect in everything you do, everything you say, every letter that you write, and indeed, to whom you write.'

'What you mean is,' Manu said, 'that I must have no contact with anyone who might at any time have offended the Company, or could even be considered to have a reason to do so.'

'That is certainly the wisest course.'

'Which means just about every prince or princess in northern India,' she pointed out. 'Not content with robbing me of my inheritance, you now seek to rob me of all human intercourse, and make me a prisoner in my own palace.'

'*I* seek only to help Your Highness,' Lang pointed out in turn. 'And it is only for a little while.'

'Two years,' she said, bitterly.

'A little while,' he insisted.

'And I must accept your recommendation because I have no other course. Go with your God, Mr Lang, and I will pray that you can reunite me with mine.'

But she was furious and her anger increased when she was informed by Major Ellis, most apologetically, that her favourite temple of Lakshmi, just outside the city, was no longer to be maintained by Company funds.

'They are swines,' she announced. 'Swines! Oh, my dearest wish is to lead an army into battle against them, to defeat them, destroy them, drive them from Hindustan for ever.'

'Please,' I begged. 'Remember what Lang said. If they ever even suspected you thought like that . . .'

'They would probably hang me,' she said, contemptuously. 'I shall be circumspect, dearest Angel. But one day . . .'

I reflected that dreams never did anyone any harm. Certainly where I could not imagine them ever coming true.

The rest of that year passed peacefully enough in Jhansi, and for me more than most others; as my body thickened and I could feel the stir of life within me. Manu took as much interest in my well-being as I did myself, and I like to feel that it was her concern for my pregnancy that kept her from any political excesses at that time, however bitterly she might stand at the windows overlooking the polo field, either to watch the Europeans at play or their military reviews. But these dwindled as the garrison dwindled. Matters in the Black Sea were coming to a head, even if there had as yet been no major battle. But the British army sent to Rumania was suffering far more heavy casualties than they could ever have taken in the most desperate encounter with the Russians because of an outbreak of cholera. Thus men were being called in from all over the Empire, the situation not being helped by the fact that Great Britain had also managed to get itself embroiled in a war in China. But the troops required had to be British. This was because by the Hindu religion to cross the sea meant loss of caste, and most of the sepoy army was of high caste. The British were well aware of this, and that it would be very unwise of them to upset the sepoys, yet, as will happen, and as British casualties escalated, the rumour grew that the Raj would indeed seek to send sepoy regiments overseas, and the troops became correspondingly agitated. Our palace guard was of course not involved, but Abid was friends with many of the soldiers in the garrison, and he told me their fears and resentment.

I replied that the Raj would never be so insensitive to Indian opinion, forgetting for the moment the business of the greased cartridges, but the new muskets had not yet been issued, being required against the Russians, suggesting that the government was adopting a cautious approach to the matter, while in fact no sepoys were ever employed in the Russian War, but as British regiments were withdrawn from their various cantonments around the country, they had to be replaced by the sepoys. As Jhansi was regarded as the most peaceful of the states, and as its nearest neighbour, Gwalior, had been entirely pacified, the Scindhia, following his mother's attempt at rebellion, having sworn eternal allegiance to the Raj, our garrison was reduced more quickly and more thoroughly than any other, and by the year end was down to hardly a thousand men, of whom only the officers were British.

By this time it had become apparent where the war was going to be conducted. As the Russians could not be forced to fight in Rumania, and as the men were dying like flies, in September the British and French armies were transported across the Black Sea and set ashore on the Crimean Peninsular, with the avowed intent of capturing the major Russian port of Sevastopol.

The Russians naturally defended their country with spirit, and by the year end there had been three major battles: at the River Alma, where the Russians had unsuccessfully attempted to prevent the Allies from crossing; at a seaport called Balaclava; and at a place called Inkermann. All of these were represented as Allied victories, although in one of them, Balaclava, a confusion in orders caused the British to lose virtually their entire brigade of light cavalry. Perversely, the British seemed to regard this catastrophe as of greater importance to the national pride than any victory, and the poet laureate wrote an epic about it.

However, these goings-on did not bring the fall of Sevastopol any closer, and the armies then had to settle down in their cantonments to see out the winter and, of course, call for more reinforcements. I would imagine Mr Dickinson chafing at being stuck in a place like Jhansi instead of being able to lead his lancers into battle. No doubt Mr Wilson felt the same, but Vima, who brought me all the gossip from town – in my condition I no longer visited the bazaar myself – told me that both officers were still in residence.

Naturally, these international affairs, momentous though they were, were of far less importance to me than the birth of my daughter at the beginning of January. Bhumaka was considerably more efficient at childbirth than he had been when dealing with smallpox or broken ribs, even though, according to the strange ethics of the court and as had been the case with Manu's delivery, he was unable to look upon my naked body. Instead I was covered in a voluminous sheet, beneath which he could insert his hands, while his head remained outside, beaming at me. I have to say that I found this blindfolded fumbling far more disturbing than if he had been able to see what he was doing, but in actual fact he had to do very little; I am a strong woman, and when I was required to push I did so with perfect success.

I would have named her Victoria, after my memory of the young queen, but I felt that might upset Manu, whose antipathy to the Raj and therefore everything British save me – seemed to deepen almost daily, so I settled on my mother's name, Alice. Abid raised no objection, nor was christening her a problem, as we could not have a christening. I temporized on this, and determined that my daughter would be christened at a suitable later date; I refused to contemplate the possibility that she might die and be condemned to everlasting damnation for not having entered the Christian Church, both because I refused to contemplate the possibility of her death and because it seemed less urgent in this totally un-Christian society.

Manu was delighted, and treated the baby as if it were her own. I am sure I can be forgiven for doing some more dreaming of my own, of perhaps my babe being married to Damodar

Rao, restored as Rajah of Jhansi. There would be a reversal of fortune.

However, not even the first stage, the restoration, seemed likely to happen, as winter dwindled into spring, and while Mr Lang continued to write us encouraging letters, the rani's case seemed very little advanced.

It was in May that Major Ellis came to see me. 'I have two pieces of news for you,' he said. 'And Her Highness, to be sure. You may consider them both good news, but one at least makes me very sad.'

'Tell me.'

'I am to leave Jhansi.'

'Oh! Because of your support for the rani?'

'I don't think so. I have been here for several years now and it is Company policy to rotate its people.'

'Who will replace you?'

'Major Skene. I will bring him to meet you before I leave.'

'Do you know him?'

'We have never met. But I am informed he is a straightforward and reliable person.'

'I hope so. And the other news?'

'The Earl of Dalhousie is to give up the governor generalship.'

'Now that is good news!' I cried. 'When?'

'Actually, not until next year. But he is definitely going.'

'Thank God for that. And who is going to replace *him*?'

'A man called Canning. He is well connected; his father was prime minister thirty-odd years ago. He is regarded as being far more liberal in his outlook than Dalhousie.'

'That is splendid,' I said. 'Do you suppose things will work out for us after all?'

'I simply cannot say. I hate to sound pessimistic, but you need to bear in mind that once Dalhousie is out of office and back in England, he will be able to take up the defence of his actions here personally, and will certainly seek to justify them. So I can only repeat Lang's warning, that the rani be patient and give no cause for offence.'

Manu was as relieved as I that Dalhousie was going; as he had been in India four years already I felt we were justified in considering that he had long outstayed his welcome.

The year of 1855 was like the calm before the storm. The war in the Crimea had settled down into a regular siege of Sevastopol, and indeed this dragged on until September, when the Allies finally stormed the port and to all intents and purposes brought the conflict to an end, although the peace negotiations went on for some time yet. India was very quiet. There was the occasional eruption of violence, but none close to Jhansi. Manu occupied herself with her various pursuits, and even more with her various dreams, and continued to prove herself a good and interested mother to young Damodar. I continued to tutor the young prince and spent all the time I could spare with my Alice, who as she approached her first birthday I foresaw growing into a great beauty.

And Major Ellis came up to the palace to say goodbye, bringing with him his replacement, Major Skene. Skene seemed pleasant enough and sympathetic to our cause, but I did not feel he was as strong a character as Ellis.

It is of course when one is at one's most relaxed that one stands the most chance of encountering catastrophe, and so it was with me. I had adopted the habit of taking Alice for a walk in her pram in the early evening, when the heat of the day had left the sun and there was generally quite a pleasant breeze. I took these walks by myself, enjoying such chances to be absolutely alone, and I never ventured into or even near the town, but went to the west of the palace, crossing the polo ground and proceeding into the rolling country beyond before returning.

I was well aware that my perambulations were overseen, and certainly noted, by various people, but this did not concern me in the least. All of Jhansi knew who I was, and that I was the close friend and intimate of the rani, as well as being the sister-in-law of the general of the army – even if there was no longer an army, everyone felt this was a temporary situation – nor was there any risk of my being mistaken for some lesser mortal, with my height, my full figure and my flowing auburn hair, which I invariably wore loose upon these private occasions, allowing the cowl of my sari to lie on my shoulders. I could not imagine there was anyone in the entire state who would dare interfere or even interrupt my progress.

And thus I was taken by great surprise one summer evening

when, having about reached the limit of my usual walk, and all but out of sight of the palace, I was suddenly confronted by a man, and realized that it was Major Dickinson.

The Decision

He wore mufti, and I realized immediately that he must have been waiting for me for some time as he could hardly have come all this way on foot, and I had heard no hooves. His horse, in fact, was tethered to a bush a few yards away.

'Why, Major,' I said. 'You gave me quite a start.'

'Then I apologize. Mrs Hammond . . .'

'My name is Kala,' I reminded him.

'Were you married in a church, with a Christian ceremony?'

'Of course I was not.'

'Then . . .'

'But I am still married, before God.'

'The Hindu god.'

'He is real enough, to many more people than there are in England.'

'Then I apologize again. Believe me, I did not come here to quarrel.'

'Why *did* you come here, almost like a thief in the night?'

'I wanted to see you. You have refused to receive me in the palace . . .'

'I did not think it was proper.'

'And was it not proper to answer any of my letters?'

I frowned. 'What letters?'

'I wrote you every month over a period of two years. Did you not even read them?'

'I did not even receive them.' I was aghast. 'To what address were they directed?'

'Well, I did not suppose it would be a good idea to address them to the palace. I sent them to the agent and asked him to let you have them.'

'Sleeman,' I said.

'You mean . . .'

'I have said, I never received them. Any of them.'

'Damnation,' he remarked.

'Yes,' I agreed. Because if I had received any of those letters, who could tell what decisions I might have taken, so at variance to those I had actually made.

'But why?' he asked.

'I suspect because I refused to act the spy for the Company within the palace. There can be no doubt that Calcutta regards me as an evil influence upon the rani.'

'And are you?'

'The only influence I have ever had on the rani is that I think I have completed her education. She now requires me to do the same for her adopted son, and hopefully, future rajah.'

'What a damnable business. Mrs Kala . . . Emma.'

'May I ask what was in those letters?'

'Well . . .' Even in the gathering gloom I could see his flush. 'I felt emboldened sufficiently to tell you how much I cared for you.'

'Then I am truly sorry I did not receive them.'

'But if you had . . .?'

'It can make no difference now.'

'Because you're married? To an Indian?'

'Because I am married, Mr Dickinson.'

'Do you love him?'

'We have been married for three years,' I said, carefully.

'Did you ever love him?'

'The marriage was arranged by the rani.' I spoke more carefully yet.

'And does he . . . did he . . .'

'We have a child.' I indicated the pram.

He bent over it. 'He looks like you.'

'Which is not unlikely. But he happens to be a she.'

'Ah,' he said. 'Well . . .'

'I should be getting back,' I said.

'You come out here most days?' he suggested.

'When the weather is fine, yes.'

'It looks as if it will be fine tomorrow.'

'It is a good time of year.'

What inanities. I was reminded of what Gangadhar had said when we first met, that the British always scouted around what they wanted to say, and never actually said it.

'Would you object if we met again?' he asked.

'Entirely by accident, as today?'

At last, he smiled. 'Of course.'

'Accidents will happen,' I agreed.

Utter madness. But try as I might, I could not submerge that secret desire to reach back into my European past, to speak English, to be with someone who, like Deirdre had at least in part the same cultural background. I swear that when I made the assignation I looked no further than that.

We met the next day, as planned, and did so several times during the following weeks. We talked, and he brought me such news as he had. None of it was very interesting to me, save when he told me that Captain Wilson had been transferred to Cawnpore. If I was sorry to hear of Deirdre's departure, it had long been obvious that we could never be close friends, and I had no doubt she would enjoy life in the far more cosmopolitan city.

'I also have been offered a transfer,' he said.

'Where to?'

'Gwalior.'

'That is not so far away.'

'Too far. I have refused it.'

'I have always been told that for a serving officer to refuse a transfer could be injurious to his career.'

'In my case, certainly. It was to carry a colonelcy.'

'And you turned that down to stay in Jhansi?'

'I turned that down to remain near you.'

'Oh, Mr Dickinson. That was surely unwise of you.'

'I don't think so. A man has only one life to live.'

'And you intend to live yours in solitary . . . I don't know what word to use.'

'I wish to live mine in hope.'

'As I have said, that is unwise of you.'

'You mean there is no hope?'

We had seated ourselves upon a sloping bank, where I could move Alice's pram with my foot. Now I got up, ostensibly to make sure she was comfortable, but really to hide my confusion.

He rose also, and stood behind me. 'You will have to tell me.'

I turned. Perhaps I meant to tell him. But he was closer than I had realized, and I was in his arms before I knew it.

He kissed me, lightly at first, as if as surprised as I that this was happening. But then he held me more tightly and my mouth opened to his, while his hands began to roam. A sari, I may say, is the least protective of garments when it comes to physical contact, and of course with the physical contact I soon no longer wished to be protected. Because here was a new experience. Stroking, caressing, had not been in Mr Hammond's nature. Abid had always been a great stroker, but from the first touch his caresses had been directed to a single objective, that of preparing me to receive him. James's movements had a quality of delighted surprise, like a young boy presented with a new toy, at once eager to possess but afraid of hurting, or even losing, should I demur, while at the same time unsure where it would end, or whether he wished it to end at all.

I felt the same way, compounded by even more disturbing emotions as I was by far the more guilty, and yet I was not sure that I wanted it to happen at all, while being quite unable to prevent it. So there we were, like the youngest and most inexperienced of lovers, for all that we were both rushing at middle age; as James was several years older than I he had to be well past thirty. But the outcome was inevitable, and in only a matter of minutes we were both stretched naked on the grass, and I had committed adultery.

'Oh, my dearest, dearest girl,' James said, kissing me time and again. 'I have wanted this for so long.'

I didn't know what to say. If I had undoubtedly considered it more than once, that had been in my midnight hours, thoughts to be rejected with the rising of the sun. But now it had happened.

'We'll have your marriage annulled,' he said, becoming forcefully masculine. 'That will not be difficult, as it was not a Christian ceremony.'

'It *will* be difficult,' I told him. 'The rani will not recognize divorce.'

'There is nothing she can do about it,' he insisted. 'She no longer has any power. If you just walk away from Jhansi, well . . . she can snap her fingers.'

'She is my friend,' I said.

'She is your employer.'

'My friend. I have promised to educate her son.'

'Her adopted son.'

'To her, he is a son. He was adopted under Hindu law. And don't tell me that is not recognized by the Raj. There, as in so many other cases, the Raj is wrong.'

He sat up. 'One would almost suppose you have become a Hindu yourself.'

'I think in many ways I have.'

'I am asking you to marry me.'

'And as things are at present, I cannot accept.'

'You mean . . . after . . .' he looked down my body.

'Even after,' I said. 'I have committed a sin. More of one in Hindu eyes than in Christian, I think. I wanted it. Oh, how I wanted it.'

'Well, then . . .'

'But that it happened has not altered my situation.'

'So you will not marry me.'

'I can only do so after obtaining permission from the rani, firstly to divorce my husband, and secondly to leave Jhansi.'

'Will you forgive me if I say I find that point of view absurd? This woman has no power, no standing. She is merely a pensioner of the Raj. She . . .'

'She is my friend, James. And no matter what the Raj says or does to me she is, and will always be, as the Rani of Jhansi, as much a queen in her own right as ever Victoria. I owe her both my loyalty and all the help I can provide until this business is sorted out. I have sworn to support her for as long as she needs me.'

He stared at me with his mouth open.

'So you see,' I went on, 'I think we both have a great deal to consider. You would like to marry me, I presume because you find me physically attractive and, again I presume, because there are sufficient aspects of my personality that you admire. I may say the same about my feelings for you, in reverse. But each of us has other aspects of our personality which are *there*, and cannot be carelessly dismissed or forgotten. They must be accepted. You are an army officer, with all that implies. Your entire life is built upon discipline and service, honour and loyalty to the crown. Those are admirable qualities, believe me. I am a woman who has only known the friendship of these people amongst whom I now live, and in particular of the rani. I can only abandon that friendship with her full acceptance. You also need to remember that as I am not well regarded in Calcutta, to marry me could well limit your career.'

'Do you suppose I would let that restrain me?'

'No. Not now. I would not have it a cause of conflict between us in later years.'

'You consider matters too deeply,' he grumbled.

'It is the only way to consider anything,' I pointed out.

'So what would you have me do?'

'Consider your proposal very carefully, for a period of a week. As shall I. At the end of that time, if you still wish it, I shall approach the rani and put the situation before her. I should think I have every chance of a sympathetic hearing.'

Actually, I was not at all sure of that, but I had to say it.

'And we will continue to see each other?'

'No. I don't think that would be a good idea. It would undoubtedly affect our decision. I will meet you here one week from today.' I kissed him. 'Now I must be getting back.'

I left him gazing after me as I walked the pram back to the palace. I moved very slowly, less to remain in sight of him than to collect my thoughts and regain my composure; one cannot have sex with a man who is not one's husband but who one has considered as a possible sexual partner for a long time without being powerfully affected. James was only the third man ever to have the use of my body, and this too was a reason for a considerable mental problem.

What was I to do? I remained rational enough to keep my thoughts in a kind of controlled progression. The first decision was, what did I *want* to do? Right then I wanted to run away with James. But that could not be done in isolation. Even more important than my relations with Manu I was conscious, as I had endeavoured to spell out for James, of the effect our elopement, for it would come to that in British eyes, might have on his future career. Presumably British officers *could* marry divorcees. Whether they could marry a woman who had, from their point of view, been sleeping with the enemy, or at least a potential enemy, might be another matter and could, as again

I had endeavoured to have him consider, present a serious source of discord between us once the first flush of sexual desire had passed.

Then there was the matter of the relationship between James and Alice, and even more, between Alice and the society in which she would be required to live and grow up. Eurasians were accepted in British India as more likely to be on our side than theirs, as it were, but there could be no doubt that they were considered an inferior species. I had no intention that anyone should so regard Alice, at least to her face.

And lastly, there was the question of the situation which could arise when I became a mother for James, as he would certainly wish to have happen. Again, I had no intention of Alice ever being regarded as inferior to any other children I might have.

Thus it will be seen that I had a great deal on my mind when I returned to the palace and fed Alice her evening meal with Vima in attendance. I do not think there can be any doubt that Vima, who was a quick-witted and alert woman, very rapidly deduced that I had had what might euphemistically be called a tumble; I do not know if there were any semen stains on my sari, but there were certainly grass stains. However, as she was utterly loyal to me, I did not think that she would ever betray me. I now know that Abid was fully conscious of all of my actions, and that he had been having me watched.

But at the time I suspected none of this, save for the mere fact that everyone knew I took these walks, and was no more than mildly surprised when my husband appeared. That I was surprised at all was because Abid seldom visited me nowadays. That he had probably come for sex was inconvenient but not disastrous. And that he had come for that reason seemed obvious when he dismissed Vima with a wave of his hand. As was her custom, she looked to me for confirmation of the command and I nodded. 'Leave us.'

She bowed, hands pressed together, and left the room.

'I shall just put the baby to bed,' I said. 'Although it would be best to wait until I have had a bath; I am not clean after my walk.'

'You mean you wish to wash away the evidence of your lover,' he suggested.

I had been bending over Alice's cot, wiping away the last of the food round her mouth, and now straightened, slowly, aware that I might have a crisis on my hands. At the moment I still considered the word might to be appropriate. But of one thing I was immediately determined: there were going to be no confessions, or even admissions, much less apologies or pleas for forgiveness.

'You will have to explain what you mean,' I said.

'Do you suppose that I do not know what you have been doing these past few weeks?'

He spoke quietly and even calmly, but I could tell from his breathing that he was in the grip of a powerful emotion.

'Tell me what I have been doing these past few weeks,' I countered.

'You have been meeting with the English officer, Major Dickinson.'

There did not seem any point in denying this. 'We have met, yes.'

'He is your paramour.'

'That is nonsense.' I bent over Alice again, and settled her.

'You have betrayed my bed,' Abid said.

I straightened. 'And if I have, have you not betrayed mine?'

'That is my right. I am a man.'

'You are my husband.'

'As you are my wife.'

'Well, then,' I suggested. 'Let us leave it like that.'

'You will suffer,' he said, and drew his tulwar.

My immediate idea was to get as far as possible away from Alice, to make sure she was not involved in the coming fracas; I certainly was not going to submit to being mutilated without a fight, or indeed at all. I was aware of a peculiar and yet strangely exhilarating emotion, compounded partly by an awareness of my guilt, certainly, but also by an understanding that this moment had had to come if I followed the dictates of my heart rather than my head. This was sooner than I had anticipated, and perhaps more critical than I had anticipated, too, but I was pleased that I was not afraid; thanks to the proficiency with weapons I had gained at Manu's behest, I felt perfectly able to take care of myself. So I backed away from the cot and round the room to reach the table on which there lay my pistols.

'Stand still and submit,' he commanded.

'Lay down your sword, and I will happily discuss the situation with you,' I replied.

'Bitch!' he snarled, and ran at me.

I gathered my sari – not the best garment in which to fight a duel – and sidestepped, at the same time reaching the table and my pistols. The guns were of course unloaded, but the balls lay in a box beside them, as did the powder horn. I released my sari to pick these up, almost falling over it as I had to make another hasty leap away from the tulwar, which now came crunching down on to the very table.

'Submit,' he shouted, his lips drawn back from his teeth.

My hands remained steady as I backed towards the door, and although some powder fell to the floor as I poured, this was because of my movements; sufficient got into the touchhole. But I did not intend to rely on the pistol alone. I was now close to the entrance arch. 'Vima!' I shouted. 'Come in here. Bring Kujula!'

I pushed the bullet into the muzzle and rammed it down, watching my husband, who had paused for breath after striking the table, but now turned towards me again.

'I am going to cut off your breasts,' he said. 'We shall see if your English lover wishes you then.'

The pistol was charged, and I faced him. 'Come one step closer,' I said, 'and I will shoot you.'

He hesitated, and I heard footsteps behind me.

'Memsahib!' Vima gasped.

'Memsahib!' Kujula panted.

'Disarm him,' I commanded.

No doubt they looked at him in dismay, because for a moment nothing happened, and I dared not take my eyes off him to look behind me.

Then I heard what in the first instance was the happiest of sounds: Manu's voice.

Someone had thoughtfully summoned the rani, and she came hurrying down the passageway.

'What is going on?' she demanded.

Shamefacedly, Abid lowered his sword. I kept my pistol levelled, however, as he had not dropped the weapon.

'He means to mutilate me,' I said.

'That is madness,' Manu declared, coming right up to us.

'She has betrayed my bed,' Abid said.

Manu turned to me, and I had never seen such an expression before.

'Say this is not true!'

I bit my lip.

She stared at me for several seconds, then she held out her hand. 'Give me the pistol.'

I hesitated only a moment, but I knew I could not defy both the rani and my husband at the same time. Thus I reversed the pistol and handed it to her, not at all sure, from the expression on her face, that she was not about to use it . . . on me.

She wrapped her fingers round the butt. 'Name the man.'

I opened my mouth, but Abid beat me to it.

'The English Major Dickinson.'

Manu looked at me, and I hung my head.

'I have the right,' Abid said.

'You did once,' Manu said. 'Now we are ruled by the British. You would be hanged.'

'You will let her go unpunished?'

Manu looked at me again. Then she said, 'Leave us.'

They filed away, Vima casting me an anxious glance, Abid one of pure hatred.

Manu waited until we were alone, then she said, 'Would you destroy me?'

'I can only say that I am sorry. You must know that I have never loved Abid.'

'He is the father of your child, and whether you loved him or not, he is your husband.'

'You made him so, Highness.'

'To save you from Nana.'

'And for that I am grateful. As I am grateful to Abid for being the father of my child.'

'But you could not resist the temptation of the flesh. Are you then a bitch on heat?'

'I have known Major Dickinson for six years. It was he who brought me here.'

'And he was your lover even then?'

'No. He was never my lover before this afternoon.'

'This afternoon? But you have been meeting him for some time.'

Proving that she too had been having me watched.

'We have met on our walks, yes. He has asked me to marry him.'

'And you believed him? Do you not suppose he just wished to get his hands on your body?'

'I believed him, because of the sacrifice he had just made.'

'What sacrifice?'

'He has been offered a transfer, which will carry with it a colonelcy. He would decline it to stay here with me. As my husband.'

'You are already married.'

'It is his opinion that my marriage to Abid would not be recognized by the Christian Church, and that it would be a simple matter to have it annulled.'

'And you agreed to this?'

'I asked him for time to consider. Time for him to consider as well.'

'That at least was sensible of you.'

'But now . . .' I sighed. 'I have no choice. I must leave Jhansi.'

'And I must ask you again, would you destroy me?'

'How can my actions harm you, Highness?'

'I may no longer have the power to make the laws in Jhansi, but I still have the power to judge them inside my palace. You have broken the law, most seriously. If I condone this, if I permit you to walk away from here with your paramour, I will lose all authority over my people. What is worse, your husband is a captain of my guard; his brother is the commander of my guard. If I allow this incident to go unpunished, I will lose all authority over them as well. My assassination will be only hours away.'

I stared at her in horror. 'You would be protected by the British.'

'In my own palace? And do you not think the British would be far happier to see me dead than alive? Besides, if they did protect me, where would my authority be? I would be humiliated in the eyes of my people.'

'Then what would you have me do?' I cried. 'Submit to mutilation?'

'No,' she said. 'I could not ask that of you, and that would certainly bring British intervention. The matter must be settled within the privacy of the palace, but must yet be settled as to leave no doubt of my authority. I am sorry. But you have brought this on yourself.'

'Can you not just expel me?' I asked.

'No,' she said.

'Not even if I wish to go?'

Her eyes gloomed at me. 'Do you wish to go? I thought you have been happy here.'

'I have. More happy than at any time in my life. But . . .'

'I thought you loved me and were sworn to serve me.'

'I do love you, Manu. And I would serve you if I could. But if I cannot . . .'

'What is to prevent you?'

'You said I must be punished.'

She nodded. 'You must be punished,' she said. 'But the punishment will leave you unscarred. You have my word. I will also see that you do not have to live with Abid, although you will remain his wife. This is legal, in circumstances such as this. But the decision to put you aside must be his, you understand. I will see that he makes that decision.'

'And my child?'

'As long as you obey me, and remain with me, Alice will be yours. If you attempt to abscond, then she will belong to her father, as in law she already does. This is something else I will have to make Abid accept. But I believe I can do this.'

There was the crowning blow. I supposed I *could* escape the palace and flee into Jhansi, to the cantonment, screaming for help. But what then? James might wish to help me, but no one else would. Had Major Ellis still been here, there might have been a chance. Or even Deirdre. But for the rest, I was a woman who had deliberately severed herself from all association with her own kind, the ultimate renegade, who had transgressed every rule in their book, and who was now appealing for them yet again to break Hindu law, and this was domestic law, nothing to do with the state.

It would also ruin James.

'What will become of Major Dickinson?'

'I would hope nothing. You say he has been offered a transfer and promotion. He should take it.'

'I do not think he will.'

'You will write to him,' Manu said. 'You will say that having given the matter due consideration, as you promised to do, you have determined that it would be very wrong of you to abandon your husband and child, that it would ruin your life and his career, and very possibly cause trouble between the European and Indian populations here in Jhansi.'

I swallowed. 'Am I allowed to say that I love him?' I asked.

'I think that would be most unwise.'

A girl ten years my junior, reading me the riot act! But she was the queen. More importantly, I knew every word of what she had said was true. I had behaved abominably, seeking only my own gratification. I deserved everything that was going to happen to me.

As perhaps James deserved everything that was going to happen to him.

'It will break his heart,' I said.

'It will be an experience he will not forget. But, contrary to what is written in books of romance, men seldom die of broken hearts. He will grieve, then he will buckle down to his new position, and in time he will meet some young lady who is free of previous attachments and marry her, and together they will raise a family. It may please you to feel that he will never love her as he loves you, and you may well be right. But few of us are fortunate to marry the one we love above all others.'

She spoke with considerable feeling. I raised my head. 'Have you ever loved, Manu?'

'How should I love? I am the Rani of Jhansi.' She stretched out her hand to stroke my cheek. 'But if I ever loved anyone, it would be you.'

We gazed at each other. 'I shall write the letter,' I said.

'It must be done, now.'

'I will do it now. Then you say I must be punished. What will you do to me?'

'Short of mutilation, the only punishment possible for adultery is the lash.'

My head jerked in consternation. 'You cannot be serious.'

'I am afraid there is no alternative.'

'You promised . . .'

'I promised you will not be marked, at least permanently. It will be painful, but the pain will fade.'

'And the humiliation?'

'Will fade also, as you bask in my favour.'

We gazed at each other.

'Where will this happen?' I asked.

'It should take place in public.'

'No!' I cried.

'But what is public?' Manu asked. 'The Raj has taken away my country. My domain is this palace. Your punishment will take place within these walls.'

'Who will be present?'

'Your husband and his family must be present, so that they can see that the law is being carried out.'

I licked my lips. 'And when I have been punished, I will be divorced?'

'No, you will be separated. Abid will have no rights over you, either conjugal or disciplinary.'

'Thank God for that. And the child?'

'He is her father, and must be allowed access to her on a regular basis. But you may always be present, and he will have no rights of education.'

'I can bring her up as a Christian?'

'If that is your wish, yes.'

She waited.

I drew a deep breath. 'You understand, Manu, that in doing as you wish, I am placing my very life, and that of my babe, in your hands.'

'Your life has always been in my hands, Angel. It is my responsibility. Now write the letter.'

Once I had done that, the die was cast; I would indeed have severed my very last link with the British community. With the Raj.

Had I ever intended to take such a vast step? But had I not done so, whether I had realized it or not, when I had refused to act the spy for Sleeman?

I was, to all intents and purposes, a Hindu. And so I must behave as one, and accept the concomitants of that. I was to be whipped, before my husband and his family, and no doubt most of the residents of the palace. The news of what had happened would certainly leak out and do the gossip rounds of Jhansi. Now I was actually glad that Deirdre had departed, although no doubt the story would even eventually reach Cawnpore.

Closer to hand, I wondered what Mrs Mutlow would make of it? And Annie? Both would no doubt say, she had it coming.

But the event itself! Once I had spent a sleepless night wondering what Zavildar the thug had been feeling, knowing that he was to be impaled in the morning. How *could* any man contemplate that without going mad? Now I had to contemplate . . . nothing so catastrophic, certainly. But it was still going to be both humiliating and painful, and I suddenly realized that Manu had not specified the number of lashes I would receive.

My hand trembled as I wrote the required letter to James. If he supposed I was in the grip of a considerable emotion he would not be wrong. I could only hope that he would already have left Jhansi before he learned of my fate, else he might well do something stupid. Perhaps because of this fear, I wrote in somewhat more bleak and determined sentences than I might otherwise have chosen, making it plain that we could never see each other again, and that, indeed, I did not wish that to happen.

Then there was nothing to do but wait and try to sleep. Vima was a great comfort, sharing my bed and endeavouring to maintain my spirit.

'It is nothing,' she promised me. 'It will be over before you know it.'

'Have you ever been whipped?' I asked.

'Oh, yes. For stealing. When I was a girl.'

'How many strokes did you receive?'

'Twelve.'

I shuddered.

'But I soon forgot them,' she assured me.

'What did you do when you were receiving them?'

'I screamed,' she said. 'As you will scream. But it is good to scream.'

Perversely, that made me determined not to scream. As if one really has any power over one's actions in these circumstances.

The circumstances were actually worse than I had even anticipated. I was awakened at dawn, surprised to have slept at all, to discover that Vima had left the bed, and indeed the apartment. For all her comforting words, even she had abandoned me. Kujula, looking very doleful, escorted me to the underground stream, to be bathed and thus purified, then I was taken to the schoolroom, where it seemed the entire palace had assembled, although thankfully Damodar was not present. Abid was, however, with his mother and father and sisters, and naturally Risaldar Khan.

Also present, of course, was Manu, seated in one of her high-backed chairs, her father standing at her shoulder, her women around her.

In the centre of the room a triangle had been erected, its legs anchored in heavy pots to prevent it moving. To this I was escorted, trying to ignore everyone, trying not to think and certainly not to feel. But I kept my gaze fixed on Manu, as my only hope.

When I stood in front of the triangle, I was formally disrobed, my jewellery was carefully removed and then equally carefully my hair was pinned up . . . while the assembly gazed at me. Then I was made to stand beneath the triangle, and Kujula lifted my arms above my head and secured them to the apex. This was just high enough for my outstretched wrists to reach, but I was pretty extended. He then secured each ankle in turn to the bottom of the waiting uprights. This distended my body even further, so that I was held absolutely rigid between the sloping posts.

I closed my eyes, but could not prevent myself from opening them again as I heard a swishing sound and discovered Abid standing in front of me, slashing the cane to and fro while he grinned at me. I raised my head to look at Manu. To my enormous relief I saw her stand up and come towards me. 'I will carry out the punishment,' she said.

'It is my right,' Abid protested.

'And it is my privilege to override your right in this matter,' Manu said. 'This woman is my handmaiden. No one can gainsay my right to punish her.'

Abid looked to his brother for support. Risalder chewed his lip; he wished to see me punished as much as anyone. For a long moment he and Manu stared at each other while I held my breath. Was I about to witness a revolution, of which I would have been the cause?

But at that moment there was a huge explosion of sound, overlaid by the tramping of booted feet on the corridors. All our heads turned to see Major Skene appear. James was at his shoulder, carrying both revolver and sabre, and behind him was the squadron of lancers, dismounted of course and thus without their lances, but every man equipped with musket and bayonet.

I all but fainted with the sense of salvation that overwhelmed me.

The men marched up to us, while the court stared at them in consternation.

Manu was the first to recover. 'You have no right to invade my palace, Major Skene. This an act of . . .'

'War?' Skene inquired. 'Will Your Highness permit me to correct what is clearly a misapprehension of the situation. Jhansi is now a possession of the Company, and I, as the Company's representative, am required to oversee every aspect of the law and its consequences. That the Company has elected not to interfere with your laws and customs, as obtain within the country, and providing there is no evidence of injustice involved, is an acceptance of the fact that these laws and customs have been practised for many years, apparently fairly and impartially. But it is not an irreversible decision. And you, no Indian ruler has the right to arrest and put on trial, much less mistreat, any British subject. Were the news of what has happened here today, or even worse what was intended to happen, that a white . . . a British woman should be humiliated and brutally mistreated to become known in Calcutta, the perpetrators of this crime, all of them . . .' his gaze swept the entire assembly before returning to settle on the rani, 'would be liable to arrest, trial, and imprisonment. Major Dickinson.'

I felt James beside me, touching me as he released me. His sergeant had joined him and they wrapped me in a greatcoat. Déjà vu, I thought. These same hands had wrapped me in a blanket six years before, on the road from Cawnpore. And launched me on a dizzy career, which had now ended? In my heart I knew that could not be so.

'This is beyond even your jurisdiction, Major,' Maropant Tambe declared. 'This woman is married to a citizen of Jhansi. Thus she has forfeited her right to benefit from British law and must adhere to Hindu law and custom. And she has committed adultery, which in our law is the most serious crime that a woman can commit. Her husband has the right to mutilation. That Mrs Kala's sentence has been mitigated to a flogging is by the express generosity of the rani.'

'Your Excellency must permit me to correct his misapprehension also,' Skene said. 'To commit adultery, a woman, or a man, needs to be married. Mrs Hammond is a widow.'

'But . . .'

'That she has chosen to indulge in a liaison with Captain Kala, while it may not be to everyone's taste, is a matter for her. Living as someone's mistress is not a crime in British eyes. If she chooses to consider herself Captain Kala's wife, that again is her choice. But again, a British citizen can only be married by an ordained priest and in a consecrated church or chapel. In certain circumstances it may be possible to apply for a special licence to overcome these requirements, but such a licence can only be granted by a magistrate. In Jhansi that magistracy is vested in me as the Company agent. I have never granted such a licence, nor has there ever been an application for one. Therefore her 'marriage' to Captain Kala has no validity in law, nor has it ever possessed such validity.'

Maropant opened his mouth, looked at the waiting lancers and then closed it again. Manu remained as if frozen.

Skene nodded, and the squadron prepared to escort me from the room. I turned my head and gazed at Manu, who gazed back. Never had I beheld such a tragic expression. But I do not think I looked very different.

I found myself in the house of a local Englishwoman, Mrs Holmes. 'My dear,' she said. 'Oh, my dear. Clothes! I will have my seamstress in immediately. Meanwhile, a dressing gown.' She bustled off. James sat beside me on the settee. 'There is nothing more for you to fear,' he said.

I was certainly shivering uncontrollably but it was delayed shock. He poured me a glass of wine. 'How did you know what was happening?' I asked.

'Vima came to see me, last night. I had to get Skene out of bed. She seems a most faithful young woman.'

'Yes,' I said. Vima!

He studied my expression. 'Will she be in danger?'

'I do not know.'

He held my hands. 'Will you marry me?'

I gazed at him. 'I would be happy to do so, if you still wish it.'

'It is the only thing I have wished for a very long time.'

'But . . .'

'No more buts, my darling. Listen to me. As I told you, I have been ordered to rejoin my regiment with my squadron, as soon as my replacements arrive, which will be any day now. It seems they need more cavalry to combat the Pathans and, as you know, just about all of our British troops have been called to the Crimea. So the plan is this: you will remain here with Mrs Holmes until the next caravan to Calcutta.'

'Calcutta?'

'There you will stay with a lady I know who will give you the best of care until I can come for you. It will not take longer than a year to complete this campaign. Then we will be married, and buy a house, and . . . be happy ever after.' He paused, anxiously.

With good reason. Calcutta, I thought. My least favourite place on earth. Besides . . . my brain was starting to work again, causing me to realize the truth of the situation.

'Emma?'

'I must return to the palace.'

'In the name of God, why? They hate you. Are you worried about Alice? We will demand her surrender to you.'

'Alice is in no danger, although I certainly have no intention of abandoning her. And they do not hate me. They undoubtedly resent your intervention, but that will be greatly reduced if I return of my own free will. Besides, Manu needs me.'

'But . . . she commanded you to be flogged. To be humiliated.'

'I broke Hindu law. At great personal risk she reduced the punishment as far as she dared, from mutilation to whipping, and she intended to handle the whip herself, to ensure that I was not injured or even marked. After what happened . . . I don't know what her position will be. But my return must alleviate that. Besides, I swore an oath to remain at her side at least until her lawsuit is settled, to help her understand the nuances of English usage. I cannot desert her now. Anyway, the case should be settled in at most a year, and you have said that we cannot be together for a year. Allow me to spend the year doing something worthwhile, rather that sitting and knitting.'

'And your own personal danger? As you have just said, I will no longer be here.'

'After this morning, I will be in no danger. Certainly as long as Major Skene remains the agent.'

He sighed. 'Emma . . . you *do* wish to be my wife?'

'More than anything else in the world, James. Save at the compromise of my honour. Women can have honour just as much as men, and contrary to what most men appear to think, it is not merely to protect their chastity. You swore an oath to fight for queen and country. Would you break that oath because I asked you to? *Could* you, and ever look at yourself in a mirror again? I swore to stay at Manu's side until the matter of her sovereignty is resolved, and to assist her in every possible way in maintaining her position as Rani of Jhansi. I cannot, I *will* not, betray her now.'

He gazed at me for several seconds, then kissed me. 'You are a woman to admire as well as to love, Emma. I will count the seconds until I can return for you.'

I resumed my sari, and walked up to the palace. People stared at me and then stepped aside to let me through. The guards at the gate did the same, clearly uncertain what, if anything, they should, or might be required, to do.

Abid was at the top of the great staircase, staring at me as if I were a ghost. I returned his stare and he stepped aside, as bemused as anyone.

I made my way along the halls, meeting the same response, or lack of it, from everyone. Then I entered the royal apartments, going straight to the throne room. Here Manu sat in her great chair, alone. She raised her head at my entry. 'Have you come to take your daughter and announce my final deposition? Or simply to gloat?'

'I have come to serve you, Manu, as I have done for six years, as I will continue to do for as long as you need me.'

She stared at me. 'You expect me to believe that?'

'I do. Because it is the truth.'

'I am disgraced, and have lost all authority amongst my people.'

'Your people love you, Manu. Their anger will be directed only against the Company.'

'Then they will hate you.'

'I care nothing for that, as long as I have your love and support, as you shall have mine.'

'And if I ordered you to submit to your punishment, now?'

I took a long breath. 'That is your right. I broke the laws of Jhansi.'

Another long stare, then she held out her arms and we hugged each other.

'There is one question I must ask you,' I said.

'Then ask it.'

'Vima.'

'She is in prison on a charge of treason for acting against the state.'

'You mean, she saved the state from catastrophe. Had my punishment been carried out, and word of it had leaked out, your hopes of regaining your throne would have disappeared for ever.'

Manu hunched her shoulders.

'Your father gave Vima to me,' I reminded her, 'to be my servant. She has served me faithfully and well for six years. Now she has, even if perhaps inadvertently, served the state as well.'

Manu sighed. 'My people will regard her release as a sign of weakness.'

'On the contrary, Highness – magnanimity and generosity are signs of strength. Now summon your court and resume your rule.'

'Can I do that? Have I the power?'

'Highness, at this moment you have more power than ever in the past. Skene will back you to the hilt to minimize any unrest he has created. His only aim now is to restore tranquillity to Jhansi, and only you can do that.'

'I shall never give Jhansi up,' she said. 'No matter what I have to do.'

'And I will be at your side,' I promised. 'No matter what.'

A last hesitation and we walked to the doorway together. Neither of us had any idea of what lay ahead, because no one in India, or indeed in Great Britain, or the world, had any idea of the abyss lying at our feet, at the feet of all India, of the storm that was about to arise. We only knew that we would face the future together.